Beneath the Surface

Matt Hebert

This second edition copy includes a reformatted
interior and new cover art by local Omaha artist
Tim Mayer.

ISBN: 1489545638
ISBN 13: 9781489545633
Library of Congress Control Number: 2014921284
LCCN Imprint Name: Omaha, Nebraska

Part One
The Illusion

Chapter One
A Day in the Life

Another line of waves broke against the rock. The salty spray shot high into the air, its green mist reaching to the sun. Generation after generation of surging madness had beaten against the rock. It had taken hundreds of years, but the rock was on the brink of defeat. Its hard roots had been eaten to the core, and the water had carried off what was left of its stony resolve. A thunderous crack rang from the rock, but the sound was lost in the deafening roar of the sea. The volcanic remains cried out as a great fissure expanded, a painful divide down its middle that drove right through its heart. The shearing surfaces let out a final roar as the elephant-sized mass slid down the cliff face and struck its brothers below. With a sickening crunch, the rock pivoted at its base and plummeted the remaining distance to the churning surface of the sea.

The water exploded with the next line of waves, adding to the spectacular victory dance. The rock descended into the foamy cavitation, frantically hissing as it took its last breath. Sparkling rays of sunshine shot down through the murk that the fallen rock had created. Soon the disturbance would settle, and the depths of the peaceful, blue world would return to their crystal calm.

***

One hundred meters below, a masked figure watched the rock with growing interest. Thousands of bubbles billowed off the giant boulder as it slowly accelerated. The figure started to fidget nervously. Sembado Grey had never seen such a large piece of surface debris, and he did not know if the containment net would hold. The government had installed the heavy steel mesh years ago to ensure protection against such things, and also to keep younger swimmers from going too close to the surface.

In fact, Sembado could not legally be at this depth normally, but he had just acquired his class C3 license. He rolled the license over in his hands as he waited for the rock to fall. The thin plastic card had his picture on one side, his flaming red hair nearly obscuring his pale face. He sat in his submarine, an Atlantis Mark-III, which had the watertight seals that qualified it as a class C. He had the cockpit open, and his breathing mask was on, since he could not see the falling object through the glare of the sub's guard shield.

His anticipation heightened as the rock's current course carried it toward the center of the closest net cell. The net was stretched over a hexagon-shaped grid of cells, which mimicked the complex layout below. It was rare to see an object fall from the surface at all, let alone something as big as this boulder. The rock plummeted closer; Sembado held his breath. Within seconds the large volcanic mass collided into the steel web. Just as Sembado feared, the mesh took up a lot of slack before the full impact of the rock had taken effect. But to his surprise, the flexibility of the net had absorbed the vast majority of the shock, and the frame above, although releasing an eerie, whale-like creak, had only shifted a couple of inches. The net itself had barely deflected the height of the rock and soon was recoiling to bring the rock back up to rest in its taught, neutral position.

Sembado suddenly gasped. He had not breathed for nearly thirty seconds. The rush of oxygen hurt his head and lungs. He blinked away tears as he pressed his tank's warning button with frustration.

What good is a breathing sensor if it only goes off after I've nearly passed out?

Sembado continued to watch the rock, although his interest had soon shifted up to where it had come from. He watched from below, three hundred feet down, as the glaring sunlight sparkled off the tumultuous ceiling above. He had heard many foreboding stories about the surface, most of which he guessed were true, but despite being warned many times throughout his youth, he had never stopped being curious.

I wonder what it's like to skim the surface. See the sun, the moon, the stars.

But that required a class A sub with airtight seals, and the coveted class A license, which most people could not afford, let alone earn.

Sembado was older now, and that was what his new license was all about. Being eighteen was one of the requirements for the class 3, and he had wasted no time getting the permit barely three weeks after his birthday. This was the first opportunity he had taken to navigate this high using his new freedom, and he could not help but notice how much lighter the pressure was at this level. He was usually swimming down at the four hundred mark, with a pressurized suit of course. A class 2, the first unaccompanied-minor license, would allow a person to roam free down at four hundred.

Despite his new independence, he was careful not to make any mistakes. There was bound to be a penalty officer watching from somewhere, if not a camera. He gave the fallen rock one last glance as he pulled the guard shield down and began the evacuation process. He concentrated as he balanced the submarine. Voiding the cockpit of water was one of the more difficult challenges of piloting a submarine and had nearly cost him a failure on his license test.

If a pilot did not keep the air balanced with the ballast water taken in, the sub could sink unevenly, or worse, shoot to the surface like a cork. That was another reason for the containment net. Most new submarines had an auto balance feature, but the Swimbler Submarine Company was famous for giving people an affordable submarine, not a fancy one. These older Atlantis models were the rule, not the exception.

Okay, sixty-four for the water, and the cockpit is twelve cubic feet. I need seven hundred sixty-eight pounds.

Sembado had memorized the conversion right away, but that was the easy part. He had to transition the water out without releasing the valve completely, or he would risk blowing out the cockpit seals. He did not want to ruin the new seals he had just replaced.

Submarines required updated seals and other maintenance to be logged with the proper authorities, and that was just for the watertight cockpits. It seemed like a pilot had to know somebody in the approval department to get the airtight cockpits approved for surface rides, or so Sembado had heard.

As the salty water fell down past his head, his shaggy red locks stuck to his face and across his goggles. He smeared his bangs to one side, revealing his hazel eyes that were bloodshot from the chlorinated goggle treatment that filled his eyewear. He finished sealing out his exhaust ports before taking off his mask, and the odorous liquid splashed on his lap. He breathed in the stale, tanked air that he knew so well. He wrinkled his nose; his oxygen filter needed a change, but it should be good for a few more weeks.

Besides, he had just blown nearly all his savings on those new seals.

He executed an awkward, vertical two-seventy, three-quarters of an overhead loop, and shot down to find an open lane. It would be getting dark soon, and his curfew permit, although awarded, had not been processed yet.

As Sembado approached the bustling rush hour traffic flow, his submarine's display monitor transitioned to play the voice of his onboard guidance system.

The OGS chimed. "Please approach transition forty-six and prepare for velocity matching procedures."

Sembado followed the onscreen prompts and was soon accelerating to his Atlantis's maximum speed, just under forty miles per hour. The OGS had directed him to the area of traffic with vehicles similar to his. His speed was being controlled by the system, but he was still responsible for steering and keeping his little Swimbler about fifteen feet away from any other submarine: above, below, and to either side.

His nervousness showed as he overcorrected from time to time, swerving slightly. The less attentive passengers around him paid little notice; most of them were busy reading, letting their autopilots steer for them, a feature not available on the baseline Mark-III. A four-passenger Beranius slowly passed Sembado on the left. Beranius was the most posh line of submarines available, and this appeared to be the brand-new Melville Luxury Class, an all-new standard in style and excess. Sembado admired its mirror like finish, which shined proudly, even at this considerable depth. The fluid, austere lines combined with the oversized viewing shields gave the vehicle a kind of haughty, proud beauty. The pilot, sitting front and center, appeared to be a hired hand. He looked onward stoically, while the young lady in the backseat glared at Sembado contemptuously. He broke eye contact when the OGS warned him of his next suggested maneuver.

Chapter Two
The Attack

Sembado walked back to his family's front door. His best friends, Meligose Feldman and Kreymond Matroid, had apparently gone down to the Aquarics to look at the new Mako Z. It was the first enclosed single-rider Mako had made. Some said the cockpit would ruin the hydrodynamics, but others were excited to finally see some developments in the sport/racing class of the submarine market.

With his friends already gone, Sembado decided to spend the day visiting with his grandfather, Hyron. He drove his Mark-III down to the Gold Sector, where his grandfather lived. He could have walked through the passages that connected his grandfather's older sector with his family's newer one, but the lifts were extremely congested today, and Sembado was taking every opportunity he could to use his new license.

Grandfather lived in one of the oldest sectors in the district. "Gold" had been around forever—at least seventy years—and by the looks of it, the council had not done much to improve it. The metal around the windows was rusted over, more than a dozen of the dormitories had imploded, and an entire floor had had to be sealed off at one point to be remodeled. Sembado's parents had tried to convince his grandfather to come and live with them in the new Madisen Wing, but he wouldn't have it.

Every time they brought it up, he'd become stubborn and start to lecture about memories, respect, and devotion, leaving the room with tears in his eyes. Sembado's parents had given up since then, but he still liked to visit the old man from time to time.

He slowed down as he approached the depressurized landing pod. When the last of the water had drained out, he took off his mask and scuba gear and left it with the Mark-III. He finished drying off as he walked down two flights of stairs to his grandfather's level.

Boom! Boom! Boom!

Gunshots! That's something rare to hear, even in these parts.

He had just opened the door to the floor's hall when two men ran past, knocking him back into the stairwell. They were both dressed in black with tactical harnesses. One had a mask; the other's face was exposed and sported a patchy mustache on his pale, worried face. He was clutching his bloody shoulder.

Sembado listened to their footsteps go up two flights, followed by a slammed door. They were probably headed toward the landing dock. There were always hoodlums and criminals running these halls. Most were petty thieves. Sembado collected himself and continued down the hall. It was rust-covered and soggy from nearly a century of leaks and corrosion.

When he got to Grandfather's dorm, the door was already cracked open. He went inside immediately; the place had been ransacked. The entire apartment had been turned upside down. He ran from room to room franticly, trying to ignore the horrible thought in the back of his mind that the worst had happened. Those two guys he had just passed probably had something to do with it.

He ran down the hall and tripped over some debris, colliding with a door. The hinges gave way with a horrible crunch and he landed hard on the bathroom floor. Head pounding and out of breath, he slowly rose to one knee. He reached out for support and gave a shout when that support grabbed him back. He gave another shout when he looked up to see Grandfather holding a pistol pointed straight at Sembado's face. The old man's grip was crippling as he bore down on Sembado's arm with his other hand. His appearance was far worse than Sembado's. He had a large welt on his gray, wrinkled forehead, and a deep gash bled on his left arm. He seemed to be winded, but held the gun firmly. He was propped awkwardly against the wall.

As the old man's pale blue eyes focused on Sembado's face, the fire behind them faded. All at once, he collapsed into Sembado and started sobbing, something that Sembado had never seen before. The tears carried on for several minutes as the bewildered boy wrapped his arms tightly around his sorrowful grandfather.

After several minutes, the old man spoke.

"I told M'Gereg those bastards were back. I think they've been hiding in the technicians' closet all week." He tried to gain his composure, unsuccessfully. "I tried stopping them; didn't do that great of a job, did I?" he said quietly, thumbing through the tattered remnants.

"You mean those were mutants?" Sembado asked excitedly. He had heard all sorts of stories about the unfortunate people who hadn't gotten underwater soon enough. They suffered all sorts of horrible mutations and disfigurements, and because they carried the radiation with them, they were not welcome in the underwater communities. From time to time, one would make a sudden public appearance and would be headline news for days. Sembado had heard the stories his entire life, but had never actually seen a mutant.

Grandfather slowly looked up at Sembado with vastly disappointed and hopeless blue eyes and dropped his head back down.

"Yeah…the mutants," he said in a very quiet and dejected voice.

"What were they after?" Sembado queried. "What's that?" he followed up, indicating the rough old book under his grandfather's arm.

"It's nothing," Grandfather shot back, making a poor attempt at hiding the book with his other arm.

"Were they trying to get it?"

"Yes."

"But what would mutants want with an old book? What's it about anyway?" Sembado asked, genuinely curious.

"It's about me," Grandfather said coldly, "and my life before this wretched place." He indicated the space all around them. "It's my journal."

"Journal? Someone wrote a book about you?"

"No, dammit. A journal is something that you write for yourself. It's like a blog on paper, only you don't share it. We had to do it for a school project. We were experiencing life before computers. I enjoyed it so much that I kept doing it for myself."

"Oh wow, you mean when you lived on the surface?" Sembado inquired excitedly, ignoring his grandfather's remark.

Before computers? Ha. Blogs are so obsolete.

"Yes. Me and your great grandma and great grandpa and..." He trailed off, beginning to cry again. Eager to change the subject, Sembado followed his curious intuition.

"Well, can I read any of it to you? Perhaps it'd cheer you up," he asked apprehensively.

"No!" Grandfather choked, slamming the cover shut on Sembado's prying fingers. "No."

"Okay," Sembado said. "I guess we should get going then; you should probably come to our place for tonight at least."

"Eh, you're probably right. Lemme grab what I need," Grandfather said, running one hand through his streaky, gray beard.

The old man started to shuffle aimlessly through the mess and pick up random articles in no apparent order. He picked up a metal container and placed the journal inside, locking the box with a key. He then promptly hung the key around his neck, tucking it carefully under his shirt. As he wandered out of the main chamber, Sembado started to have his own look around. He realized that a good portion of the clutter on the floor was pages from his grandfather's journal.

Very interested in what the old journal might contain, Sembado started frantically collecting pages. He grabbed two more just as his grandfather came back in the room.

"What are you doing? Put those down!" the old man barked.

Sembado immediately dropped the pages as if they were contaminated.

"I don't want you goin' through those pages, and I don't want you back around this place again, ya hear." It was not a question.

He then piled a number of funny old appliances and some clothes in Sembado's arms and ushered him out the door. Sembado's heart raced with excitement, but he did not bother mentioning the journal pages already in his pocket.

Chapter Three
April 9

That night found Sembado in bed, a fistful of beef jerky in one hand, and the stolen journal pages in the other. He stuffed his face, wide-eyed with horror, as he read of his grandfather's history and the history of the entire complex. He had learned of the beginnings of the complex when he was still in school, but it had been brief, and did not compare to the personal narrative that lay before him.

March 30, 2021
Journal,
The president announced the opening of the new SAO complex today—Dad says it means Sub-Aquatic Observation. That's the fifth one this year already. The president says it's a positive step in taking the American peoples' minds off of the war, but still stresses that terror attacks are looming more than ever. Americans still aren't allowed to leave the country. He's starting his peace campaign with the Chinese any day now and will have a treaty summit with

the heads of state for the European Union. This whole thing's been going on for twenty years by Dad's count. Anyway, Dad's impressed with the way President Brandt is handling things in such a crazy world. He says he is handling the war much better than the Madam President before him, or even the guy before her. He's only been in office for two months and has already fulfilled his six-month sea-exploration program and pulled the rest of the troops out of France. We learned all about the War this past week in history class. The War on Terror. It started off right at the beginning of the century and got out of control in North Africa and Eastern Europe. Mom says that it's the same thing, but in a different decade. She said in 2005 it was Al-Qaeda, and in 2015 it was the Islamic State, but that it's just the same. The unrest then spread into Europe, India, and China. A whole bunch of oil refineries were blown up, and soon even the most developed countries were battling over what little fuel was available. Eventually the UN had to pull all their health care troops out of Africa to stop the war. This let the warlords in Africa run rampant, using the virus outbreak as a weapon. The publishers of our history book are still waiting for the title of chapter thirty-eight to be okayed as "World War Three." After seven years, the public impeached the president, and his vice president took over for the last few months, but he was nearly assassinated, and wasn't seen much on TV after that. In 2016, this really popular lady was elected who my history teacher, Mr. Sense, says did a really bad job of pulling out troops, but managed to keep the war from escalating any more, or at the times it did, it wasn't her fault. Some North Korean dictator named Kim tried to enter the war on China's side and began fighting with the rest of Southeast Asia. To take the public and news' eyes off the war the president made many failed attempts at a public service research campaign called "Mars: the Next Frontier," which consisted of ships full of researchers, astronauts, and sometimes random civilians being shuttled up to the International Moon Base and then rocketed to Mars. Four times in as many years and over two hundred deaths later, there was no success, and by 2020, which was last year's election, the public was fed up with space, the war, and especially political extremists. So they elected the most moderate candidate possible who went for a more realistic research program, including underwater labs and some living facilities miles underwater. Today, we're still at war and Mom says it's a more depressing and dangerous world than when she grew up. Yea, back in the Nineties. But she seems happy to see that gas went down below ten dollars a gallon. Dad says Brandt has innovative ideas and says he really won over the votes with his proposal for a "Discover the World" approach to research rather than continuing with more Moon colonies and another trip to Mars. I guess anyone would have given up on that after the fourth failed attempt. I wouldn't have done it if I were those astronauts. Anyway, Ben Ryder at school said this new SAO complex is the biggest one yet and can house more than 15 million people! I'd say that's quite a bit. David says that brings the total to more than 750 million with all the world's complexes added together, but the numbers don't seem to add up.

I hear all the adults saying stuff like, "Seems fishy that Brandt'd wanna build so many of these complexes so quickly," followed by a "Yeah, you'd think he knew something we didn't. Ya know I hear North

Korea set off another TDD." David says it means "Total Destruction Device," and Mom said she's glad they changed it, 'cause if she heard WMD one more time she'd scream—it's the third one this week. I hear those things can clear a place out completely, like not a damn thing left for almost a hundred miles! Most of these comments are usually cleared up by a simple, "Yea, but didn't you hear, 'cause of Brandt's complexes going so deep, they discovered two more species just last week!" Then they go on about the new creature and how many fins or eyes it has. I think it's pretty cool. I heard from Ben Ryder at school that the Chinese are already building two, but David thinks he's full of it. I don't care. I'd love to go see one someday. David says Mom and Dad are planning on a vacation to one. He says one of 'em is completely set up for living quarters now and people from all over the world are coming to see 'em. He reckons Mom and Dad'll take us next month for holiday. I think he's full of it.

March 31, 2021
Journal,

David was wrong about Ben. I heard the news guy say today that China has started building two sea labs already and are designing a third. Australia is also starting their own—though Dad says that'll fall through. And to top that, the Japanese are already done with one and onto another. He also said the Scandinavian Union is working on designs, but with little success as their waters are significantly colder than ours. He finished out the report with a live feed from some car factory where his affiliate was interviewing an auto designer about the rumor of plans to build an underwater car, a mini-sub kinda thing that would be affordable, and it would be designed for personal use rather than scientific use. He continued to report about two more detonations in Eastern Siberia, three in West China, and one in our own North Alaska. The White House released a statement saying the test was for research purposes only and was not directed at anyone.

But guess what? I found out I was wrong about David. I went into the kitchen to find Mom and Dad looking at pamphlets for one *of the SAO complexes! They tried to hide it, but Dad gave up—I think he wanted me to see— and told me all about it. "Consider it a fourteenth birthday slash holiday gift," he said.*

I read the pamphlets front to back about a dozen times today. I memorized all the "Sectors."

"Black Sector" is the five-hundredth through the four-hundredth levels below sea level. "Red Sector" is from four hundred up to three. "Gold" is from three to two hundred. "Green" is from two to one. And from there up is "White Sector."

Today was a good day. I can't wait to see Ben's face when he hears I get to go to SAO complex number two, as the pamphlets says.

April 1, 2021
Journal,

Happy April Fool's Day! Ryder wouldn't believe me. Thought I was trying to fool him. I finally convinced him when I showed him the pamphlet. He's so jealous. I talked to David on the phone; he's in New York right now. He told me he wasn't lying, and I found out he gets to take a break from school and his new job to go with us to the SAO complex. He says he's getting excited and can't wait to look at all the cool science things with me and says we'll have a ton of fun. Mom says we leave next Friday to allow for a little travel time. We get to spend my birthday there, April ninth, so we're going to leave early. Dad says we get to spend two weeks there because his big deal with the Samoan client went through. Oh, and I overheard Mom and Dad arguing about the news. Apparently Brandt left the summit unexpectedly, and there's been nothing but news analysts for the past twenty-four hours speculating what it might mean. But, who cares...seven more days!

April 8, 2021
Journal,

We're in Hawaii! We're spending the night here because it's pretty late. Tomorrow we'll pick David up at the airport, and then we all go to the SAO complex! Can't wait.

Sembado paused. He was finding great delight in hearing of his grandfather's memories of the surface, but he knew from his history classes what the next date's entry held.

April 9th, 2021
Journal,

It's nighttime. No one is sleeping. We still haven't received any official news, but everyone's saying it's the end of the world. Or it's the apocalypse or something. Dad says the peace treaties fell through, and that someone fired a TDD. He heard from an older man down the hall that any country with TDD capabilities fired everything they had. Apparently the North Koreans fired at us first. We returned fire. With all of the alliances and treaties, the whole world was soon dragged into the fray. Everyone was bound by what the man referred to as "Political Obligations." For anyone that survives, there won't be anything left to defend. The war is finally over. No one won. Everyone has completely annihilated each other. I imagine only those in remote places escaped the blasts. All the major cities were targeted first: Los Angeles, Chicago, Miami, a number of Texan metropolises, and even worse, New York. David's plane wasn't to leave until midday. The attacks came at daybreak, and his plane couldn't have departed yet. He's lost. He's gone. Mom still hasn't stopped crying. Neither have I, to be honest. I tried not to cry so I could appear strong like the other men, but I think my dad was onto me, because he told me to never, ever hide my feelings, and he cried too. After the announcements and warnings, we were rushed by the authorities with everyone else to the SAO complex for protection from the fallout. I didn't want to go in without David, but Dad forced me. I tried so hard to get away from those men as they helped us into the pressurizing chamber, but it was no use. Dad helped them drag me inside...

Sembado's eyes welled with tears. He had heard his grandfather complain of the complex before, but never with such utter resentment. He pitied his grandfather, for he already felt claustrophobic from the description, a sensation he'd never felt before...

They've had us in lockdown for five hours now. Dad volunteered to help the other men. Every so often, he comes back to check on me and Mom. He updates me on how many new people have arrived in the past hour. They're arriving by the thousands. They're fleeing from the reported fallout from the TDDs. They have to be decontaminated. I keep hoping that by some impossible chance the next time Dad comes back, he will have David with him and say, "Look, Hyron! Look! I found your brother. He escaped the blast and found his way to Hawaii to come stay with us! Isn't that wonderful?" And then David and I will get to go explore the complex, and we'll get to help the men usher people around and greet them aboard, but it doesn't happen. Each time he arrives, his face is more troubled and sad than the last. Every time he comes back, an unchallengeable wave of disappointment washes over me, and I fall deeper into a dreadful state of depression. There's a pit in my stomach that aches. I miss David so much, and I feel helpless against the truth. Why did this have to happen to him? Why did this have to happen to us? Why did this have to happen to me? Why? If I could do something to fix it, I would. A million other older brothers could die in his place if I could only have him back. But I know that's not right, wishing that on someone else. I feel alone in this dark room, with its thick windows and gloomy water outside. I feel trapped. How long will we be here? I need to get out immediately. Then I can go to New York and find David. As soon as I can get out...

There was an ear-ringing silence. Sembado now realized that David was the great-uncle that his dad had mentioned only once in passing. Grandfather never spoke of him, and now Sembado knew why. There was one final entry, but by this point Sembado almost did not want to read it. He pressed on in hopes that there would be some uplifting news.

> *April 10, 2021*
> *Journal,*
>
> *There's no chance of escaping. Dad told me the entire complex has been placed under lockdown until further notice. We might have to live here forever. I'm already starting to hate this place. I hate the stupid metal walls, and the stupid submarine doors, and I especially hate those stupid guards who patrol the halls, giving out friendly advice in a sad attempt at brightening the faces of those who have lost. What do they know?*

Sembado stared at the pages blankly. That was it. There was nothing else on the page but angry little sketches and doodles.

It was obvious that the younger version of his grandfather did not understand that the complex government only wanted to protect them, and that they were safer in the complex than they had ever been on the surface. Crime was so well controlled by the penalty officers that even the smallest incidences made the news. Mostly it was an occasional mutant attack like his grandfather's today.

As he was setting the pages back under his bed, a small scrap that had been stuck on the passages came loose and fell to the floor. Sembado picked it up and examined it. This piece of paper was much newer than the old, yellowed journal entries. To his surprise, the little note had a date that was just days away. It read:

WEDNESDAY

AUGUST 13, 2084

20:00

T.M.—CIVILLION

What could T.M. mean? Probably Terranean Memories.

Terranean Memories was a shop down in the Civillion that specialized in different products that were used back when people use to live on land. Some of the interesting things Sembado had seen there were a bicycle, a kite, and a potted tomato plant.

Grandfather spent a lot of time there if he was ever down in the Civillion. The man who ran the store was just as old as Grandfather, and they would frequently reminisce about the past. That had to be the place.

Sembado studied the note a little longer before tucking it away with the other pages and falling off to sleep.

Chapter Four
Pale Yellow Lines

It took a few days for everyone's excitement from Grandfather's attack to subside, but eventually Sembado was the only one still interested, and even he couldn't keep his full attention on Grandfather when he was awakened suddenly the next morning. He opened his eyes to see grinning faces hovering in and out of his vision. His two best friends, Meligose and Kreymond, were standing over his bed making ugly faces. Kreymond had just started to lightly smack Sembado's forehead when Sembado realized he was not dreaming.

"Stop it!" he snapped, annoyed but amused. "What are you guys doing?"

"Watchin' a sea cow sleep." Meligose laughed, pushing his long, blond hair back over his head. He sat down on the foot of Sembado's bed, his tall fame still towering over Kreymond as he sat. He barely dodged the pillow Sembado threw at him.

"We're gonna go 4D," said Kreymond, catching the pillow before it knocked over a lamp. His bright smile contrasted greatly against his dark-brown skin. "Get out of bed, floater. We're meeting Jean Paul for the four-by-four. Remember?"

Sembado mulled it over. They had signed up for a four-by-four tournament weeks ago, but he hadn't thought they would be chosen. And in the excitement of Grandfather's attack, he had completely forgotten about it. He still wanted to look into Grandfather's journal pages, but he loved 4D, and before he could say anything, Kreymond beat him to the punch.

"Your mom already told us you don't work today. Don't be fresh, Sem. The tournament starts in forty minutes."

Grandfather's journal was thrown to the back of his mind at the prospect of the tournament. The three friends were some of the best in the local complex, and they often had their old schoolmate, Jean Paul Midreaux, round out their team for a tournament. Sembado was dressed and out the door in three minutes with a sandwich in each hand. He arrived at the arena empty-handed in less than five.

The arena held the 4D events. It was two passages away from the Civillion, and when the boys arrived there was a line out the door. Those waiting either did not have a reservation or were there to watch the tournament. Sembado followed Kreymond and Meligose past the crowd and up to the registration desk. The attendant, Zetvez, was only slightly older than them, and he recognized his best customers right away. His brightly colored, spiked hair and flamboyant earrings shuddered as he nodded to each of them in turn.

"What's wet, fell's?" he said casually, tossing a visor, vest, and plastic gun to each of them. The equipment behind the desk was shared by all patrons, but Zetvez had made a habit of setting their preferred gear aside for them.

"Who we versin' today, Zet?" asked Kreymond, his afro bouncing back into place as his vest fell over his head and onto his shoulders. He was well-practiced at maintaining an air of coolness for the younger patrons who were listening in.

Sembado and his friends continued suiting up while Zetvez replied.

"Well..." he said, looking over the tournament brackets on his screen, "those fish from the far-south end of the complex lost yesterday, so I guess it's your group versin' that crazy Japanese squad."

"Great," said Sembado, eyeing his friends nervously.

"We got this," Meligose said. "And Jean Paul's been practicing all week," he added, pulling his yellow mane through the straps on his headset.

"And we're gonna drown every one of 'em." Jean Paul added, pushing a nearby bathroom door open into a crowd of young boys. He was fully suited with his visor up; his beady black eyes surveyed the younger onlookers proudly. After greetings and handshakes, he offered his advice.

"Zet said the arena's been reconfigured for this round, but we can't scout it out until fifteen minutes before."

"Rules are rules." Zetvez chimed in without looking up from his monitor. "You got about five more minutes." He tossed them each half a dozen mobile sensors and began booting up the system.

"Let's calibrate one last time before doing the recon walk," Sembado said.

The four teammates took turns lowering their helmet visors and looking at the calibration board next to Zetvez's desk. Their visors held a projection of a virtual world in a contoured screen that enveloped their vision. Sembado watched Kreymond square his bulky frame to the wall, his head twitching as he went through the calibration process. To Sembado's right, Jean Paul was using his reflection in one of the arena monitoring screens to preen his meticulously manicured hair.

Sembado shook his head in disapproval as he took his turn standing in front of the calibration board. He did not appreciate Jean Paul's vanity in the slightest. The board was a man-sized rectangular panel that hung on the wall. It had a multicolored target at its center. He stood with his feet on the blue footprints on the floor and squared his shoulders with the panel just as Kreymond had. He pulled his visor down over his eyes. The visor was blank for a moment before the familiar loading bar and calibration symbols began to dance in front of Sembado's eyes. White shapes popped around his peripheral vision. No matter how hard he strained to look up, down, left, or right, the shape and size of the visor kept its extreme edges out of his vision. The configuration process required him to follow the dancing shapes with his eyes. Despite the fact that Sembado had completed this process over a thousand times in his life, it never failed to make him slightly nauseous. After the initial calibration, the weapon configuration took place. A panel, identical to the calibration board, was projected into Sembado's vision. Along with the board, boundaries of the walls, ceiling, and floor were projected as pale yellow lines. These lines kept the players aware of their real world limits, so they did not accidentally collide with them. The virtual board and the wall it was on slid away from Sembado, so that it got smaller as it moved away. As usual, the faint yellow lines stayed in place because the real-world boundaries they represented remained static. The virtual board stopped at what was supposed to represent fifty feet. Sembado pointed his weapon at the center of the board, and a red dot appeared near the edge of the target. Sembado carefully moved the dot to the center of the target, took aim, and fired. The target flashed green and moved ten feet closer. This process was repeated until the final shot was taken at point blank range where the virtual board had started.

The final step was to calibrate the body equipment's movement-capturing capability. Sembado performed a series of familiar callisthenic-like movements. After the other teammates had finished, Zetvez gave them the go-ahead to enter the arena.

Being familiar with an arena was one of the most critical steps in a 4D match. To stress this point, players were given fifteen minutes to scout the arena together. This time was often spent identifying good cover points, possible sniper positions to be wary of, and other ways to take advantage of either the real or virtual boundaries. Teams would also typically use this time to come up with terms and code words to refer to various features so that they could rendezvous or identify an opponent more efficiently. As they walked they flipped their visors up and down to see the different spaces and rooms as real and virtual. The theme of this tournament was an industrial one, and the virtual arena was presented as a rough, steel-clad factory. The four young men had just turned into a hallway when Sembado put down his visor again. To his surprise, this hallway had been turned into a catwalk in the virtual world. The walls were replaced with pipe railings, which overlooked the floor below on either side. He looked at the virtual projections of his friends. Each one was represented by avatars that they had customized over the years. Kreymond and Jean Paul ran back the way they came. Sembado saw them reappear one level down on either side of the catwalk. They moved around pieces of machinery, which were outlined in the pale yellow lines. He knew that the rooms they were moving through were shaped like the spaces between the machinery. A hallway between the two sides connected them directly below the catwalk a few feet ahead of Sembado and Meligose. Sembado could see virtual representations of his friends waving up at him, but if he pushed his visor up, he would be staring at the floor of the hallway. Their Japanese opponents were scouting an identically configured arena in their own complex. These opponents would be virtually projected into Sembado's team's visors, but they could not interact physically. This feature not only allowed teams to play remotely and long distance, but it also kept players from physically hurting each other. Suddenly, they heard Zetvez over the intercom.

"Just a warning guys—we have seven minutes until go. It looks like the other bracket will be between the European team that beat those south-end fish, and those tricky Australians."

A four-by-four tournament was a special kind of 4D match. The first round consisted of two simultaneous matches. This was the first bracket. Sembado and his friends were playing the Japanese team in the first round. The European and Australian teams would begin their match at the same time. As soon as each first-bracket match was over, the winning teams would immediately face each other. This meant that the team who won first would get a break to catch their breath, as 4D was very physically strenuous. The disadvantage usually came for the second winning team, because they could sometimes be playing continuously for an hour or more between two straight matches. Some teams would try for the paced endurance strategy and play at a consistent speed the whole time. Sembado's team had a different strategy. They would go full-out and play aggressively through the first round. This full offensive took most teams off guard and could usually win a match relatively early, giving them a lot of breathing room between matches. However, this also meant that their second round had to be played more defensively. They would find a room or space that could be defended and hold out as long as possible.

This worked well in four-by-four matches because each team was allowed one ghost player. Ghost player status was swapped to a new team member every two minutes. For those two minutes, the player with ghost status was invisible to everyone on the opposing team, except for their ghost. This would lead to interesting strategies and techniques, but there were consequences for the ghost. If a ghost player was shot by the opposing ghost then that team lost any ghost status for a full minute. This made the ghostless team extremely vulnerable to the opposing ghost, because none of them could see it. The only thing to do in this case was to fortify the team in a room with a door lined with proximity mines, which even exploded for ghost players.

When a player was shot, whether he had ghost status or not, he had to run back to the team haven to reboot. He would be invisible to opponents, and could also not see or hear them either. This kept a "dead" player from running around to scout opponent locations for their team.

The audio system used in 4D made it important to be stealthy and use nonverbal signals. If Sembado was discussing strategies or battle movements with a teammate, microphones in their complex would play that conversation in the corresponding location of the opponent's complex. In this way, people could play as teammates from long distances and have conversations between avatars if necessary. This remote system for teammates was used in the bigger ten-by-ten matches that happened once a month. It also meant that if two players were talking in one arena, a player in another arena could eavesdrop like they were right around the corner. This phenomenon was often exploited by a team that was trying to cause a noisy distraction to take the attention away from their clandestine ghost. Ghost players would often eavesdrop as well.

"Heads up lil' fishies—two minute warning."

Zetvez played an important role in the match; he could direct his announcements only to his local arena if he wanted. He could also communicate with the other arena attendants, but typically only did that to announce a kill by their local players. Because most attendants had a similar relationship with their best players like Zetvez did with Sembado and his friends, they would typically get more animated and dramatic for their home players' kills.

The boys finished up scouting the arena before returning to their team haven.

"Here we go, boys. This is it. Match beings in 3…2…1…Go!"

"All right, boys," said Meligose. "We're gonna get to that catwalk and go from there. We can use the high line of site. Whoever gets ghost first will roam and hunt down below. Shout out if you see the other ghost. Let's hit 'em hard and fast. We're gonna drown 'em!" Meligose often took the lead. He was the best at keeping morale up.

The four teammates stepped out of their haven in single file. Sembado was third in line, and when he stepped out of the haven, the edge of his visor blinked and glowed black.

"All right guys," Sem said. "I have first ghost, keep an eye out."

He ran off to the left as the others quickly plodded to the catwalk. Sembado soon found himself on the factory floor. He carefully avoided the pale yellow lines as he darted in and out of hissing, sparking machinery. He had just enough time to glance up to see his friends setting up position at the end of the catwalk before he trotted on through the main floor. As Sembado's teammates disappeared from his line of sight, he caught a glimpse of another player running past a three-way intersection ahead. Was it the other ghost? Sembado looked down at the status monitor on his wrist; he had one minute and twenty seconds left in ghost mode. He would need at least twenty seconds to get back to his team, which meant that he had about a minute of his ghost status left. He approached the three-way hallway intersection carefully, and gave a startled twitch when one of the Japanese players rounded the corner and ran right through his avatar. It was one of their nonghost players, and he was followed by the other two. They hugged the walls in a crouched fashion as they moved at a cautious, yet confident pace. Sembado smiled as he activated one of two grenades each player was allotted and rolled it after his opponents. He would get more from the equipment crates scattered about. They had little time to react and merely scrambled before the blast took them.

"And the Sea Tones get a hot start with a triple-kill! Booooom!"

Sembado smirked at Zetvez's theatrics. His dead opponents quickly disappeared, surely heading back to their haven. Sembado peeked at his status; he had about twenty seconds before he had to head back. He rounded the corner the three Japanese players had come from in time to see their ghost player taking aim at him from about ten feet.

It was a trap!

A clean head shot left a vibrant skull laughing in his visor, the same death alarm he had just given his three opponents. Sembado berated himself with obscenities as he sprinted back to his haven, reluctantly listening to the other team's announcer as he went.

"And the Hikiro Supreme ghost gets a stunning ghost kill!"

This was salt in the wound for Sembado's already bruised ego.

Experienced players would have never rounded that corner so wildly. They were just setting me up. I can't believe I fell for that!

He was rebooted in a moment and snuck back toward the catwalk. The three kills he had gotten were not enough to outweigh his own death. A ghost-to-ghost kill was worth four times as many points as a normal kill. His team was already losing thanks to him, but the winning team had to score a significant amount of points to end the match, and neither team was even close at this point.

Sembado shrugged off the embarrassment as he approached the catwalk. It was hard to ignore the feeling of vulnerability since the other team had the only player with ghost status for the next minute. He found some cover on the catwalk where the open railings were replaced by solid panels for about six feet. Suddenly, a barrage of fire came from the lower level of the arena. He listened for any kill announcements. To his amusement, Zetvez made a kill notice.

"Oh, and another point for the Sea Tones—"

But before he could finish, the other team's commentator interrupted.

"And that kill is countered by the Supreme for another point. Keep up the lead, men!"

Sembado smirked at the thought of Zetvez rolling his eyes. Then he spotted two of his teammates appearing from where he had been killed. It was Meligose and Jean Paul. They were racing back across the factory floor. He would meet them back at their haven. Forty seconds left with no team ghost. He stood quickly and reached for the catwalk railing for support. He rolled his eyes at himself when his hand merely smacked the flat wall of the hallway he was actually in. He reprimanded himself again.

Amateur mistakes, Sem. Get it together.

He backed away to the end of the catwalk. Before he could turn to leave, he caught a glimpse of the other team cautiously entering the other end of the catwalk. He laid down some intimidating fire before running back to his team haven.

38

He found his whole team waiting for him. He recognized the blue glow around his teammates' avatars that indicated their visors were up. He pushed his visor up to join the conversation, butting in to offer his apologies.

"I'm really sorry, guys. I can't believe I fell for a three-for-one."

Meligose responded first, leading the conversation as usual.

"Don't worry about it; we have thirty more seconds of no ghost left, but we're only down five to four. When you were out scouting we got another, but Krey got hit. He just got back with us before you."

"Yea, I saw you guys from the catwalk."

Jean Paul joined in with strategy advice.

"So we're gonna head out to the catwalk again. Before we leave the haven, let's have everyone switch over to proxy mines and throw those out ahead of us to guard against that ghost. We gotta keep our heads down in the big spaces in case of a sniper. We've killed another ten seconds, so let's get ready to go out. Heads down, eyes up, boys. Let's do this!" The teammates dropped their visors and lined out of the haven.

They stopped every few steps to throw proximity mines ahead. By the time they had approached the catwalk, Jean Paul's avatar had acquired the black aura that indicated ghost status to his teammates. He dropped down and headed to the front of the line, constantly scanning for the opposing ghost. The other three boys took turns tossing out the proximity mines. They were down to five as a team.

Sembado, bringing up the rear, had both of his mines still available. They took turns moving from one cover point to the next. Each one covered the one ahead as they made their move. Jean Paul was midway across the catwalk when he held up his fist, indicating the others should stop. He extended all five digits and wiggled them animatedly. Sembado hunkered down for cover. He'd spotted the other ghost.

For some reason, this made Sembado think to check their rear, one of his responsibilities at the back of the group. Just as he was swinging his head around, Jean Paul took aim at the other ghost and fired.

"Grenade inbound!" Jean Paul yelled, but he was able to kick it off the catwalk before it detonated. Sembado jerked as the grenade exploded more loudly than expected. He then realized that one of the proximity mines behind them had just exploded simultaneously with the grenade.

"We got floaters at our rear!" he shouted. He steadied his gun in anticipation of an opponent appearing around the corner. Then the kill announcements came in. Zetvez couldn't have sounded prouder.

"And that's one ghost and, count 'em, three regular kills! The Sea Tones get an instant team wipe with a ghost-on-ghost bonus! Seven points and a power play!"

"All right guys, we have one minute for them, and I have about a hundred seconds left," said Jean Paul excitedly. Jean Paul was the most efficient ghost they had, and having him on a power play was even better. Sembado could not believe their turn of fortune. They were suddenly beating the Japanese team eleven to five. The match ended at thirty points.

Jean Paul took off across the catwalk as cavalierly as possible, an attitude indicative of a player with the sole ghost status in a match.

"All he has to do is steer clear of any proxies, and I bet he drowns the whole team again." Kreymond laughed.

Sembado, Meligose, and Kreymond spent the next minute cautiously patrolling the arena. They felt confident in their newly won lead, but they all knew from the recent turn of events how fickle leads could be. Their worries began to fade as they received two more points by the time the other team had reclaimed ghost status. Sembado and his two current companions had just rendezvoused with Jean Paul, the winner of the two additional points, when his ghost status was transferred to Kreymond. Kreymond continued on with the other three while his ghost status continued.

The match started getting hectic after that. Within five minutes, ghost status had been given back to Sembado, and the score was eighteen to thirteen. Sembado's team still held the lead, but five points did not constitute a comfortable margin in a four-by-four.

The next fifteen minutes were a blur, with each team stepping up their aggression. This resulted in three more ghost-to-ghost kills, only one of which went to the Sea Tones. Soon the score was twenty-six to twenty-four, and Sembado and his friends were trying desperately to hold their lead. This was one of the longest four-by-four matches he had ever played. The team had just converged in their haven after Meligose had given up the most recent ghost-to-ghost kill. His only redemption came in the form of a double-kill shortly before dying himself.

The no-ghost status had just expired, and it was Jean Paul's turn again. Sembado and his friends had repeated the strategy throughout the match to cover the catwalk first before launching a hard offensive. They had been using this technique as a long-term strategy; they had been luring the Japanese team into a rhythm and then switching it up at the last minute. At Meligose's orders, they split up into teams of two and swarmed the lower level of the factory floor. One team, Meligose and Kreymond, went to the right, while Sembado followed closely behind Jean Paul as they ran past the site of Sembado's death at the beginning of the match. Before they trotted into the hallway, Sembado took the chance to toss a proximity mine to the underside of the catwalk, hoping to get an extra kill later on. Jean Paul was only a few inches taller than Sembado, but his legs were disproportionately long, and Sembado had to jog briskly to keep up with his teammate. Suddenly, the Japanese announcer came in over the intercom.

"Oh! The Supremes get a hard double-kill with a frag grenade. Boom!"

Sembado swore under his breath, but shook it off with Zetvez's additional announcement.

"But the Sea Tones answered back with a quick kill of their own before going down! They're still in the lead."

Then Zetvez's voice came in on their visors, which meant it was a message for their team only.

"Guys, I'm sorry I didn't get to you sooner. I only just heard myself, but those Aussies were caught cheating and were disqualified a half hour ago. The Europeans are just waiting for ya. You're gonna need to lock it down and catch your breath before the match is over.

Sembado could not believe it. He was already near exhaustion; another match against a fresh team would be impossible.

"This is porpoise spray!" spat Jean Paul angrily. The two were doubling back to their haven to discuss their strategy with their recently killed teammates. He continued protesting as they ran. Jean Paul's complaining was one thing that would normally annoy Sembado, but he shared his friend's heated sentiment this time.

"It might be easier if we had heard the news a half hour ago, but now the match is nearly over. At least if we had a healthy lead, we could let them get a couple easy kills to drag it out and get some rest, but now they're near thirty too. We can't afford any giveaways!"

They got back to their haven right after their teammates, and Sembado pushed up his visor angrily as Jean Paul whipped his off in a dramatic fashion.

"What are we going to do?" he said furiously. He was pacing.

"We'll have to hold out in the haven as long as possible," suggested Meligose disappointedly. Holding up in a haven was not illegal in 4D, but "camping" was highly frowned upon, and teams could lose a great deal of respect from their peers for hiding out.

"No. We aren't camping this match, or the next one!" Sembado said. He was picking up some of Jean Paul's indignation, but he had his own feelings of betrayal as well. He took the lead as he channeled his frustration into an attack strategy. The others, emboldened by his example, listened intently and reinforced his passion. "We'll split up, all four individually. We only need three more kills, so whoever sees an opponent first, use a grenade if you can. If you get shot, then we've only given them one kill, and the others can give it another try. We can worry about the next match when we get there."

The team went out seething, but focused, and Sembado's strategy worked like a charm. The match was soon over with Sembado getting a double-kill before being shot himself, and Meligose sniping an opponent from across the factory floor for the final kill.

The four teammates sat in their haven with their visors up, breathing hard and sweating. The only spare time they were afforded between the matches was the time it took Zetvez and the European attendant to synchronize and load the new game.

Familiarity with the arena layout would not have normally been an advantage for one team over another, but Sembado's team had played a long, difficult match. That kind of burning experience offered a more intuitive environment for a player compared to the kind of analytical walkthrough that the European team had been limited to.

The European team had been waiting nearly forty-five minutes for Sembado's match to end. Their fresh lungs would be a very strong advantage, but they did not have the pace and momentum that Sembado and his friends had, and they had spent that whole time overanalyzing the match to come. Despite these psychological impediments, the European team, The EuroPact, had a diverse and skilled team that was not even remotely as exhausted as Sembado and his teammates. Meligose voiced these very concerns as they sat and savored their break for as long as it lasted.

"This is going to be crazy intense, but I really liked that last strategy Sem thought up. I say we stick with it, and see how far it takes us." Kreymond and Jean Paul nodded in approval, each smacking Sembado's shoulder in admiration. These characteristics were very indicative of the four friends: Meligose took the lead, Jean Paul got heated and passionate, Kreymond kept things lighthearted, and Sembado thought things through. They were the perfect foursome, and that realization inspired Sembado to look past the overwhelming challenge ahead. He shared this with his friends, and soon they were passing motivational anecdotes. Soon, they were completely exhilarated; they jumped and yelled as if they were children again. They had gotten their second wind, and it came with a high that enveloped them in an energetic euphoria. Their rally came at the perfect time, as Zetvez had just announced the beginning of the next match. Nobody had to speak. Nobody could speak. They were feeling loud, proud, and energized. They ran out of the haven at full speed, pulling down their visors as they went.

It could not have been more obvious how much the Europeans had overestimated the Sea Tones' fatigue. It took ten whole minutes of the Sea Tones attacking with Sembado's strategy before the Europeans wised up and developed a defense. By that time, Sembado and his teammates had used sacrificial kills to work up an early lead of eighteen to ten over the EuroPact. Unfortunately, the Sea Tones' endurance started to fail them just as the Europeans were gaining their own momentum. Neither the loss of stamina nor the opposing team's momentum shift would be a fatal challenge by themselves, but together they made a deadly combination. Soon, the Sea Tones felt downright oppressed. They were trying to keep up with Sembado's newfound guerilla technique, but their exhaustion had them waiting up to thirty seconds in the haven, the longest time they could bear waiting without feeling like cheaters. Sembado had just trotted back to the haven from a death when Zetvez's voice was heard over the speaker again.

"Hey! I told you little eels to...oh deeks! Boys, we got a prob..." As the feed cut out, the equipment deactivated. Sembado pushed his visor up to see the emergency lighting directing him and his friends to the exit. Meligose was close by. He and Sembado exchanged puzzled looks. Kreymond and Jean Paul could be heard rounding a corner nearby.

"What the depths! I know we did not lose!" Jean Paul whined, clearly stressing each syllable as he did when he was upset.

The teammates were about to begin their speculative discussion when a new voice was heard over the intercom. It was definitely not Zetvez.

"You will vacate the four-dimensional training arena immediately or face penalties."

"Snaps! What the S?" said Kreymond, trotting away instantly.

"Yea, this is bad," said Sembado, and he and Meligose followed close behind.

"This is the most inconvenient experience ever," Jean Paul declared, bringing up the rear. His tirade continued right into the control chamber.

As they rounded the corner, the three remaining boys found a room full of penalty officers, two of whom were commandeering Kreymond's equipment. Kreymond looked terrified.

One of the two officers turned to address Sembado and the others.

"We are utilizing any available equipment for mandatory government training. Hand over your guns and visors. They will be returned to the attendant's stocks when we are finished."

As Sembado listened to the decree, he caught a peek at the other main officer's face. The man looked very familiar, and while Sembado could not put his finger on it, seeing the man made him feel very uneasy. He then realized Jean Paul was marching right up to the officers.

"The government doesn't have its own equipment?" He protested. "This is ridiculous. This is entirely unprofessional. I will not be giving you my…"

In an instant, the second officer had grabbed Jean Paul by the back of the neck and had his face pinned again Zetvez's countertop. After the initial impact, he continued to smear the boy's face to one side; his perfect hair was ruined. The man bent down so his face was only inches from Jean Paul's.

The room, training officers included, took a collective gasp, but before any more was said, the first officer was between them, pushing the assaulting officer away and consoling Jean Paul to a minimal level. The officer that accosted Jean Paul braced the arm with which he had attacked.

"Why don't you four get out of here? Zetvez is it? Set up a five, ten, twenty match for my twenty-five guys."

Sembado, Kreymond, and Meligose quickly ushered an increasingly furious Jean Paul out of the control chamber.

Chapter Five
Nighttime Reconnaissance

Despite all the excitement the past few days had offered, Sembado still kept his grandfather's appointment note fresh in his mind. The date on the note had arrived, and Sembado's heart raced as he hurried off to work.

Sembado worked for a man named Mr. Fenguino doing small civil service projects. Mr. Fenguino was an old man, older than Sembado's father, but still much younger than Grandfather. He was a short, squat man of mostly Italian heritage, as he liked to boast, with big arms and a big head. He always let you know that he was one of the very few Americans left in the complex with a distinguishable lineage. He looked not unlike a gorilla, and had a very similar attitude. Sporting a long, deep scar across his chin and having suffered a very bad burn on his left arm, he reminded Sembado of the pictures of pirates he had seen in history books. Despite all these intimidating qualities, Sembado had come to know him as an honest and fair man, regardless of whose feelings he hurt.

The two of them had been working for two weeks on a civil service project updating some lower-grade housing units. Mr. Fenguino was a contractor, and bid for the lowest prices on civil service projects of that type. The lowest bidder then won the contract from the complex government, and fixed up the housing facilities or whatever else the project involved. Some parts of the complex were more than sixty years old, and many such projects were now springing up everywhere. The government auctioned off the work in order to create more jobs for the thousands of young people like Sembado who were now old enough to join the workforce. Mr. Fenguino and Sembado won many of the auctions on the smaller projects because their operation was small, so they didn't have much labor cost or overhead. This particular project involved a group of housing units only a dozen or so levels above Grandfather's place. Sembado had been rushing through work that day. He had much to do that night, and very little time.

"What the hell are you doing!"

Sembado had been resurfacing one of the walls of a master bedroom, and had accidentally cut an inch too deep for the last foot and a half.

"Oh, deeks! Sorry, Rick. I didn't realize I—" Sembado started. He was completely distracted by what he was planning to do that night.

"That's the third time today, Sem! Didn't taking a lunch clear your mind at all? Damn, boy!"

Mr. Fenguino was always quick to erupt, but he never got nasty. If he was ever yelling at you, you probably deserved it.

"I…I guess not, sir, sorry."

The truth is, taking that lunch had only given Sembado more time to think over the night's plans and walk through them a couple more times in his mind. He had never snuck out before.

Mr. Fenguino sighed. An honestly fed up sigh, not the dramatic ones Sembado's brother, Herbert, let out when he had to expel the garbage.

"Eh, it's almost seven anyway. Just get here a half hour early tomorrow and throw some filler compound in there, huh? And don't forget to let it dry this time. And get some sleep kid. You've been weird all day." He turned around to put his tools away. "And Sem, watch out for those mutants, huh? I heard they were spotted down in the Civillion again—"

By the time he looked up, Sembado was gone.

"Damn kids."

***

Sembado raced back to his house. He jammed his arm in the doors of two different lifts so he wouldn't miss them, and ran out first, completely ignoring the glares and mutterings. He closed the door quietly when he got home. He had oiled the hinges the night before with some solvent he borrowed for Mr. Fenguino. He didn't want to attract anyone's attention. His dad was not home yet, and his mother was busy in the galley getting dinner ready. Herbert was probably over at Jamboid's place. Grandfather must have already left. Back in his room, Sembado dropped his tools on his desk and went under his mattress for the journal pages. With a quick glance down the hall to see if his mom was still occupied, he dashed toward the door and slipped out unnoticed.

***

Sembado got down to the Civillion entrance at five after seven. He entered on the north side, which was connected to his side of the complex. He was very used to the sights, sounds, and smells he encountered when first coming out of the tunnel entrance.

As he walked in, the ceiling rose to its fifty-foot-high glass top. Sunlight would have shown down through this glass ceiling if it did not have the numerous expansions of the complex crisscrossing above it. The many living quarters looked like interwoven fingers, allowing only a small amount of sunlight to get through.

Dozens of light ports had been installed decades ago to solve this problem. These ports were hubs that brought sunlight from the surface down to deeper levels with fiber optic cables. This type of lighting was used all over the complex. Presently, the sun's bright rays shined down around the Civillion, casting shadows under the many awnings.

All around the rim of this dome were vines that had been allowed to grow up the dome or down, whatever the shop owners would allow. The Civillion itself was approximately three hundred feet across; there were a few dozen shops around the perimeter. *Terranean Memories* was one that had allowed its resident ivy to over grow on itself and its neighboring courtyard. The courtyard was used for the customers of the shop's previous dwellers, who ran a restaurant of some sort. It closed before Sembado was born, and you could no longer see anything in the courtyard. Its wrought iron skeleton had grown an ivy skin, but Sembado's mother had once said that the courtyard used to be accessible through a back door.

He stood for a moment and scanned the Civillion. The evening's vendors had already set up shop in three-tiered pits that sat at the center of the plaza. The ever-growing crowd slowly circled the pits with an organic pulse, each of its members craning their heads for a glimpse of the barterers' goods.

There were a few present-day restaurants around the Civillion, including the Thai place, *Siamese Sunrise*, which was one of the first shops you passed on the way in from the north side. Every time Sembado passed through, he was overwhelmed with the smells of peanuts and garlic. He had eaten there many times and liked it very much, although Grandfather said it was not what it used to be. He would not take his grandfather's advice tonight. With a steaming bag of spring rolls in hand, he made his way to the center of the Civillion.

On any busy day, musicians would set up along the pits or outside some shop that needed more customers attracted. Most would set up near the Aquarics. This is where the wealthy young people who just received their class A certification would go to look at their first real vehicle, unlike the dinky, one-man Swimbler that Sembado's parents had purchased for him at *Jet Setters*, the used personal-sub dealer. The musicians would set up their computers and sample their various electronic mixes; some even brought real instruments.

The real residents in the center pits were the barterers. These were the merchants that would either haggle for the price of their steady line of goods or pawn various random things that they either found underwater or scavenged from the garbage. One time, Sembado had heard one of them barking out to the highest bidder for something called an anchor, whatever that was.

Sembado continued to scan the crowd as he finished eating his cabbage-filled treats. A large crowd was convened at the Aquarics. In the display window was the object of affection for most of the young, and old, men in the complex: the Beranius X Series Model 230. Sembado had been lucky enough to score a chance to sit on it the week before. But even if he had his class A, he would never be able to afford a fraction of the ten thousand coin price tag. He admired it from afar for a few minutes before returning to the task at hand. He continued toward his preplanned watch spot.

He settled down on the top rim of the eastern center pit. He was positioned with his side to *Terranean Memories*, but from there he could keep an eye on its entrance and the three main entrances as well. He didn't know if his grandfather would be coming from the north side for sure.

There he sat, and waited.

7:18.

7:35.

It was 7:55 p.m. and still no sign of Grandfather. The crowd had surged in the last half hour. The trade school had probably just got out. After a long day of troubleshooting malfunctioning robots or learning to bind glass, most of the students would come down to the Civillion to relax.

Was this one of the reasons the appointment was at this time? To provide cover for Grandfather?

Having to now stand up to keep *Terranean Memories* in sight through the crowd and even craning his neck to see all the exits, Sembado grew nervous as the minutes ticked on, hoping not to miss Grandfather making his appearance.

7:58.

7:59.

"Sembado! What's a goin', drifter?" Meligose's head came bobbing over the surrounding crowd as he forced his way into Sembado's view of *Terranean Memories*. Sembado's heart raced as he tried desperately to see around Meligose and the others that were crowded around. They were apparently trying to get a good look at a set of new ultra-compact oxygen tanks a nearby vendor was trying to sell. Sembado's efforts were in vain. He lashed out at his friend.

"Deeks, Sem, I didn't mean to squid ya," he said, nervously running his fingers through his blond hair.

"You didn't squid me!" Sembado snapped. "I was trying to…" He trailed off, now aware of how strange it would be to say he was stalking his grandfather, which was exactly what he was doing.

"To what?"

"I was trying to get a look at that fishie over there." He lied, indicating a group of girls nearby.

"What? Which one? In the green scuba?"

"Uh…no. She must have gone into *Saren's* there."

"Deeks, oh well. So, what are you down to? Ooo, *Siam*!" Meligose said excitedly, grabbing the bag out of Sembado's hand. When he realized it was empty he balled it up and threw it at Sembado's head.

"Huh?"

Sembado was still trying to steal a glance at the shop entrance. Meligose apparently caught this.

"Oh, is she back?" Meligose asked, pushing his hair behind his ears.

"What? Oh, no, sorry man."

He was forced to give up. He'd have to figure something else out. He instead joined Meligose, whose attention had turned to the nearby merchant. He was still trying to find a higher bidder in the growing crowd.

"Come on, folks!" He barked. "It's got a thirty-six hour supply, can fit in most of your PS storage compartments, and still only weighs a little over ten pounds. Look. I'm holding it with one hand."

"That is pretty cool," whispered Meligose, afraid of being accosted by the oxygen salesman.

"I'll give ya one hundred coins!" yelled a man in the crowd.

"Ten coins? Sir, this is an investment here. What can you get for a hundred coins? Do I hear a hundred? Ninety-five?" he asked patronizingly, turning to any other potential clients.

"I can take your mother and all your sisters out to dinner, you overweight sea horse!" spat the man, as he turned and stormed off, followed by a few laughs.

"Anyone else?" the merchant asked, looking around more desperately. It seemed this last interaction had turned off many in the crowd.

The boys moved on, leaving only a handful of genuinely interested customers to talk to the vendor.

"Class was so shallow tonight," Meligose said as they walked through the crowds of people, skirting around the larger crowds to see who or what they were giving their attention to. One man was selling puppies of some kind, a very rare and expensive luxury these days. They were snaking their way to the Aquarics. They always passed by at least once, just out of habit.

"Me and Akio, that Japanese dude I told you about, we had to fix this little humanoid we got stuck with. A practice model of course, but it wouldn't stop running once it was turned on. It's almost two feet tall, so it's kind of hard to keep under control. It kicked Akio in the face twice. Man, that thing looks so nice."

They had reached the display window of the Aquarics and the new Beranius was polished to an extra-high shine today.

"You don't know what I'd do just to ride one…" Meligose began, fogging the glass with his breath.

"Oh, yes, I do," Sembado replied, cracking a wide grin.

They continued on looking around for a few more minutes before leaving.

***

"All right, man, I'll see ya tomorrow. Keep it deep," said Meligose as he got off the lift. His family lived on the opposite end of the level from Sembado's.

"Night," Sembado replied. He was partially distracted with the job of sneaking back in unnoticed, which would be difficult now that he'd been gone for more than an hour. Someone would have definitely noticed his absence by now.

He was on his way to the end of the corridor when he heard voices approaching the next corner. His heart's pace quickened as he recognized one of the voices as his grandfather's. He crept close to the edge of the corner and peeked around.

Sure enough, there was Grandfather walking up the corridor, deep in conversation with a tall, pale gentleman. They had their heads close together and weren't paying attention to where they were going; they were looking back over their shoulders. Sembado stuck his back flat to the wall so that as they walked by they didn't notice him. He caught a bit of their conversation as they passed the T-intersection of corridors.

"I don't care what Mohr thinks, this surface release is just their way of rooting out the rest of us," Grandfather snapped.

Sembado jumped across the corridor and peered around the corner. He could now see that the tall, pale man was so thin that his pants were folded over where his belt was. The man was trying to reason with his grandfather. When he spoke, he had a very bad stuttering speech impediment.

"I kn-kn-know, H-Hyron, b-but he wouldn't l-l-lishin to me, and itsh b-b-b-been really hurd t-t-trying to get that guy t-t-to shee your shied of the sht-shtory. Y-you kn-know how optim-mistic theash young guysh are. Th-they don't shushpect…"

Sembado couldn't make out anything they were saying after that. By the time he came around the corner, the tall man and Grandfather were gone around the next one, down to his family's place. Sembado hurried down to the next corner; Grandfather was already inside and the tall man was on his way back toward Sembado. He ducked back around the corner and then walked around it casually, like he'd been walking all along. He made brief eye contact with the man as they passed. He was nearly a head taller than Sembado, but was hunched over and now Sembado could see that he looked sickly with sunken, nervous eyes. Sembado turned to get another look at the man, only to find that the man was looking back. They both snapped their heads back around, and Sembado quickened his pace toward his front door. He opened it slowly. It was still silent from its recent oiling.

As he expected, his mother was waiting for him right in their entry tunnel.

"Where have you been?" she said, accosting him. They moved into the living room where Sembado's dad and grandfather were already sitting. They looked up, but soon went back to their respective reading materials.

"Well?" she asked; she was extremely persistent.

"I was down at the Civillion." He began honestly, unable to ignore the quick look front his Grandfather. Even more noticeable was how suspiciously quick he seemed to go back to his reading, while Father's attention was completely Sembado's now.

"What were you doing down there?" he asked, with a tone of frustration. "And why didn't you tell your mother or me?"

"I was meeting Meligose; he gets outta class at eight. You know, his robotics class. Deeks. I'm sorry. I rushed there after work; it didn't even cross my mind."

"That's just fine, Sembado, but there have been a lot of those mutants spotted lately, and not just in the bad parts of the complex."

"I'm not the only one who's vulnerable. I wasn't the only one out this late," Sembado whined. He was confused and frustrated.

Why wasn't Grandfather being scolded? He was the one who was just attacked the other day.

Mother suddenly became short. "Well, I'm not that boy's mother. I'm worried about you."

"I'm not talking about Meligose!" he shot back, giving his grandfather an indignant glare. Grandfather shifted nervously in his chair, but glared right back, cold and stony.

"Your mother's right, Sem," Father said. "I know you heard about those sightings at the Civillion just last week. We're not as mad as we are scared, you know?"

"I do. I'm sorry. I'll let you know next time. Sorry, Mom. Sorry, Dad. Good night. Good night, Grandfather."

"Night," the old man mumbled back.

What in the ocean was that about? What was with Grandfather?

Chapter Six
A Future Unveiled

Sembado walked quietly down a corridor, his thoughts consuming him.

Why was Grandfather acting so suspiciously?

"Shtop!" Sembado heard up ahead. He looked up to see a tall, thin man standing at the next corridor intersection. It was Grandfather's companion from the other night. His voice was much more commanding than Sembado remembered. He froze as the man pulled a gun from his side and pointed it right at Sembado.

"I shed shtop! I'll chute!" the man bellowed. He cocked the pistol.

"I did!" Sembado pleaded; he cringed.

Boom! Boom! Boom!

The thin man fell to the floor. Sembado looked behind himself and saw two men running at him full speed. The same two that had rushed past him on Grandfather's level the other day.

They have guns!

Sembado turned and ran for his life. His two pursuers were gaining on him. He passed the thin man on the floor as he ran. His face looked sallow and gaunt. His eyes were lifeless. Sembado stomped his feet as he slowed down to make a quick turn at the next junction. Every footfall splashed on the wet floor of the hallway. He made the turn and looked back over his shoulder to see the two continue on straight. Apparently they had not seen him. As he directed his attention forward again, he realized the tunnel he was now running down was made completely of glass, and all around it there were people riding the new Beranius Model 230s. They spiraled around the tunnel and did overhead flip-roll combinations that Sembado had never seen done in a regular personal submarine. Nevertheless, he kept running down the pipe and at the end he found a door.

He slowly opened it and found himself in *Terranean Memories*. Extremely confused, he continued to run through the store, knocking over a stand piled with old, holey umbrellas as he went. As he stumbled out into the Civillion, he stopped short in surprise. It was completely empty. There was always a store or two open, with customers to match, even in the middle of the night. He walked out to the middle of the atrium and looked around, overtaken with the feeling of loneliness.

He then realized that the entire floor was littered with loose papers. He reached down and grabbed a handful. As he looked them over, he realized they were pages from

Grandfather's journal. He was about to start looking them over when something wet hit the top of his head. He jumped out of the way as the dripping water turned into a steady stream. He looked up in horror as a huge crack in the glass ceiling, spanning the width of the dome spread its fingers across the surface. Before he could react, the ceiling exploded, and tons of glass and water rushed down on him. He was crushed in an instant.

***

Sembado woke with a start. He was completely soaked in sweat, his heart still racing from the terrible dream he just had. He turned on the light next to the bed. It was 6:21 a.m. He didn't have to leave for work for a couple more hours, but decided to get up anyway, not sure that he could get back to sleep after that strange dream. He continued to calm himself down as he walked into the living room. There he found his father watching the morning news. He looked up with a grin on his face.

"I was just about to wake you and Herbert up. Look at this," he said, turning up the television.

On the screen was a huge red headline that read:

IFCG ANNOUNCES SURFACE RELEASE TO TAKE PLACE
WITHIN THE YEAR

Sembado stood and stared, dumbstruck with a combination of excitement and the early morning stupids.

"That's right," began the woman on the screen. "Today, the International Federation of Complex Governments announced its plans to have a mass surface release of all complexes. This is after years of successful radiation testing and environmental analysis that has apparently been done in secret."

Father dragged a disgruntled Herbert into the living room and sat him down next to where Sembado had just seated himself, and then sat down next to them. All three listened on.

"We now go to field correspondent, Gillian Minero, who is eagerly waiting to hear an IFCG representative, possibly ECC Hurlock, make an official statement at any moment. Gillian?"

"Eagerly is right, Theria. The entire conference room here is literally buzzing with excitement. As you can see behind me, there are at least a thousand people packed in, waiting to hear more on this unexpected announcement."

Sembado and Herbert exchanged looks of excitement and disbelief as this surprising news had now woken them both. The man on the TV continued.

"As you said before, Theria, the seals on the surface chambers were finally and completely sealed in the final months of 2021. There are very few who won't be looking forward to this announcement. Though some have already voiced concern as to whether the radiation problem is completely resolved with all the past 'mutant' sightings, many are hoping, myself included, that these and many other questions will be answered here today."

The conference room burst into a dull roar as many journalists realized that the IFCG representative had made his way out to the podium. Gillian signaled the camera man to focus in and turned around to listen.

The man was older, with a thick head of sandy white hair. Sembado read the man's title across the bottom of the TV screen.

FREDRICK HURLOCK:
IFCG ENVIRONMENTAL COALITION CHAIRMAN

When he spoke, his voice was thick and gravelly.

"Good morning, ladies and gentlemen. Thank you for joining me. I'm here to confirm that the IFCG is in fact planning a surface release within the next seven months."

There was a murmur among the crowd.

"This decision was made after very careful and meticulous testing and surveying. The release will not be worldwide immediately. The West Pacific Complexes will open first, followed by the Hawaiian Complexes some time shortly after. The European districts have decided to postpone their release for another two months, and the other complexes have yet to reach a decision. But you can expect all of the complexes to be released to the surface by the end of the year. I have no time for questions. I'm sorry. No. No time for questions."

The crowd of reporters broke into an excited hum as Hurlock was escorted offstage.

The camera focused back on a giddy Gillian Minero. Just as she began to analyze the ten-second speech excitedly with newswoman Theria Trench, the TV turned off. Sembado, Herbert, and their father all whipped their heads around to see Grandfather holding the remote.

"Come on," he said sternly. "Let's go to the Civillion for some breakfast."

He spoke in a way that didn't invite argument. Sembado and Herbert got ready, and soon the four of them were off toward the lifts.

Grandfather's been acting awfully strange, He was talking about the surface release with the tall, pale man yesterday. How did he know before the news? What's he hiding?

Chapter Seven
Deep Secrets

Sembado was anxious to share what little he had learned with someone. Even these small secrets were eating at his insides, but for some reason he couldn't bring himself to share them with anyone. Every time he was about to tell Meligose, he would think of his grandfather and how disappointed he would be. After a week of no developments the thrill of investigating had all but run its course.

It was a Friday afternoon, and Sembado was down at the Civillion with Meligose and Kreymond. The three boys were back together for the first time since the incident at the arena. Meligose and Kreymond shared Sembado's growing impatience with Jean Paul's snooty attitude and refused to invite him out. Today they were checking out the week's latest releases in entertainment and industry.

The light ports from the surface were all but black. At this time of day, that meant that there was probably a monster of a storm up topside. Bright flashes through the ports suggested lightning. Sembado watched as he walked along absentmindedly; he was glad to be done with his stressful week. Next to him, Kreymond and Meligose continued an hour-long argument.

"I don't care what your dad says, Krey," Meligose replied. "The Poseidon line is for the eels, the whole school of 'em. Besides, how could you argue for anything else after seeing the new Beranius? It's practically a sex object. Look. Look at those contours. I don't care if your dad had a Poseidon ten million. It can't compare. Quit bein' a floater about it."

"I'm not bein' a floater, you slime!" Kreymond shot back. "I'm just sayin'. The Poseidon line was at the top of its class in its day. Sem, would you tell Mel I'm right? Sem. Hey!"

Sembado had stopped dead in his tracks. Just as his detective streak was running cold, he spotted his grandfather and his tall, pale friend walking into *Terranean Memories*. He would have tried to ignore it, but they both looked extremely suspicious; they checked over their shoulders at least a dozen times before sneakily shooting into the store.

"Sem! What are you doing?"

"What? Oh. Sorry, guys. I gotta make warm water. I'll be right back," he lied.

"Okay. We'll be in the Aquarics," Meligose said smugly. Kreymond rolled his eyes as he followed.

Sembado made for the bathroom, which was conveniently located just near *Terranean Memories*. He made sure his friends were inside the Aquarics and distracted before he broke his walk toward the bathroom into a double-time pace to the store. He slowed his gait as he got closer, slipping into the store behind a group of older ladies. They veered right toward the old cookbooks unexpectedly, forcing Sembado to hide behind a rack of old postcards. He scouted out the store as best he could. His heart raced. The longer he looked, the more anxious he got. After a few minutes of spying and seeing neither Grandfather or his tall friend, Sembado stopped peering, came out from behind the postcards, and gave the store a thorough once over. Neither of the old men was there.

They couldn't have got past me. I'm right next to the door.

Sembado was puzzled. Feeling determined, he made one more, good lap through the racks and shelves until he caught the store attendant's attention.

"Can I help you find something, kid?" the man asked irritably.

"No, thank you. Sorry," Sembado offered. He left quietly.

I blew it. Well, maybe it wasn't them. No, it had to be. No one else looks quite like that old pale fish. And I'd know my own grandfather anywhere.

Sembado began to walk away dejectedly. As he did, he passed the old courtyard next to *Terranean Memories*. He idly played with the top layer of ivy as he passed. It was at least a foot thick. Most of the undergrowth was dead or dying, but decades upon decades had created a thick, heavy padding over the old cast iron, which could no longer be seen or even felt. Just then, he heard a voice, and not just any voice.

"Thish ish sheariush men!" the voice whispered. "We haven't g-g-got mush t-time."

I'd know that voice anywhere, Sembado thought, *but where is it coming from?*

He looked around. There weren't many people nearby at the moment, except for the older group of cook bookers who were presently leaving *Terranean Memories*. The bags they carried suggested they had each found a book of interest. Then it hit him. Sembado leaned the side of his head gently into the ivy wall. Sure enough, the voice got louder!

"Hyron'sh right. We've g-got to g-g-get the boysh together, and sh-shoon!"

"Well, all of the sector leaders anyway," said an old, familiar voice.

Grandfather.

"The IFCG is getting serious," Grandfather whispered in a solemn tone. "They don't want a surface release any more than the oxygen dealers, but they know it's their only way to get the rest of us to come out of hiding. There won't

71

be a man, woman, or child allowed to see the sky who isn't thoroughly checked first. And they know it's only a matter of time before we all give in for a chance to breathe fresh air again."

There was a very soft murmur among a few others behind the green, leafy wall. Grandfather continued in a very firm tone.

"We're going to hold the next meeting in the J-Vents two hours from now at exactly twelve; don't be late, and bring everyone you can. All right men, let's head out in ones and twos. Lebby, you have somewhere to be. You take off first."

Sembado couldn't believe what he had just heard. He stood up straight and away from the wall, just realizing how foolish he must've looked for the last minute or so. He quickly adopted what he thought was a casual stance. Just then, a man walked out of *Terranean Memories*. He had a thick head and neck with a thick, black goatee. Sembado hadn't seen him enter and was suddenly aware that the man must have been Lebby.

The gorilla of a man eyed Sembado suspiciously as he quickly walked out of the Civillion; he looked like he was in a hurry. A few moments later, two more men came out. Sembado was sure they weren't in the store beforehand.

They must be more men from the meeting.

If this kept up, Grandfather was sure to come out too. He quickly made his way to the Aquarics, sure that Kreymond and Meligose were still there.

I'll come back.

Sure enough, when he got to the PS dealer, his friends had convinced the showman to let them sit in the Beranius that was on display. Apparently they had failed to mention that neither of them could afford the price of the sleek machine on their present student income, let alone any monthly payments. The man was a high-strung little person. He was always scaring clients off with his high-energy offers or angry accusations.

"I'm sorry?" the smiling salesman offered through the cockpit glass. "Did you say a fourteen-hundred-coin down payment?" The vehicle was so well sealed that Kreymond's pitiful offer of a forty-coin down payment had been misunderstood. Sembado stood by, doing a bad job of keeping a straight face.

"Nooo," Kreymond stated slowly. "For-ty. Four, zero."

"What did he say?!" the salesman said, jerking his head up at Meliogse; the smile quickly faded from his face.

"Umm, forty shells," Meligose said meekly, realizing their luck had run out. "Do you think I could hop in it for a second?" he asked bravely, a cheap smile on his face.

"Get outta here, you punks. I have real customers to take care of," the man demanded proudly.

"No, you don't," Kreymond retorted, getting out of the Beranius. "Deeks, ya old fish, we're the only ones in here."

"Shove off, you two!" the man snapped. "Are you with them?" he asked, eyeing Sembado indignantly.

"Uh, yeah. Sorry." Sembado fought back a nervous laugh at the anger his friends had worked out of the little man.

"Then get out!"

"Take a breather, ya crab!" Kreymond shouted back after they were at a safe distance. "You were right, Mel, that thing was totally deep. Sem, you shoulda felt the curves inside."

"Neither of us got to feel anything with you in there the whole time," Meligose said bitterly, pushing his shorter friend away by the head. "Who do you think you are? Launa Guna?"

"Ha! I wish. Did you see him in last week's race? He beat that Japanese fish, Sakira, by twelve and a half seconds," Kreymond replied excitedly, fixing his afro.

"I know. That guy's so fast his bubbles break surface before the competition can reach 'em. Wait. What time is it?" asked Meligose, suddenly cheering up.

"Uh. Quarter to eight. Why? Where're you goin?" Kreymond asked suspiciously.

Sembado's mind had wondered back to the ivy covered courtyard.

I have to check that place out. I have to find out what this J-vents place is. I'm not missing another one of Grandfather's secret meetings.

"I'm meeting Lissy Lebick. We're gonna go hook a show, that new one about those airplanes they had way back when," Meligose said smugly.

"You eel, I wanted to see that," said Kreymond, a bit put off.

"Then go see it, but I'm goin with Lissy," Meligose said smoothly.

Sembado wasn't listening.

I'll have to sneak in behind some other customers like earlier or that store clerk will be even more suspicious. But then what? Where's the door to the courtyard? The only door there is the front—wait. Of course!

"Eh, whatever. I'll just sink with Sem tonight. We can see that one about the ancient queen's affair with her servant. I'd love to be that lucky fish who is playing the servant. Can you imagine playing the royal bodice boy opposite Camilla Jones's Madame Malaria? He was close enough to smell her. I'm not bubblin'!" Kreymond said, pretending to sniff the air around him. The sound of his name brought Sembado's attention back to the conversation.

"Oh, uh, sorry, Krey, I can't tonight," Sembado lied.

I've got to get back in there.

"What?" Kreymond said indignantly. "It's Friday night! Some friends you two are. You're a couple of floaters!" He walked away dejectedly.

"What's that about, man?" Meligose asked. "I really am goin' to the theater with Lissy. What's your excuse?"

"I gotta—do something for my grandfather," Sembado lied quickly, slightly humored by the irony of his statement.

"All right, whatever man. Keep it deep. I gotta swim."

"Yea. You too, Mel," Sembado said automatically.

His thoughts were already at the hidden courtyard. It was almost eight o'clock. *Terranean Memories* didn't usually close until ten or later, but Sembado didn't have much time to find the J-vents. He knew there was a clue to its whereabouts in that hidden courtyard, but he would have trouble finding a place he had never been to; a place whose location he wasn't even certain of.

I have to get to that back door and into that courtyard.

He approached the store cautiously. It was starting to get busy around the Civillion; it was 8:00 p.m. on a Friday night. Sembado was surprised it wasn't busier already. He hung back from the entrance; he wanted to avoid being seen by that suspicious clerk. A barterer nearby was selling a wall-mounted body drier.

"Never worry about towels again. Swim without a wetsuit? Be dry in minutes. Buy one for every depressurizing chamber in your home," he suggested.

"Who has more than one?" protested an onlooker.

"Well, buy one for a friend or family member?"

Sembado stood toward the back of the crowd so that he could keep an eye on *Terranean Memories*. He spotted a familiar group of women, the recipe book buyers from before, walking back into the store. They looked disgruntled. Perhaps they were unsatisfied with their purchases.

This is my chance.

Sembado waited only a moment, making a quick pace toward the store and dipping in behind the women. Sure enough, as he shot past the group of protesting old ladies, who were conveniently blocking the clerk's view, he heard them complaining about the authenticity of their cookbooks.

They were the only clients in the store, and Sembado reached the safety of some taller shelves as the disagreement at the front of the store broke into a full-blown argument.

"What do you mean these were printed a year ago? I'll have you know these hail from 2003 Kentucky. Fine American cooking ma'am."

Sembado got to the back of the store safely, but there was no back door there. He knew his mother had described the back entrance from the store to the courtyard when she was young and the property was a restaurant. More vivid was his memory of the door from his dream only a few nights ago, but that had been just a dream. He scoured the shelves all across the back wall, moving some random objects aside to see behind them. A group of old, glass soda bottles stood in a bunch on a shelf to his left. They just fit in the shelf space, touching bottom and top. He stuck his hand in the middle of them to push them aside. Four bottles moved one way and three the other, but one newer-looking cola bottle did not move.

What's this?

He carefully pushed the others bottles away to single the new one out. He grabbed it around the middle and jerked. It held fast; it was adhered to the shelf, top and bottom. Sembado shot a quick glance over his shoulder; the angry cookbook club was raising enough commotion to draw spectators.

It's now or never.

He gave the cola bottle a nice, even pull. Amazingly, the shelf swung out silently toward him about a foot. He gave it another heavy tug and opened the secret door just wide enough to slide in. On the other side was a real door handle, a sterile metal one. He gently pulled it shut behind him.

It was quite dark in the small space he was in now. He stood with his back to the door, allowing his eyes to adjust. His heart beat with excitement. To his right was a newer brick wall. It seemed to partition off a path to the rest of the nearby business.

Probably an old service corridor.

The hall was about five feet wide. It had a cement floor. To his left, Sembado could see the source of the only light in this space. He turned to look squarely at a high iron gate.

It was at least ten feet tall and extremely intricate. The light that he saw was what little light could make it through the thick ivy ceiling of the courtyard beyond. He walked up to the gate and placed a hand on it; it swung open silently with the slightest push.

Grandfather must keep this thing well oiled.

Sembado looked around. The courtyard was much less colorful from inside. Most, if not all of the ivy on the interior walls was dried and dead from lack of sunlight, but the outer vines lit the area with a warm green glow. As the lights from out in the Civillion shined through it flooded the courtyard with eerie flashes of green light every time the storm on the surface flashed through the lighting pods. The space was about fifteen by twenty feet. It had a brick floor. A long, tall table sat in the middle. It was littered with papers. Sembado went to work. He looked around for a paper or map that might refer to the J-vent place. Most of them were notes from one person to another. Sembado was still trying to make sense of what all of this was. He recognized a few of the papers with his grandfather's handwriting—new ones, not the old faded journal pages from the past. Most of the papers, however, were quick notes from one person to another.

I'll never have time to check all of these.

Sembado hurriedly scanned everything he could, hoping that something would jump out at him. He could hear the muffled commotion of the mad cookbook brigade through the thick ivy walls; apparently they had drawn a crowd.

Then he saw it. He quickly picked up a note that he saw a capital *J* on. It read:

KLISK

SOUTH END

GROW HOUSES

INCUBATION CHAMBER J3

FAR FLOOR VENTS

Klisk was Sembado's mother's maiden name, and Grandfather's last name.

That must be the J-vents! I've never been there before. I better take off.

Sembado quickly gave the note one last looking over before leaving; he didn't want to forget the details. He set the note back down and made sure that the table didn't look too disturbed, as messy as it was. He walked back to the iron gate and shut it quietly. He got to the hidden door and slowly pulled it open. Sembado cracked the door slightly and looked through—no one could be seen. He pushed it farther.

"What the hell are you doing!" shouted the store clerk in Sembado's face, ripping the door open and grabbing the boy by the shirt. Apparently the cookbook club was gone. He slammed Sembado into a nearby shelf. Sembado fell to the floor.

"You're gonna spy on us? You IFCG rat!"

This old fish is insane!

He kicked Sembado in the ribs, knocking the wind out of him.

My God!

"I thought I've seen you lurking around here before."

Sembado took a chance, reaching up and punching the man in the knee as hard as he possibly could.

"Son of a bitch!" the clerk yelled, grabbing his leg as he went down. Sembado jumped up, confused and breathless, and ran toward the entrance of the shop. Something caught his foot and he slammed hard onto the floor. He had tripped over an old bicycle.

Why not?

He could ride; his grandfather had taught him once before. It was incredibly similar to riding the water trike he had as a child, but with much less resistance. But did he still remember how? He picked up the bike quickly and mounted it on his way out of the store, speeding past a crowd of spectators. They were watching a musical performer.

That's what the commotion was—not the book club.

He turned hundreds of heads as he awkwardly pedaled through the Civillion. He looked over his shoulder just long enough to see the store clerk running back inside *Terranean Memories*. Sembado headed south.

I've got to get to that grow house.

***

After riding for a few minutes, Sembado slowed to a stop as he approached a public information booth. These booths had maps and directories for the public.

He brought up a map of the southern greenhouse sector. The incubation pods he needed to get to were accessible by only one lift, which was two miles away, unless he swam from a nearby public pressurizing chamber to one close to the greenhouse.

I'll have to swim, but it should be much quicker.

He sped away toward the local pressurizing chamber, one that he'd used several times before. He dumped the bike in the corridor as he opened the first chamber door. Inside, like most PPCs, was an attendant whose job it was to sell oxygen tanks to potential clients. The distance Sembado was going only required about thirty minutes of air. Sembado gave the young man behind the counter five coins for flippers, swimming gloves, pressurizing muffs, and a tank of oxygen that was about as big as his forearm.

"Right here in tank three." The attendant signaled for Sembado to climb into one of the smaller, secondary chambers that was marked with a yellow three. The chamber was about the size of a large closet, maybe four by five feet.

Sembado sat down once inside; there was a small bench built into the wall. He quickly slipped on the flippers and adjusted the oxygen tank. He put on the pressurizing muffs, which kept his ears from exploding, before putting on the swimming gloves. They were typical diving gloves, flexible plastic with webbed fingers.

He gave the attendant a thumbs-up to signal that he was ready. The attendant adjusted settings on the computer screen behind him, and a tone signaled the imminent air evacuation of the tank. Sembado sat impatiently as the air in the tank was pumped out and replaced with the salt water from outside. He regulated his oxygen tank one more time as the water crept up his legs and spilled onto his lap. He stood up and the water rose past his waist, his chest, his neck. The cold Pacific Ocean water felt nice and soothing as it enveloped his body, like a good friend he hadn't talked to in a long while. He was now completely submerged. Sembado became momentarily lost in the comforting feeling, pushing the water with his hands back and forth in front of his goggles. A red light flashed; the chamber had pressurized to the outside water pressure. Sembado felt his chest being pressed tightly, a feeling he had grown used to. He heard a sharp, tinny knocking noise and looked over to see the attendant tapping on the thick glass window on the door. He mouthed the words "You okay?" Sembado gave the kid another thumbs up and the door to the outside ocean opened.

Sembado sat and paddled idly for a moment as he got his bearings, then he was off. A lifetime of swimming in this deep open water had given him strong legs and arms, and good swimming stamina. He passed many people on the way. He passed a father giving his daughter submarine lessons; her first it seemed, by the way the submarine lurched forward. He also saw some government officials taking water samples as he desperately swam toward the grow houses. He knew from the map he had looked at that even this shortcut would take a good twenty minutes; after all, he could only swim his fastest, about four miles per hour, for so long before cramping up.

He swam as hard as he could, pushing his arms and legs to their extremes. He spotted the incubation chambers in the distance through the briny deep. They appeared in tall columns, a countless number in all. They jutted away from the main structure in a radial fashion, like an open hand with its fingers spread at wide angles. These arrays were stacked with each level rotating about fifteen degrees from the one below. There were hundreds of pods in all. Even with its size, this incubation center could only provide for a small fraction of the denizens of the complex. The scene was illuminated briefly by another shot of lighting overhead. The ocean lit up blue and green and dark.

Sembado shifted his attention a bit left where some movement caught his eye. Outside the pressurizing chamber, he was looking at three people who were waiting. By the rush of bubbles leaving the chambers, he could tell they were waiting for the chambers to fill and open, which happened momentarily. The three swimmers floated into their own chambers and the hatches closed behind them. Sembado slowly swam closer, giving the occupied chambers time to be evacuated. He took this time to observe the large incubation center some more. Bright lights were mounted on the outside of the pods and shone along their sides. Each had a large yellow number-and-letter combination printed on the side. He saw that the letters correlated with the level the pods were on, and that the numbers coordinated with each chamber on each individual level.

He spotted the J level, but could only see chambers one and two.

Number three must be out of sight. On the other side of the pod, perhaps.

He was startled, for a moment, when the pressurizing chamber to his left began spewing air bubbles rapidly and flashing its red warning lights.

Within a minute or two the lights stopped flashing and the hatch opened. He swam inside. Looking back as the door closed, he saw more swimmers approaching. His chamber's hatch sealed and began evacuating the water, replacing it with air. As soon as the water level was beneath his chin he removed his mask.

His chest heaved as he fought to catch his breath, tired from the intense swim. He looked through the door's window into the larger chamber as the water fell below his legs. The swimmers ahead of him were just leaving; the last looked suspiciously over his shoulder as he dipped out of sight. Sembado threw the door open as soon as the water had drained from the small chamber.

He stripped off his gear and left it on the floor; this was an automated chamber and had no attendant. He could hear the compression chambers pumping full of water again. As he slipped out into the corridor, he looked back and was startled to see four faces staring at him, one through each of the windowed doors. He was horrified to recognize one of the faces as the crazy store clerk that he thought he had lost. He looked absolutely livid. Sembado took off toward the grow houses. He wasn't sure who the other men were, but something told him they were with the angry clerk.

His fatigued legs would only run so fast after the long swim, and he felt helpless as they slumped along. From his observations outside, he saw that the J area was going to be two levels up. He hobbled to the end of the corridor and up a stairwell to his right. As he suspected, a large sign by the stairs indicated that he was on the L level. His legs were getting sorer every moment. He began to cramp up halfway past the K level and had to stop.

Ugh! I wonder if I lost that crazy old fish for good this time.

As if to answer his question, the stairwell door two levels down slammed open and a number of feet started to stomp up the stairs.

Desperation took over Sembado's body as he scrambled to his feet and ran up the remaining steps. He slammed the door open and paused momentarily. Yellow letters on the wall ahead of him read:

GROW CHAMBERS →

He took off in the direction indicated, passing a startled looking man who had a mobile phone plugged into a public communication port halfway down the corridor. Because the old wireless phones didn't work underwater, public communication ports were installed all over the complex. If you had a mobile phone you simply plugged it in and were then connected to the system. Shortwave radios were available as well, but they were a very rare commodity and extremely expensive. Few people owned them, but most penalty officers carried some kind of walkie-talkie. As Sembado passed the man, he caught just a moment of his conversation.

"I told you I'm not sure. M'Gereg said he ran off this way. He's some young kid."

Sembado looked back to see the man ripping his phone out of the wall. The old clerk and his three accomplices had just kicked open the stairwell door.

"That's him, you idiot!" shouted the clerk, pointing at Sembado. "After him!"

Sembado raced to the end of the corridor. It curved slightly to the right as he went so that he could not see his pursuers when he shot a glance over his shoulder. There was a solitary door at the end of the corridor. A sign over it read:

GROW CHAMBERS—KEEP DOOR CLOSED

He jerked it open and jumped inside, looking for somewhere to hide. Anywhere.

Far floor vents. Where are those vents?

This particular grow house was filled with corn plants. Rows and rows of corn plants. Sembado could not see the other end. He cut around the plants and ran on the outside path along the side of the chamber. The room opened up as he went farther in, reaching a maximum width of about twenty feet. It must have been at least five times that long. He ran toward the other end, scouring the floors with his eyes for the vents. Then it occurred to him.

If that's M'Gereg chasing me, he knows where I'm headed already. I can't go into those vents; he's ready to kill.

In a flash Sembado stomped to a halt, just a few yards from the other end of the chamber. The door at the front of the chamber slammed open. He quickly jumped into the rows of corn, carefully trying not to break any of the stalks as he worked his way deeper into the small patch, stopping in what seemed like the middle of the corn. The plants were at least seven feet tall. He could see nothing, but heard the men that chased him coming down the chamber on both sides.

The men reached the far end of the chamber and met around the end of the corn.

"Where the hell is he?" Sembado heard the old man, M'Gereg, shout.

There was a sound of metal scraping and then many more voices could be heard.

"Quiet men!" M'Gereg shouted. "We have an intruder! And if I'm not mistaken, the dirty little squid has taken to the corn."

Sembado's stomach dropped as the pain returned to his legs. He fell to one knee, hoping to better hide from his pursuers. Old M'Gereg could be heard yelling again.

"You three! Hurry to the other end and make sure he doesn't escape. The rest of us will spread out and comb the corn. Let's see that scumbag get back to his IFCG friends now. Don't miss a single stalk! Go!"

There was a great commotion and a growing number of voices as many feet could be heard marching along the sides of the corn. Sembado felt close to vomiting as his sorry fate started in toward him from every side. He heard the snapping of corn stalks all around him as the group moved further into the small field.

"Break 'em all down! We don't want him moving back around us."

Sembado's heart raced and his stomach turned. Through the corn he could see more and more light as the stalks a dozen rows down began to twist and fall. He wet himself. Sitting pitifully in the engineered soil matter, he wondered why all of this was happening.

Where's Grandfather in all this?

Desperation took over as individual legs could now be seen through the corn. Sembado shot up and took off, ready to plow anyone over. He ran past two men and approached a third.

"There he is! Get him!"

He lowered his shoulder and knocked the man down. He landed on the outside walkway that ran along the outside of the corn. Four men were running straight for him. He jerked to his left and back into the corn, moving from row to row as fast as could. The sweet smelling leaves cut his face and arms as he ran past them.

"He's back in the corn! Someone guard the door!"

His clothes were soaked with urine and the moisture from the corn stalks. He heard huffing and puffing as someone came up on his right. He dove on the ground in that direction, catching the man's foot in his ribs, but successfully tripping him. He fought to his feet and just caught a glance of the man lying in a heap before he caught a small rod in the back of the legs and went down. Six hands forced him against the soil; a seventh smeared the side of his face into the sweet corn leaves.

"We got 'im! Everybody over here! We got 'im!

From this angle, he could see the man he tripped turning over to face him. It was his grandfather! They exchanged looks of horrid surprise.

"Get off that boy!" Grandfather bellowed. "That's my grandson!"

Chapter Eight
A Guilded Truth

A whole minute passed before anyone could process what Grandfather had said. A good five more minutes passed before Grandfather could convince M'Gereg to take his chunky knee out of the small of his grandson's back. Sembado got to his feet quickly and stood behind his grandfather; the rest of the men faced them, crowded around in a half circle.

"I can vouch for this boy. He's no trouble at all," said Grandfather, calmed but breathless. As he stood and straightened himself, he quickly tucked the key around his neck back under his shirt. "And if my word's not good enough for you, then you've no right bein' here."

"You say he's your grandson, Hyron? Then why the hell's he been spyin' on us?" retorted a red-faced M'Gereg. "At least three of our men spotted him outside the courtyard earlier. Said his ear was buried a foot into the ivy. What's with that, eh?"

There was a murmur of agreement through the group.

"I was curious!" Sembado interjected boldly. The crowd fell silent. This was the first they had heard out of him.

"I found strange notes about meetings," Sembado continued. "And...and I was curious!" The sudden change in events had made his head swim. He felt ill.

"Don't ya see, Jean? The boy's here for the same reason you and I were sixty years ago. His curiosity got the best of him. That's all."

"Hyron'sh right," said a voice, as Grandfather's tall, pale friend stepped out of the group.

"I t-told Klisk that I was sh-sh-sh-shushpicioush of the boy overh-h-hearing our conversh-shation about the shurfacshe r-r-elealsh. Wr-r-ong place, wrong t-time."

"Ya see?" scolded Grandfather, when he had the chance.

"Now, we've made far too much noise as it is," he continued, now in a commanding tone. Sembado noticed how well he could direct these men. "We can discuss more downstairs. We have no choice but to induct the boy. Gentlemen, take a look at our newest member," he said seriously, slapping Sembado on the back.

"Now get down into those vents; we have a lot to cover."

The men obediently turned and began to shuffle toward an open grate on the floor. They quickly descended a ladder into the vents below. Sembado hung back nervously with his grandfather, who was now talking with M'Gereg and the tall, pale man as they filed toward the vents. Sembado, now testing his new found listening freedom, leaned in to eavesdrop on the old men.

"We're all here tonight," Grandfather said to the other two men. "Briars brought that electronic copy of all our documents and we're going to do an official briefing to the boys about the release. We'll just have to take care of Sem first. That way, he's up to speed."

They all looked back at him. Grandfather gave him an endearing smile. The tall, pale man also gave Sembado what he figured had to be a smile, but it came across as more of a twitchy grimace. Old Jean M'Gereg, on the other hand, gave him a cold, steely sneer.

Grandfather waited at the grate as the other two old men disappeared below.

"I'll go in last. Now get down there, and be quiet."

Sembado got to his knees and slowly crept down the ladder. The rungs were cold, wet metal bars. Sembado's eyes strained through the dark in vain; light from overhead snuck through a crack or two, but it was mostly pitch dark. He moved aside as his grandfather slowly made his way down the ladder. When he was all the way down, one of the younger men hopped up the ladder to shut the grate. It had four locks on it and he latched each of them carefully. As he came back down, there was a snap as someone flipped a switch and the entire area was lit.

Sembado's eyes again focused for a moment under the new bright light, and he suddenly realized how large this space really was. It was more of a mechanical room than just a vent, with large machines all around and pipes running up through the ceiling. The area in the middle of the ceiling was extruded down, with a lower clearance.

This accommodated the corn roots no doubt. As Sembado looked around he realized that everyone was staring, at least four dozen eyes in all, right at him. His grandfather ushered him forward as everyone took seats on the equipment around the room. Others sat on the damp floor. Three guarded the ladder. They had guns. It was silent as Grandfather brought Sembado deeper into the room and then turned him around so that everyone could see him, and he could see everyone. Sembado felt hot. Grandfather's voice broke the silence.

"It's been quite a while since we have inducted a new member into our guild. Many decades more since it was someone by the Klisk bloodline."

A soft chuckle could be heard throughout the room.

"I am Hyron Edward Klisk," he began, in a ceremonious tone. "And I am here to elect Sembado Metchell Grey into the Elephant Guild. As all of you know, except for our member-elect here, the elephant is our symbol."

He then turned to Sembado, to imply that the following information was for his ears.

"Sembado, we are the Elephant Guild. As I'm sure you learned in school, the elephant is a very large land mammal that lived in Africa and Asia. We chose it as our symbol many years ago because its traits are also characteristics that we as a group try to emulate. The elephant, as I said before, is a land creature, like us. They are not meant to survive underwater, and neither are we. They have long trunks to breathe from, but eventually they surface and indulge in their land habits. The elephant is a smart, proud, and strong opponent. We strive to be the most clever, noble, and fierce adversary the IFCG has ever had."

"But why are you against the IFCG?" Sembado asked.

"That is my next point. And it's not me, it's us now," he said, grabbing Sembado by the shoulder. "There is an old saying: 'an elephant never forgets.' This long memory is the pillar on which this brotherhood is based. The IFCG did our families wrong many decades ago, and we will not rest until they are brought to justice, or until the truth is known. We will not forget what they did."

"I don't understa—" Sembado began.

"Shut up and listen!" barked M'Gereg. "We don't have time for your questions. Go on, Hyron."

"Sembado, you learned about the big catastrophe in school right? At the end of the war, those huge explosions killed millions of people."

"And David…" Sembado said quietly.

"What? How do you know about David?" Grandfather asked.

"The day of your attack…I…put some of your journal pages in my pocket when you weren't looking." Sembado said. The group of men looked at each other nervously. Grandfather looked into Sembado's eyes. As tears welled in his old blue eyes a smile spread across his wrinkled face. There was a long silence that even M'Gereg did not interrupt. Finally, Grandfather spoke.

"Then you know. How about how me and my friends started to rebel and sneak out?" Sembado confirmed with a nod. Grandfather chuckled, continuing to fill in the pieces.

"We pretended to spy on the administration and break into places we weren't supposed to be at, just to mess with the people that were locking us in. It began as dumb child's play. What we found was terrifying. One night we snuck into a ventilation system, much smaller than this one. We had been sneaking around for weeks. We got so good at crawling along on our stomachs that we could move through the government workers' vents without making a noise. On this particular night, M'Gereg here, two others that are now dead, and I decided to up the ante and go as far across enemy lines as we could. As we passed vent after vent, we noticed how many fewer civilians we saw and more and more government workers there were. We had gotten past their security gates. We crawled so long, more than an hour, that our hands and knees started to bleed. We came upon a vent that opened into a records room and we decided to finally stop. I had volunteered to get down into the room and steal a folder or two, just to say I had. The room was huge; bigger than the grow room above us, but lit half as well, if that. I could barely make out the other end. It was freezing inside; the room was packed from end to end with computer servers. About twenty feet to one side was the door, which had a card-scanning access panel. A little way down in the other direction I could see a monitoring station where they kept the controlling computer. None of the information there was in physical files, it was all kept on their hard drives, so I hurried back to the guys.

"Back in the vents, I told them what I had seen and that it'd be impossible to get into their computer system. We'd never get access. One of the other boys, Claude, wanted to go home—"

"He always was a nancy," interrupted M'Gereg. "That's what got him killed."

"Well," said Grandfather impatiently, "we were just about to head back when we heard a noise. Suddenly, two government workers came into view. They both wore dark, heavy suits and glasses. We watched as they walked casually over to the computer, talking together. We couldn't quite make out their conversation. M'Gereg got my attention with a tap on the shoulder and quietly produced a small flash drive from his pocket. It was a portable memory device we used before the wireless palm readers were made. He handed it to me. And then, to my and the other boys' confusion, he started to crawl farther down the vent, which passed right over the workers and continued farther down the room. We watched as he slithered along, silently, out of sight, gradually masked by the darkness in the vents. I watched the workers cautiously as he made his way over their heads; neither was any the wiser. They were now reviewing some data on the computer screen. Suddenly, there came a bang and a crash from the far end of the room. I watched in a panic as the workers exchanged looks and hurried away from the computer toward the source of the noise. M'Gereg's genius plan struck me in an instant, and I slid the grate away to poke my head out for a look-around. The men were out of sight. I quickly got down, glancing back up at the boys' ghost-white faces painted in horror. I shot to the computer as quietly as possible. I jammed the key drive into a port and started clicking. I didn't know exactly what to look for, so I opened the file to the computer's main hard drive and began to copy the entire thing. As it loaded I looked around, still no workers in sight. I remember wondering, in that short time, whether M'Gereg had got caught or not. I heard the echo of footsteps some ways away, the loading had stopped at one percent; the flash drive was far too small. I pulled it out and quickly got back to the vent, where the boys were waiting to help pull me back up. As I got my feet up and in safely, I looked around to see M'Gereg smiling at me proudly."

"I had gotten down just far enough to kick in one of the server door's glass," M'Gereg said, interrupting proudly. Sembado looked around to see many of the men listening intently to his grandfather's tale.

"Well, our victory was bittersweet," Grandfather continued. "I had forgotten to close out of the files I had opened on the computer. I looked down through the vent as I realized this, just in time to see the workers discover the same thing. They started talking quickly to each other as they looked around for intruders. The two men quickly ran to the exit and swiped out, going to tell security, no doubt. All through the government offices there was an uncharacteristic buzz of chatter. News spreads fast in those boring offices. We hurried back to civilian territory as fast as we could without making noise.

"We came out of the vents behind what is now M'Gereg's antique shop. Back then, it was a small law office. We hurried back to Eric's place; he was one of the other boys and the only one of us with his own computer at the time.

"We collapsed on his bed and floor in exhaustion, laughing and joking about what we had just pulled off. A half hour later, we were dead silent as we read through some of the files we had stolen. What we discovered was…terrible."

Grandfather had faltered for the first time in his long story. He couldn't continue. All the men around them were quiet. They too knew this horror of which Grandfather couldn't speak

"Here," M'Gereg said, forcing a portable computer screen into Sembado's hands. "Read for yourself." He pressed a button and an official looking document appeared on the screen:

```
SGR137FY18      OP: CLEAN SLATE      6/15/21

Attn:
Commander in Chief
White Sector, Office 501
United States Facility 2

Mr. President,

There is no doubt that the population is
convinced that all of Operation Clean Slate
was caused by the escalated wartime
activities; many are blaming the North
Koreans, as we planned. Eye witnesses to each
```

of the detonation points are convinced that the weapons were nuclear in nature, and survival rates from the detonation points are a clean 0 percent. Neither our agents, nor our European or Asian affiliates, have reported any mutiny or suspicions among the civilian populations.

All seventy-nine US detonation points have been swept and cleaned. Survivors from outlying suburban and rural areas are being gathered up for transportation. Our international sources have estimated a casualty count worldwide at 5,635,000,000; only fifteen million more than was predicted in the preoperational planning. All of the informed operatives have been cooperating well, and all ignorant military members are doing an excellent job providing security for the Submarine Facilities.

In closing, Operation Clean Slate was a complete and utter success. We will now begin the public affairs campaign to get the public to reconcile its distrust with our enemies so that we can continue with our trade agreements.

On a side note, sir, I was able to speak with your public affairs chair, and you will be pleased to know that the population thinks you are doing a superior job handling the 'catastrophe,' as they have come to call it. Don thinks your reelection will be a breeze.

Respectfully,

442

Sembado was quiet. He understood what he had just read, but he still wasn't sure what it all meant. It felt foolish to push the subject that seemed to bring so much pain to those around him, but he had to know what was going on. He reluctantly broke the silence in the dank vents.

"I'm not sure what this means. Could they not stop the nuclear attacks in time?" he said into an echoing quiet.

"No, you fool! It means they planned it themselves!" M'Gereg barked angrily.

"Don't you see, boy?" Grandfather whispered bitterly. "It was a conspiracy; the controlling governments of the world were getting sick and tired of the mess that the planet was becoming. So they hit the reset. They did what people do best when something they've made gets to be too much to handle; they threw it away and tried to start over. That's why the IFCG is so intent on finding and killing us. We are the wrench in the cogs of their perfectly controlled system. With the citizens so emotionally suppressed from the artificial apocalypse, the government had no trouble keeping them under control—but not us."

"That's why it's so important for us to keep fighting," M'Gereg shot in. "If we give up or let them get us, the public will never know this awful truth. And that's something we can't let happen."

Sembado's head swam with all this information. He didn't know who to trust.

Grandfather? The Government? Certainly not nasty, old M'Gereg.

Then he thought back to all the stories from his grandfather's journal and decided to challenge his grandfather to those facts.

"Wait," Sembado began, trying to think as clearly and cleverly as possible. "So, you're saying the whole reason these complexes were built was to get ready for this planned 'Doomsday'? What about all that in your journal where they wanted to build the complexes for science? I thought these were built as an alternative to failed space flight?"

"Awfully convenient, no?" spat M'Gereg, now pacing in and out of the other men who all stared on stoically, hardened by the hate that these cold truths infused in them. "The deceit reaches back farther than one measly presidential term. The top crust had been planning this thing for years, at least two presidents back. They planned bad space trips and everything, boy. They wanted them to fail! We found out later that they had started building these things years before anyone knew. And not just the Americans; the Chinese, the Europeans—this was big, son; they were all in on it. Anyone they really wanted rid of they just left out of the secret; why, the entire country of North Korea was eliminated; most of Africa and the Middle East too. Any hot spots in the world that they couldn't handle anymore, they terminated. 'Sorry, you're not playing well with others.'"

"You read the document, Semmy," Grandfather continued. "They knew how many people were gonna die. They planned it, boy. *They planned it*. And this from a group of people who constantly preached freedom and fair opportunity to the masses. Not everyone in the world is right—but that doesn't give any of us the power to judge, not like that. It was genocide on the grandest scale imaginable."

"And these government goons have passed down their legacy of lies and deceit through the generations," added M'Gereg.

"Brainwashing the new recruits into sympathizing with 'The Only Solution.' We don't want to hurt anyone, boy, and we aren't going to ask you to either, but the people have to know, and if we have to defend ourselves, we will. We have. They've been rooting us out for decades. Anytime you hear about some damn mutant-spotting, it's either another one of us being captured, or some IFCG jerk in disguise, keeping the public afraid of 'Surface Dwellers.'"

"But…but, they've done such a good job of maintaining normal life in this place," offered Sembado, trying to find a way to stifle the empty pit of disappointment that slowly grew in his stomach. He sank to the floor.

"You're right, Sem," his grandfather said, consolingly.

"And we wouldn't have a problem if this wasn't the awful truth. We would have eventually grown up and moved on like everyone else has seemed to; but this is all one big lie. A lifetime wasted in this damn complex, all because they couldn't hack it up there." He pointed up.

"So why didn't you ever tell anyone? All these guys believed you. Why no one else?" Sembado was looking for a way out of this terrible place he had found himself in.

"We were afraid for our families. These boys came looking for us. Found out through rumors and snooping—the same way we had to discover the truth. The same way you did." Grandfather looked especially dejected after this last sentence. "I'm sorry it had to happen to you too, Sembado. I know how much of a disappointment it is, but it's not my fault. It's not yours. It's theirs. And the only way we can get back at them is by spreading the truth as best we can."

The old man turned and addressed everyone.

"That's what tonight's meeting is about. We finally got a good copy of those security pictures that Leland was able to dig up. Thank you, son."

There was a murmur of friendly recognition as the focus turned to a young man, smaller than Sembado but probably older, with dark curly hair. A few boys around him patted him on the back. He looked on sheepishly.

Old man M'Gereg disappeared back behind Grandfather and could be heard fumbling with something mechanical. After a moment there was a bang and an obscenity.

"Damn it, Hyron! What'd you do to this lock?" he shouted over his shoulder.

"I didn't do anything to it, you old cuss. You can never get it opened," Grandfather replied bitterly. The two old men wrestled with the lock for a few more minutes.

Sembado took this chance to look around, and quickly realized that everyone's attention was off of Leland and back on him. The young men stared down at him as he sat on the floor. Some had crossed arms, others glared blankly. Sembado felt very alone, despite being surrounded by so many people. And then another person caught his eye; the tall, thin man who stood and smiled weakly. His eyes pierced Sembado and yet offered no threat. The man himself seemed to give off a presence of absolute good. Sembado took a chance. He slowly stood up and leaned in to ask the man an important question.

"Is it worth it?" he whispered, afraid of being overheard.

The man gave Sembado a very sure and solemn nod, not saying a word.

It was at that moment that Grandfather and M'Gereg finally came back with the small object that had apparently been locked up.

"Bring me that computer screen," Grandfather said, taking the screen and inserting the small chip he had into a port in the side. He touched the screen a few times, bringing up the files of the portable hard drive. As he did this, Sembado noticed that M'Gereg was speaking to two young men who produced a large white sheet from a bag and began to attach it to some pipes and framework on the ceiling, a makeshift viewing screen. Grandfather turned on the built-in projector that was common on the type of portable screen he held.

As the sheet fell, a picture appeared on it, waving in and out of focus as the material settled. As the picture became clear, Sembado identified it as a picture of a man in a hallway. From the angle of the picture, it seemed to have been taken from a high position, by one of the countless security cameras that could be seen around the complex. The man wore a penalty officer uniform: black with dark green accents, a helmet with a visor, and a sidearm. The guard's visor was down, but Sembado could still recognize his face.

"Wait a minute!" he shouted out, drawing everyone's attention.

"That's one of the men I saw running from your apartment the day you were attacked. And…I saw him again when the Pens took over the arena. He openly assaulted Jean Paul," he said, now addressing his grandfather.

"That's right," Grandfather said proudly. "They were posing as mutants when they attacked. They had identified me and tried getting my journal, but I fought them off. That's why it's important that I stay with your mom and dad now. They don't seem to have connected your mother being my daughter. I don't think they know where I am."

"What do you mean posing?" Sembado said, interrupting a slightly exasperated Grandfather. "They *shot* at you. Isn't that illegal?" Sembado was genuinely amazed, and even a bit skeptical that the government would go to those extremes to pursue his grandfather. The young men around him erupted in sarcastic jeering.

"Shut yer holes!" M'Gereg barked. The crowd died down immediately; the boys' stony expressions told

Sembado that M'Gereg demanded their respect regularly. When Sembado looked back at his grandfather, he saw a troubled look on the old man's face.

"Sembado, I know it seems too bad to be true, but the only thing our government has control over is us regular people, and that is only by using our fear against us."

"What else should a government have control over?" Sembado asked. He agreed that he was afraid of crossing the government, something that he prayed would never happen, but he knew that the tight control they had on the masses was for their own good.

What else do they need to have control over?

"Themselves!" Grandfather answered. "Themselves, Semmy, don't you understand? They don't have control of themselves." The statement echoed in Sembado's head as he tried to wrap his mind around the concept. He voiced his conundrum aloud.

"What would the government need self-control for? It doesn't do anything wrong." This time the laugh of disagreement came from M'Gereg himself, but only a single scoff. Grandfather looked especially disgusted.

"They've been brainwashin' ya for too long!" he shouted. Sembado jumped, feeling startled and uneasy. He'd never seen his grandfather so animated or angry. M'Gereg made no effort to keep the peace this time, but Grandfather took a minute to gain composure before continuing.

"Don't you know what corruption is, Sembado? That's why we're here, in this complex and under this floor. So long ago, when I was younger than you, the people in control of the world were becoming more and more corrupt. They took advantage of their power and started to scare themselves, so they built these damn inside-out fish tanks to keep a better eye on themselves, not us. Doesn't that make any sense? People in power are still people."

Sembado felt a hole open in his stomach. It got hot, then cold, then hot again. The idea had never occurred to him. His whole life the government had been a refuge of order and control. It was referred to as a single entity, not a group of people working together. He knew that it was people; he had seen them, talked to them on occasion, but it never sunk in until now. And what was worse was suddenly realizing that those people were able to make the same human errors as everyone else. Before, he had understood the whole thing to be a flawless operation, but that comfortable reality was very quickly falling apart. Sembado's thoughts were in disarray; he felt confused, disappointed, and betrayed. His thoughts raced as he searched for some rationale to make things better.

I've been safe and happy my whole life. This can't be true; perhaps grandfather is exaggerating, or even wrong.

Sembado knew the men around him, whether right or wrong, were dangerous. He knew that if he decided to resist them now, they would, with Grandfather's approval or not, eliminate the obstacle that he would then be to them. On the other hand, he had seen the government do very powerful and absolute things. Despite his remaining doubt about some of his grandfather's details, Sembado fully believed that the government was ready to crack down on this activity. He felt that, at least for the moment, he had no choice but to stay the course with Grandfather and his comrades. If the government had any suspicions that he was associated with these men, they would take little pity. He could not deny that the local authorities made it a bad habit of shooting first and asking questions later, but the uncouth, totalitarian nature of it had just occurred to him.

There was a long silence in which the dripping water from overhead echoed loudly in Sembado's ears. He scanned the group surrounding him, looking each man in the eye. Every one of them wholly believed in Grandfather's cause, yet each one was there of his own accord. Sembado looked his grandfather in the eye.

"I understand," he said. Though barely a high whisper, the statement was filled with resolution. Even crusty, old M'Gereg seemed satisfied. The two men brought the group's attention back to the presentation screen, which was occupied by a close-up of the young government agent's face. He wore a look of smug satisfaction. The next item presented was a soundless video clip of the man swaggering down another corridor, a young lady on each arm.

"As most of you know," M'Gereg began, addressing the group, but maintaining his glare on the screen, "the dead weight shown here is Gerard Hutch. The two young fins with him are not targets, merely victims of his so-called charm. He is neither a top agent nor a high priority. He does, however, have important connections."

The video clip was replaced by a new picture of the young man named Hutch standing next to a powerful-looking woman in a suit. He was also in a smart suit, clean shaven, and haughty as ever. M'Gereg continued his briefing.

"This is Hutch and his dear mommy, Jadice Fabian, She is the wife and political partner of J.L.Fabian, the Complex's Security Czar. Hutch is the worst kind of penalty officer there is, by our reckoning or the government's. He abuses what little power he has, berating undeserving citizens: men, women, and children. His careless fraternizing would have landed him in a whole deep of trouble on numerous occasions if it hadn't been for Mother Fabian bailing him out. He is inept and sloppy, but because of his mother's position he has been granted control over his patrol sector. The penalty officers under him, however, have little to no respect for his policies or practice. Although a few have joined his crooked club, the others steer clear; afraid of the rift he has made with the public, but more afraid of his bad habit of tattling to mommy when things don't go his way."

This last statement was met by condemning murmurs from the young men around Sembado. They all wore very definite looks of the deepest disdain for Gerard Hutch. Two of these young men had been called forward to collapse and store the presentation equipment, while the two old leaders continued their briefing. Grandfather spoke first.

"As Sembado pointed out during the first slide, Hutch has been used for mutant assignments before. There's no doubt that this scum loves the thrill of terrorizing the poor victims of these contrived attacks. His name gets drawn more for these missions than anyone else. This is due not only to the fact that his stepfather is the Security Secretary, but also because he is the most convincing mutant they have. No other agent goes to the lengths he does to sell his attacks; upon capture he has been known to seriously injure his fellow penalty officers. This is supposedly to better sell the scene to the public, but I've heard that these injured officers just happen to be those he likes the least. He plays dirty, gentlemen, even by IFCG standards. The gunfire that my grandson heard was another example of his unacceptable, cavalier behavior. This infraction nearly got him arrested, Fabian's stepson or not. He's a perfect embodiment of the corruption we're trying to fight, no matter how small his role really is."

"That's right," M'Gereg said, nodding approvingly. "It's this, combined with his mother's and stepfather's positions, that makes Hutch a perfect target for the Elephants' next major operation. More important than getting a hold of these pictures and video, our Leland was able to unearth some very interesting information. Leland, would you come up here and share what you've discovered."

Leland stepped over his compatriots slowly, careful not to step on fingers, as he made his way to the front of the assembly. He shook hands with M'Gereg. Grandfather patted him on the back as he turned to face the crowd. He looked around at his friends and began to speak. He had a high, boyish voice that seemed to clash with his burly appearance. Sembado was no longer convinced that Leland was older than him.

"I'll just get down to it," he said to the group. The young men around Sembado seemed eager to hear whatever special news Leland had regarding Hutch. "Hutch is up for another mutant mission. They are being planned more frequently now, as the surface release approaches. The IFCG seems intent on keeping the public wary of the surface. His assignment is planned for tomorrow night, but we already have everything we need to prepare. He should make his appearance at the Civillion around six-thirty p.m." Leland sat down to murmurs of approval as M'Gereg took over again.

"By custom, the offending mutant is usually given several minutes to make his appearance and terrorize as many citizens as possible, making the event as personally offensive as possible. Hutch uses his parents' influence to gain a few extra minutes of performance in case he spots a particularly vulnerable mother or child; I've seen him operate. The objective of tomorrow's operation is to capture him before the Pens do."

Pen was a common nickname for the complex's security forces, the penalty officers.

"By waiting just a minute after the public recognizes his threat, we should be able to use the commotion to shadow our movement. A few of you will also distract and confuse the officers on duty. This extra interaction should throw them off as we hurry Hutch out of there. By the time they move in to escort him out, we should be long gone. He will be taken to the far east chambers where the refugees live. Klisk's already met with them and they've agreed to keep Hutch concealed."

Grandfather continued the briefing, as Old M'Gereg finished his portion.

"This capture should send a very loud and articulate message to the Fabians that we mean business. They've tread all over us for a long time, but we're more organized than they know." The room was buzzing with anticipation and excitement as M'Gereg concluded the evening's affairs.

"It's gettin' late boys, and you need to keep it down as you leave. We've jammed the security cameras in this sector, but that means that they'll be sending maintenance this way before too long so we'll be leaving in twos and threes. We will meet behind *Terranean Memories* tomorrow so arrive between five-thirty and six. We have much to discuss and many duties to assign. It's going to be a lot of work for a one-day prep, but if you show up and keep quiet, we'll get things done. Now take off, you in the back first."

The first few boys nearest the ladder slowly ascended to the corn field above. The young men awaiting their turn stood in small groups, fidgeting and whispering excitedly about the evening's main announcement. One of these groups nearest Sembado beckoned him over, its three occupants looking friendlier than when he was first introduced.

"Welcome, Grey," whispered the first boy. Sembado recognized him from school. "I'm Gin Marx, and this is Leno Brone," he continued, motioning to the tall young black man to Sembado's right. "And this is Petro Pauls," he said, motioning to the last boy who nodded smugly. Sembado was sure he recognized Pauls from somewhere, but before he could put his finger on it, Gin finished the introduction with a cool, nonchalant addition.

"You probably recognize Pete from his portrait with the detention department." Petro continued to smile smugly as his friend expounded on his outlawed accomplishments. "Pete here was nearly caught trying to get the same information that Leland brought tonight, but was able to get away. Actually, it was Hutch he slipped past. Hutchy was too busy trying to get some fin away from her friends for some alone time. The IFCG got a good shot of Pete's pretty face though, had his poster up for weeks before giving up. He's been underground ever since."

Petro continued to smile and Sembado realized that he had a very clear, soft complexion. Presently, the boys between Sembado's group and the exit were shuffling toward the ladder. A hand grabbed Sembado's shoulder and he turned around to find that Grandfather had shifted through the group. He motioned for the others to go on and exit. There were very few men left in the room; they seemed to be the oldest of the crowd. One of them followed the last younger member up the ladder and closed and locked the maintenance hatch. He returned and joined the others who remained; they were all sitting back down. Only Sembado, his grandfather, and M'Gereg remained standing. M'Gereg was fumbling with something, his back turned to the others. When he turned around, Sembado could see something like a gun in his hand. Confused, he looked at his grandfather for support a reassuring smiling on his old, wrinkled face.

"Don't worry boy, it won't hurt, but it is permanent. You're one of us now, and that can't ever change. You understand me, Sem?"

It seemed absolute. Whatever it was that they were planning on doing to him was forever, but Sembado didn't feel that he was in danger. M'Gereg approached Sembado with the small gun like object.

"Sembado Grey, let me see your right forearm and repeat after me," he said.

M'Gereg recited a handful of initiation stanzas officially and Sembado repeated each one carefully as prompted.

"I, Sembado Grey, do swear my allegiance to the Elephant's Guild, and all the truth and justice that it stands for. I will honor this pledge with my life and death."

"Hyron, would you like to do the honors?" M'Gereg asked, handing Grandfather the tool in his hand.

Grandfather took the gun in his right hand and Sembado's right forearm in his left. Sembado was shocked to see how wet his grandfather's eyes looked. He pressed the tip of the gun to Sembado's skin and pulled the trigger. A bright white light shined where the gun was pointed. It was in a concentrated beam, like a laser, and was moving around at a fast speed. The surface of Sembado's skin started to feel warm and soon it felt as if it were being burned. Just as it became unbearable the process was over. Grandfather pulled the gun away slowly to reveal a slightly blistered shape on Sembado's skin. This is what he saw:

"This," Grandfather began, "is the mark of the Elephants' Guild. All of our members have this mark on their forearms like you. You are forever branded and will be an Elephant forever. I wish we had time to celebrate, but we don't. Let's move out."

The remaining older members took turns quickly shaking Sembado's hand and began their own procession toward the ladder. Sembado and his grandfather were the last to leave. The walk home was a long and quiet one.

Chapter Nine
Disturbing Developments

The next day, Sembado and Grandfather passed their time until the big event by completely moving Grandfather into private quarters, something he had been very reluctant to do. With Sembado's dad having weekends off, the three of them made quick work of the old boxes of clothes and toys that towered in the room. They were moving Grandfather into what used to be Sembado and Herbert's playroom, but had more recently played host to an array of spiders and rats. This was the perfect excuse for Sembado's father to try out his new decellurizer.

Grandfather eyed the box with a look of utter disgust, almost loathing. When he caught Sembado's curious stare with his own glare, he quickly turned away to open the door to the room.

"This," Sembado's father explained, "is a new gadget that is designed to destroy most living matter by defusing its cell membranes. It's kinda interesting really. You can even get a special attachment that's specifically designed to destroy cell walls if the target is some sort of plant life. I read somewhere the government uses this technology for all sorts of top secret things and that they've even applied it to assault weapons."

"Yea," Grandfather muttered sarcastically. "Top secret."

Father was too excited to take notice and continued.

"And this is the first available application in the retail market," he finished breathlessly, like a child reciting aquascope specs off the back of the box. "Anyway, it says here that the setting we're going to use requires us to be fifteen feet away," he added, surveying the room. The room was hardly ten feet square and it didn't take Sembado long to realize they weren't going to be able to watch unless they rigged up something special. By the looks on their faces, he could tell his dad and grandfather had come to the same conclusion.

"Well," Sembado said, screwing his face up in concentration, "if we put the trap in that far corner there, it'll be about fifteen feet from the door, so I guess we could hang out in the hall and watch."

"That's good, but not good enough," his father said, as a mad scientist would to his assistant. Father left for their storage compartment and returned momentarily with his second latest gadget, the Black+Decker Multi-Purpose Plasma Separator. He then used it to turn the old, discolored door into a Dutch door by simply cutting it in half. Sembado watched his father carefully as the microlasers disintegrated the dust and pieces of door before they hit the ground.

"Cleans up for ya," his father said, sounding, as usual, like an advertiser pitching a product. "Guess that's the beauty of Black+Decker," he added with a wink.

"But what about my door?" Grandfather asked sharply. "I won't be undressing with people walking about."

"That door was ancient," Father rebutted. "We'll fix ya up a new one."

And with that, he snapped the separator's carrying case shut and hurried to the storage compartment and back quickly enough to be winded.

"Now," he began breathlessly, "let's see what this thing can do."

He took the device out of the protective plastic mold, set it in the corner, and clicked a large knob on the top of the unit to the left three times. He then got up hastily, as if waiting for it to explode, ushered Sembado out into the hall where Grandfather was already waiting, and began fiddling with the remote.

"Now it says in order to set it off from a distance, we'll need to synchronize the remote with the main unit," he said. "Since we set it to three yards on the main unit, we'll need to adjust it to the same setting." Sembado examined the words on the remote as his father adjusted it to the same setting as the mother unit. There were a vast number of settings on the remote, ranging from one yard to a hundred. Sembado guessed that the farther the settings, the more potent the trap would be. He then noticed the three buttons next to the dial. One was green, one yellow, and one red. Grandfather gave him a light cuff on the head to signal they were about to begin. Father pressed the green button while reading the instructions, just in case fine details were being missed. When he pushed the button, it began to glow bright green. Immediately, Sembado noticed a soft whirring noise coming from the corner. It started out soft and smooth, like a hum. As time went on, it became stronger and louder. It was a mesmerizing hum. It was dull, yet enchanting, and almost hypnotizing.

As the hum picked up to an even pace the second light on the remote, the yellow one, lit halfway up. It seemed to invite pressing. Scanning over the manual yet again, Father traced a specific line three times before proceeding. He then pressed the yellow button and sure enough, it lit to its full brightness.

As before, something began to happen. This time it was a light, which seemed to be coming from anywhere the box would allow it. Not from inside, but not from the surface. The thing itself seemed to be glowing. A soft glow that Sembado wasn't sure was there at first. Then it picked up just as the hum had, which was still keeping even all the while. As the glow became more defined, Sembado picked out a color; he could tell it was distinctly blue now. A beautiful blue, not like the sky, but a bright, unnatural, electric blue that was obviously artificial but entrancing just the same. It became brighter and more electric. His trance was broken, as he noticed movement out of the corner his eye.

Three large rats came creeping out of the closet. Completely ignoring Sembado and the others, they crept closer to the corner on the opposite side of the room. They sniffed the ground as they went, but apart from this, didn't appear like their normal cautious selves in the slightest. In fact, the closer they got to the device, the less care they took and soon were in a quick trot. Their odd behavior had completely distracted Sembado from noticing the other creatures that were making this same strange dance toward the box. A handful of mice had joined the parade, as well as many small insects. Spiders were crawling out of every crack. Fewer new members joined the fray as the existing ones piled onto the rats, who, now that they had reached their goal, seemed to be content with being in its presence.

Finally, there were no more newcomers. The last of the creatures, which had made their entrance right between Sembado's feet and under the half door, made their way to the box and joined their friends in the vibrating mass. The red button made its half-lit appearance. Before Father's finger even came close to the button, something else started to happen. The light and sounds from the box started to happen. The light and sounds from the box started to pulse. This seemed to affect its guests, as the rats, mice, spiders, and others began to vibrate. As they shook, they moved, and Sembado soon realized that they were creating a pattern around the box. The shape their bodies were making very closely resembled the patterns he saw in physics class when a magnet and a handful of iron filings were put underwater and allowed to sit. The animals made two opposite loops around the box, forming concentrated rings that grew outward. Once this choreography had ended, and the critters were all lined up, they stopped and the red button lit up completely. Machine and animals alike seemed to stop and wait. The machine continued its rhythmic pulses of light and sound, and everyone stayed in their places like stage actors waiting for the curtain to go up. Only after this repetitive show continued for a full sixty seconds did Sembado, Father, and Grandfather realize nothing else was going to happen until the last button was pressed.

Again, Father reviewed the corresponding manual pages and, after a moment's hesitation, pressed the red button. Immediately, the blue light changed. It seemed to solidify from its previous soft glow to a hard, definite light. It was more of a transparent dome that had formed around the box. It started to grow. Like a party balloon, it continued to expand until it reached nearly two feet in diameter, big enough to engulf all of the creatures around it. Sembado stared in amazement as the rats, spiders, and other animals stood as still as statues, tinted blue under their new home. After only a moment, the dome began to move again, this time inward, and extremely slowly. It reached the rats first. And Sembado watched closely, curious to see how they would be disposed of.

Did it just pull all the animals into a pile so they could be trapped together and easier to remove?

Then to his horror, he realized this wasn't the idea at all. As the dome shrank, it ate away at the rats, quite literally. As the surface of the dome continued to shrink, it burned the rats away. Hair, skin, and bone made disgusting hissing and popping noises as they burned; there was no blood; it was cooked up before it was spilled. Slowly but surely, the deflating balloon of blue death devoured the entire mass of creatures, who, even after being half destroyed, kept their stoic watch at their designated posts. At the end of its cycle, the box became quiet, lightless, and dead.

Sembado, now sure of what he thought about the death box, looked over at his father and grandfather's faces to see their reactions. Father had a disappointed look, like a young boy caught doing something he wasn't supposed to. Grandfather wasn't making a sound, but had tears steadily trickling down his face. Father slowly opened the door and entered the room; it was odorless. The box had even killed the smells that the burnt hair and blood would have normally caused. He collected it and left, to dispose of it no doubt. He returned with a handful of papers.

"I don't want you to say anything about this to your mother or brother."

"Yes, sir," Sembado replied solemnly.

"And here, Hyron. I got paper copies of your resident reassignment forms. I know you prefer paper. These should have been filled out a week ago. I have filled out what I could." When he handed the papers over to Grandfather, he kept his eyes on them, avoiding eye contact. Grandfather, staring him straight in the face, snatched the papers away without looking at them.

He turned and walked away, not saying a word.

The whole death box production had made Sembado uneasy, even exhausted. He soon became tired and spent the early afternoon sleeping off his sorrows.

Sleep brought little comfort. Sembado had an awful dream that he could not wake from. In it, he saw a troop of majestic elephants being herded into a large room, which was then filled with water until the great creatures nearly drowned. The water receded and the breathless, exhausted animals sat stooped in a group.

Then he was one of them, and a man resembling Gerard Hutch appeared with a large death box and threw it at Sembado and the other elephants' feet. He laughed maniacally as he ran out of the room. Sembado looked on powerlessly as the box began to hum and dance. As he and the other elephants shuffled toward the hypnotizing box, anxiety swept over him, and he suddenly realized that despite all of his definite thoughts of fleeing the box, his body continued forward. He wanted to be as far from the box as possible, knowing its capabilities, and yet he could not resist its call.

The horror culminated as he and the other elephants fought for the closest position and were slowly dissolved. A white-hot pain covered his entire body, making him reel and cry out, but he could not get away. Suddenly, the room was enormous, miles across. At the far end, a giant Dutch door a hundred stories high framed the face of nasty Gerard Hutch. He continued his disgusting laughter as the pain commandeered Sembado's consciousness.

***

He woke in a hot sweat and felt close to vomiting. The clock on his bedside said he had been sleeping for four hours. It was nearly four-thirty and he needed to start mentally preparing for the night's activities.

He shuffled out to the main chamber where his mother, brother, and grandfather were gathered around the television. His mother was crying, his brother Herbert looked terrified, and his grandfather showed no emotion at all. They were watching the news. Sembado entered the room and sat down next to his brother who gave him a pitiful look before looking back at the TV which was displaying the headline:

GOVERNMENT OFFICIAL MISSING, PRESUMED DEAD

"This is Gillian Minero with Complex News Channel Eight. We've been reporting this disturbing news all afternoon, and we here at Channel Eight will bring you updates as soon as possible. So far we only have limited information. What we do know is that IFCG Internal Investigations administrator, Jonah Feldman, was last seen yesterday afternoon leaving his office at the Internal Investigation Service at the Complex Government's main chambers. Suspicions of foul play arose when Feldman's briefcase and other personal effects were found early this morning with his blood on them. The Security Department has yet to comment on their investigation. Feldman's family was unavailable for comment."

Sembado sat stunned and appalled. The missing IFCG administrator was Meligose's father.

I know this man. Personally. I have to go see Mel; I can't imagine how he feels. Mr. Feldman, I mean, my God.

Sembado and Meligose had been friends for a long time, and their families were well acquainted. Sembado's mother continued to sob hysterically.

"I'm going to see Mel," Sembado said breathlessly. He had already gone to change clothes and then was on his way out the front door. Herbert was busy consoling their mother. Grandfather shot him a serious look and pointed at his watch, but said nothing.

Sembado raced to the Feldman's door and knocked quickly. Meligose answered the door with bloodshot eyes. He left the door open for Sembado, then shuffled back into the chamber without saying a word. Sembado closed the door carefully and turned to find the silent chamber quite full. At least a dozen people quietly watched the TV. They seemed to be seated around Mel's mother, bracing her for support. Sembado recognized three of Mel's aunts, but the rest of the group was made up of neighbors. Sembado just caught Meligose sulking back to his room and quickly followed. When Sembado entered the room, he found Meligose slumped on the bed, his big blond head in his hands. Sembado said nothing.

What can I say? He's only a kid like me; it's just him and his mom now; what can I say? I can't believe his dad's gone, but is he for sure dead? I can't believe it.

Sembado decided that saying nothing might be the best idea and he sat next to Meligose on the bed, one hand on his friend's back. For a long time, the two young men sat in silence. The minutes ticked by and apart from an aunt poking her face in to offer a helpful smile, there wasn't any disturbance. Finally the silence was broken when the boys' mutual friend Kreymond entered the room solemnly.

"I'm so sorry, Mel," he said quietly as he sat down on the bed. "I just can't believe it."

Despite being genuinely distraught by this turn of events, Sembado was startled to see Mel's bedside clock read 4:45 P.M. As insensitive as it seemed, he could not let this keep him from getting down to the Civillion on time. Sembado left the room quietly, gave Mel's mother wordless condolences, and headed back to his own unit. There, he found his own mother and his brother still sitting in front of the TV. His grandfather stood behind them as Sembado entered the room. Grandfather was the only one to take notice. He left for his room to collect something and returned quickly to lead Sembado out to the corridor. They walked quietly for a long time until they reached a more vacant side corridor.

"Sembado, listen." Grandfather's tone was not sullen, but calm. "You realize that the weapons used in the…eradication all those decades ago were not nuclear, right?"

The question struck Sembado as odd. He had a hard enough time focusing on tonight's mission after the news of Mel's father, let alone on the secret files from last night. He nodded his head.

"There is more to that rat trap than you—and especially your father—realize. M'Gereg and I have more files that we haven't shown many people that explain that the weapons used for Operation Clean Slate were of the same technology used in that damned death box."

Sembado became dizzy as his grandfather's last statement sunk in. He tried in vain to block out the morbid pictures his mind began to paint. Just as another million faceless victims poured into this awful scenario, his grandfather brought him back to the present with more words.

"They're gettin' desperate with this surface release, Semmy, and they're not afraid to play nasty again. They have dozens of jerks like that Hutch ready to pounce on anyone who isn't playin' by their rules. Now, we need to get down to the Civillion."

Chapter Ten
Captured

Grandfather decided that it would be better for him and Sembado to enter the Civillion separately, and he had Sembado hurry ahead. Sembado's instructions were to wait casually around and contact any of the other young men while Grandfather went to rendezvous with the senior Elephants behind Terranean Memories.

Sembado walked into the Civillion and paused to take in the familiar view. As usual, there was a dull roar of commerce and gossip. This used to be the most comfortable place on Earth for Sembado, but now it felt completely different. It was like being lied to. It felt dirty, foreign, and cheap.

He wasted no time getting lost in the throng. He bumped into people and turned this way and that, instinctively moving toward the PS dealer. He started to falter, halfway there, realizing that it was not that busy and offered little cover. He came to a complete stop and started to panic as his confused, awkward pause became more obvious. Just as his clumsy shuffle had started to attract attention, two hands grabbed either arm and pulled him back into the crowd and into a salesman's unoccupied storage space between two vendors.

"You look like an idiot. What the depths are you doing?" Gin Marx was shaking his head in disapproval as he whispered harshly; Leno Brone was busy looking around for anyone whose attention was still theirs. It appeared for the moment that total distraction had been averted.

"I'm sorry, I didn't—" Sembado's excuse would have been inadequate.

"Whatever, listen: just keep your eyes peeled for anything. No matter what, we need to move before they do."

Leno started to move through the crowd in an uncommitted fashion much like Sembado had attempted to. Sembado, at Gin's orders, followed second. He tried to keep up without bumping into Leno or anyone around them. It was a difficult, irregular dance, but Sembado was soon moving fluidly behind his leader as Gin gracefully brought up the rear.

He found it easier to anticipate Leno's movements if he periodically watched the other boy's face between scanning the crowd for inconsistencies and looking for visual clues from his eyes. As Sembado did this, he was able to pick up on more than his guide's next turn. It appeared, more obviously by the minute that Leno, and most assuredly Gin as well, was making purposeful eye contact with a number of other figures in the crowd. Sembado confirmed his suspicions when he started to recognize some of the men from the meeting in the vents just last night. He had to make sure he didn't let his jaw drop when he realized that a dozen or more of his secret conspirators were moving amid the tumult of commerce. The individuals snaked this way and that, all but avoiding eye contact as they shuffled and stepped into what soon became an autonomous web, slowly leaking through the crowd in no particular direction. It seemed to Sembado that although his allies were moving in a group, some of the individuals continued to break off in new directions. Then it struck him: despite knowing that Gerard Hutch's farce of a mutant attack was to take place in the Civillion, the brotherhood did not know which, if any, of the many entrances the offender would use. After all, there were many vent hatches in the Civillion floor, which were surely accessible to anyone in Hutch's position.

This thought moved Sembado to start taking a grander view of the Civillion, and to inspect any of its intricacies that he was aware of. In doing this, he realized that not only were there now nearly twenty Elephants drifting through the crowd, but many of the senior members of the brotherhood, Grandfather included, were now posted in ones or twos all around the perimeter of the circular space. Sembado was nearly distracted from the task at hand by how impressed he was with the combination of control and improvisation that seemed to rule his affiliates. His thoughts soon drifted as he realized that this display may have been at work countless times during his past visits to the Civillion or any other crowded sector of the complex.

Just as his thoughts started to wander further, a wave of confusion swept from his right across the entire Civillion. Hutch had made his move and was, from what Sembado could tell, chasing a group of frantic young ladies toward the greater group of denizens.

Grandfather had told Sembado to mostly stay out of the way and try to create more confusion for the penalty officers without getting too close. The crowd began to break in different directions, but most of the terrified people, Hutch's female prey especially, moved directly away from him. Sembado saw people being knocked over and was jostled himself in the panic, but could still make out a penalty officer's pathetic attempt of pushing toward Hutch. He could also see the eight or more Elephants between him and Hutch, fighting desperately against the current to get the frenzied marauder.

Sembado was close to the attack, and in the hurried pace and confusion and thrill, decided to join the charge as nearly ten of his comrades were now rushing at a bewildered Gerard Hutch. Hutch wore ragged clothing and a mismatched suit of scrap-metal-adorned armor. His brash and reckless attitude only allowed him a brief pause for concern before he met the onslaught brutishly with a loud bang. Sembado ricocheted off of the initial contact and lay in a heap as the other young men knocked Hutch over the head with his own improvised bludgeon and carried him off.

Sembado shook off the collision and hurried to his feet. It seemed for the moment that the others had been able to distract or delay the penalty officers long enough, but the evacuation of bystanders was nearly complete, and Sembado now realized that he was one of very few people left in the Civillion, the rest of which were penalty officers. He had almost all of the Pens' attention, but few opportunities for escape. It appeared that by this point, the mission was an utter success. The officers seemed to realize at least a portion of what had happened, and they were now frantically calling on their communicators as they motioned to each other and eyed Sembado very suspiciously. He did a very poor job of acting inconspicuous as he started to back away from the majority of the officers and toward the nearest exit.

Sembado wanted to turn and run, but fear held him on the spot. He could barely manage a steady pace backward, as a dozen penalty officers started moving toward him quickly. The closest officer started toward Sembado at a trot, and released his sidearm from its holster. This gesture moved Sembado to break into a turn and pick up speed as the nearest officer shouted after him.

"Stop! Stay where you are!"

Sembado was in no way going to obey and gave one last glance over his shoulder at the Civillion as he was chased out of it for the second time that weekend. He was horrified to see more than a dozen penalty officers charging hard in his direction, three of whom were riding a Penalty-Officer-Powered Vehicle, or POP-V, with two more climbing on. He might have been able to outrun two or three officers, but a POP-V was able to do nearly twenty miles per hour when traveling in a straight line.

My only chance is to put as many twists and turns between me and that POP-V as possible.

The thought shot through Sembado's mind as he raced away. He tore down the next set of passages turning this way and that. More than once he had to double back as there were penalty officers coming down the corridor he had chosen.

At this rate I'll never lose them.

Sembado rounded the next corner as bullets whizzed past where he had just been and caused a nearby light fixture to explode. His lungs burned as he sprinted faster, losing breath as he continued. Another glance over his shoulder showed an empty corridor, at least a hundred feet.

Could I have lost them?

Suddenly, an agonizing pain caught Sembado in the throat and a stomach-turning crunch rang in his ears as his feet continued forward and off the passage floor. He slammed hard on his back, and the pain of losing his breath doubled the fiery burn on his throat, which he instinctively grasped as he reeled in pain. Somebody had sprung from a side corridor and caught Sembado right under the chin with a metal-clad forearm. Sembado's vision went black.

Part Two
The Exodus

Chapter Eleven
Elephant in the Room

Sembado was being dragged down a dimly lit hallway. His wrists were bound behind his back, and two very bulky men in dark clothes held him by each upper arm. One sported black armored bracers. They allowed him to struggle into step, as his feet had been dragging until now. He could not remember the recent debacle at the Civillion, and his immediate thought was that he was dreaming.

The dark corridor ended with a stout, heavy-looking door, which opened when one of Sembado's escorts swiped a card through a scanner to the left. Sembado's eyes strained from the light, as the next corridor was much brighter. As the glare subsided, he could see that he was now in some kind of government processing room. There was a bank of desks to the right and left, and in the middle stood a large podium and a U-shaped countertop. There were workers typing at a majority of the work stations on either side. One of the workers got up and walked to another occupied station to confer with its owner. Sembado was being led past these desks and onto the podium in the middle. A man and woman were posted behind it; the man sat with his head in one hand, reviewing files, while the woman stood expectantly.

"Dis is one we coat 'n da Seev'eon," said one of Sembado's captors in a thick foreign accent. Sembado now realized that this man was quite a bit darker than him, while the other had thick curls and shockingly yellow eyes. His stomach also turned as the memory of the capture and pursuit from the Civillion flooded back over him. He now realized that he was being processed in a government penitentiary office.

"And his identification?" the woman replied curtly.

"Couldn't find it. Musta migrated," snapped the dark man.

She replied with an exasperated sigh. This was news to Sembado.

Should I tell them it's implanted in my bicep?

Despite his panic, it was easy for Sembado to pick up on the fact that these two people held positions that were seldom required to interact. She seemed more intolerant of the dark man's presence than Sembado's, and the dark man seemed completely aware of this and was therefore even more impatient with the woman's haughty demeanor. Sembado had never seen two people interact like this. The tension fueled his anxiety.

"Then did you bring him here?"

The woman's reply was sweet and coddling, as if she were talking to a small child and was only willing to give helpful hints. "Perhaps he was just running from the mutant attack."

"An' jus 'appenin' to 'aff one o' deez?" The man shot back his retort as he jerkily yanked up Sembado's sleeve, exposing the Elephant symbol on his forearm. The woman turned her nose up even further and looked away as if a noxious smell had just overwhelmed her. Without looking, she pressed a button on the console hidden behind her podium.

"D-24," she hissed into the console.

A buzzer sounded faintly. A door behind the U-shaped desk was kicked open, and two uniformed penalty officers marched out and pulled Sembado out of his current captors' hands. At this time, Sembado let out an unexpected cough. He experienced an agonizing pain in his throat and was suddenly reminded of his capture. His throat was extremely swollen and painful to the touch. The panic caused him to start breathing harder, which in turn made him cough even more. It was a very painful experience, and soon he was choking and gasping for air.

"Get him out of here. Please," said the woman briskly, eyeing Sembado as though he were an infectious wild animal. As the slightly shorter guards ushered Sembado away, he could hear the dark man and his red-headed partner making a fuss about payment, and then the woman's stuffy response.

"Bounty can only be had in the financing department. Take this form to level four."

The argument faded out of earshot as the door that had been kicked open was now swinging closed, with a very anxiously sick Sembado on the other side. He continued choking a bit longer until one of his escorts put a small oxygen mask to his face and had him breathe into it for a minute or two. The cold gas burned, but it allowed him to breathe regularly long enough to get the coughing under control.

His new handlers were much more professional in demeanor than his previous escorts, but also just as cold, if not more so. They treated his condition as though they were afraid to catch whatever he had. They both wore standard Pen uniforms with tactical vests and helmets.

The corridor beyond the processing room had thick windows down the right side. Behind these windows was a wall of hundreds of monitors, which were being watched by several armed penalty officers. On the corridor wall opposite the windows was a bulletin board inside a glass case. Sembado was able to look it over as his escorts talked with the other penalty officers posted behind the glass. Six portraits of wanted criminals were posted on the board. Below each mug shot were security camera screen shots of the fugitives, a physical description, and a list of offenses. Sembado saw four of the six posters stamped with the word "Elephant" in bold letters. He recognized one of the four as Petro Pauls. One of the other Elephants had a red X across his picture.

A seventh poster was taped to the outside of the glass case. It was more of a gag portrait of Gerard Hutch. It had been decorated with a single thick, bushy eyebrow, a mustache, and missing teeth. The list of odd violations included "dating own sister."

A hand shot over Sembado's shoulder and quickly ripped Hutch's poster down. Sembado spun around quickly to see both of his escorts and all five surveillance room Pens glaring at him. The one who ripped down the poster was now balling it up. The men in the control room went back to watching their monitors.

One of the penalty officers took out a plastic wand and scanned Sembado's shoulder. After a moment, he became frustrated, jerking the wand back and forth.

"I thought I told you to replace the battery in this thing," he snapped at another nearby officer.

"I did. I heard the bounty hunter say it might have migrated."

"Your chip migrate?" the penalty officer asked, addressing Sembado directly.

Sembado did not reply, but instead pointed to an area in his upper arm, just above his new Elephant mark. The penalty officer made an exasperated face, scanning the area with the wand. It beeped immediately. He looked at the display on the back of the wand's paddle-shaped head. He raised his eyebrows, called his comrade over, and motioned for him to look at the display. The other officer's eyes instantly shot from the display up to Sembado's face, and then he ran off to whisper something to the officers in the control room. All of them took a moment to crane their necks and glance back at Sembado.

When the second officer returned, Sembado was hurried along to the next corridor. This corridor turned out to be a lift chamber. He waited quietly with his captors while the lift was brought to their level. When it arrived, there was a great commotion coming from inside. One of Sembado's escorts forced him against the nearby wall while the other readied his weapon. The door on the lift opened, and two penalty officers fell out on the floor with a detainee underneath them. Three more penalty officers had an even larger prisoner pinned in the corner of the lift, struggling to hold him still.

Both captives had dark, tattoo-covered skin, long hair, and dirty, unkempt beards. Sembado had never seen anyone like them. Sembado's escort, who had drawn his weapon, was now pressing it firmly against the floored prisoner's head.

"If you don't stop wiggling, I'll melt that ugly head clean off your shoulders."

As the penalty officer said this, he cocked his weapon loudly. Sembado didn't understand, but the prisoners must have because they both stopped moving immediately and were quickly subdued.

"Thanks," said one of the Pens who had knocked the man down. "These two started fighting halfway down. I guess they aren't friends anymore." He and his partner forced the first man to his feet and into the opposite corner of the larger captive.

Sembado was then packed into the lift by his two escorts.

"We're headed to D," said one of Sembado's captors, pushing the appropriate button. "What about you guys?"

"These two are going to F," one of the men replied, and Sembado's escort obliged by making the necessary selection.

The lift stopped after a moment and opened into a reception chamber with a large yellow *D* painted on the wall. The chamber had corridors leading to the left and right, and Sembado was led to the left. A sign over this corridor was marked *20-40*.

These have to be penitentiary hold cells.

Sembado was being marched past small rooms with thick glass. *22, 23...*

"D-24, unlock for deposit. No withdrawal," said one of Sembado's escorts into an intercom on the wall. A moment passed before a light above the door flashed. It was accompanied by a dull tone. Sembado was shoved inside the very bright room, and the thick glass door was shut behind him.

Chapter Twelve
The Madness to the Method

Sembado had been thrown in with a cellmate. He was absolutely stunned to be staring at a very familiar face. Sitting on one of the two bench-like beds was his best friend Meligose's father, Jonah Feldman.

Mr. Feldman was sitting on his bunk with his elbow on his knees, and his were fingers running through his thinning blond hair. He wore cracked glasses, a few days of beard stubble, and an even more surprised expression than Sembado.

Sembado had grown up with this man's son, and knew his family well. He and Mr. Feldman were not overly familiar, but they were close enough just the same. Mr. Feldman leapt to his feet and threw his arms around Sembado. He smelled as if he had not showered since he had disappeared.

"Sem! My word! Are you okay? What's going on? What have you done?" Several more jumbled questions followed. Sembado could not respond, but he gestured to his throat instead, trying to show that it was swollen beyond use.

"My word, Sem. What did they do? Can you breathe?"

Sembado nodded his head in the affirmative, and proceeded to charade the chase and subsequent forearm chop to the throat.

"I can't believe it," said Mr. Feldman solemnly. He sat down on his bed and motioned Sembado to do the same.

"Actually, I can," he added. "Our top agencies have gotten completely out of control; they are preparing to use weapon systems that violate nearly every human rights law ever passed. I've even learned of corruption in some offices that reach from the lowest ranks to the highest officials. That's why I'm here. I was preparing an internal affairs report explaining the whole thing." He paused for a moment and let it sink in. Even without his voice, Sembado clearly communicated how disturbing this news was. Mr. Feldman must have assumed it was just the gravity of the situation that was overwhelming; there was no way he could know everything that Sembado knew about the IFCG.

Sembado's disappointment was caused by something completely different. He had temporarily accepted Grandfather's and the Elephants' stories because he had no other choice at the time. He desperately wanted to find out that they were somehow wrong and that they merely misunderstood their government. He wanted to believe this so badly because the alternative was too much to take. He was not sure how to even begin to process the obvious fact that nearly every aspect of the government that made his daily life possible was corrupt. Every bit of it was being eaten alive by cancerous greed and corruption. Now he was hearing it from Mr. Feldman, an actual government official. It was undeniable.

Sembado's head swam. It suddenly became even harder to breathe, but it had nothing to do with his swollen throat. Sembado was hyperventilating and was now in the throes of his first panic attack. In his calm, surreal life, he had never been pushed to such anxiety, especially not by his own thoughts. Even this current observation seemed to make the experience more and more straining.

Mr. Feldman had responded to Sembado's fit quite rapidly. He had the boy lay down on the bunk, and for several minutes, he spoke very calmly to Sembado about nothing in particular. The kind and polite man had had his share of betrayal and stress in the past few years, and even more so in the past few days. He still believed this was the first time Sembado was learning this upsetting news. It was just the first time it had grabbed Sembado as hard as it did.

When Sembado was finally breathing evenly and the color had returned to his face, Mr. Feldman went to the single cabinet in the room and returned with a tepid bottle of water. Sembado drank it down quickly, despite the stinging sensation that the repeated swallowing caused.

After a very long time, Mr. Feldman began to speak again. He continued from where he had left off.

"The reason I'm here—" He paused to check Sembado's reaction. Sembado nodded for him to continue. "I'm here because of my reports. Me, and twelve others. If our report was released, the entire, and I mean the entire Security Branch would have to be indicted, and that's just the one department. Like I said before, we found weapons with illegal uses, even for the government. We discovered that almost all of these mutant attackers have been either scripted or have been covers for illegal government arrests of partisans."

This last piece of information had little effect on Sembado.

"Doesn't that surprise you at all, Sembado? That all these years these mutant attacks have been made up. Why? Why the deception? I mean—who knows what deeper, darker secrets we would have found if we hadn't been arrested?" Now Mr. Feldman looked a bit worn with anxiety.

Sembado wanted desperately to share everything he had learned from the Elephants with Mr. Feldman, but he could still not talk; his throat was as hot as ever. It hurt just to breathe or swallow. Then he remembered something that he could communicate to Mr. Feldman quite clearly. With the older man's attention, Sembado pulled up his sleeve, revealing the Elephants' symbol.

"My word, Sembado! Is it real?" He seemed intrigued, but wary nonetheless. It appeared as though old government biases die hard. "My word! But I wish you could talk. I have so many questions about what the Elephants actually are. I can't believe this administration has been truthful about that either. But, of course!" With this last exclamation, Mr.Feldman hurried over to his suit coat, which was folded in a corner, and started rummaging through the pockets. "I always carry an extra pen with me, but I'm not sure if they took it when they brought me in here. I usually keep it well hidden so that I won't lose it. Mel gave it to me for my birthday. I really miss him and the Sharon. Ha!" Mr. Feldman pulled a small ballpoint pen from under one lapel of the jacket. "So much for thorough security. Now, I'll try to keep this easy and not make you write too much." He clicked the pen open and handed it to Sembado. Sembado took it, but realized when he had it that there was no paper to write on. Mr. Feldman seemed to realize the same thing, and he zipped across the room to grab something else.

It was only at this point that Sembado took in his surroundings for the first time. The room was yellow-green and small, approximately eight by ten feet, with two bunks, a cabinet, a toilet, and a sink. The floor had ugly, stained linoleum with a ceiling to match.

Mr. Feldman returned and revealed a half-empty roll of toilet paper and handed it over to a grimacing Sembado. With the toilet paper and pen in hand, Sembado was poised to write. He felt strange hunkered over the roll. He had to hold it in an awkward fashion in order to gain an effective grip. Without waiting for the first question, he began to scribble away furiously. With so much inside, he needed little prompting.

I know everything you do and more, he wrote.

Mr. Feldman, seeing Sembado's enthusiasm, held his questions and continued to follow along with the awkward scrawl. Sembado kept his statements short. His tight grasp on the pen made his hand cramp.

I know about mutants—corruption—why we're here. I'm not sure about illegal guns, but have an idea what they could be.

"What do you mean, 'why we're here'?" asked the older man.

The war was planned. The devices were planted by home and blamed on nuclear war—it was a conspiracy.

Mr. Feldman's mouth hung wide open as Sembado continued.

They used the same kind of device as new rodent traps—Ive seen it—it has blue energy sphere that dissolves—

Mr. Feldman interrupted in his enthusiasm. "That's what the weapon systems are based on. They've put that technology into a bullet cartridge. It's the most disgusting thing I've ever heard."

They must already be using them—heard a penalty officer threaten to 'melt' a prisoners head off!

The two carried on for a while longer. Sembado would explain a little more about his grandfather, the Elephants, and their plans, and Mr. Feldman would react with deep interest and growing excitement. It seemed that each ensuing minute he was sympathizing more and more with the Elephants' cause. Sembado explained about Mr. Feldman being on TV, and the capture of Hutch. At this point, Mr. Feldman became very excited and was trying to respond to all of this at once.

"They said I'm dead? You guys captured Gerard Hutch? That little—I can't believe it! Where are they taking him?"

The far-east chambers...The refugees will be keeping him concealed.

"My word, you guys know about the refugees too? I've been briefed about them, but as far as the public's concerned, those chambers are all imploded and out of service."

Why? Who are the refugees?

"A group of militants who prefer to be left alone. The government doesn't want them to recruit citizens to their cause, so they agreed. They made a sanctuary for the refugees by faking a sector implosion. They've been there for a few decades, as far as I know."

My grandfather has befriended them

"My word!"

Sembado and Mr. Feldman went on for at least an hour more, and at midnight, a buzzer toned and the lights went out.

"Better get some sleep," said Mr. Feldman's voice through the darkness. "Those lights come back on earlier than you'd expect."

Sembado was just getting situated on the cell's second bunk, but just as he lay still, a voice outside the cell spoke, and a moment later, the door swung open. The bright light outside flooded in, hurting Sembado's recently adjusted eyes.

"Get on your feet, Grey, and step outside."

Sembado looked over his shoulder on his way out, and saw Mr. Feldman's face. It was distorted by the mix of dark shadow inside the cell and the bright light shooting in from the corridor.

"My word," the man whispered as the cell door shut firmly behind Sembado.

Chapter Thirteen
The Legacy

Sembado was led back to the lift he had arrived on, and taken down as far as it could go. From there, he was led down a series of corridors to a second lift that took him even farther down. When the lift opened on this new set of corridors, they were noticeably different from the rest of the penitentiary. The finishes and lighting were not only more comfortable, they were downright luxurious. Sembado tried to concentrate on his surroundings, but his throat was throbbing again, and his breathing had become more painful as his escort rushed him along at an uncomfortable pace.

The only corridor on this level seemed to be the one Sembado was currently being marched down. At the end was a large door, handsome and professional, not like the typical steel doors seen around the complex. With three quick raps on the door, the escort opened it and quickly ushered Sembado inside.

As soon as Sembado was deposited inside, the officer stepped back out, quietly shutting the door behind him. Sembado held his throat as he tried to slow his breathing. It stopped altogether when he turned to see one of the most marvelous rooms he had ever been in. The space was at least three times taller than the typical height he was used to, and the floor, walls, and ceiling were covered in dark, rich hues of wood planking; each piece seemed exquisitely crafted for its individual place. Three of the walls were adorned with painted portraits and landscapes, as well as other artifacts that Sembado recognized from *Terranean Memories*. The fourth wall was not a wall at all, but a giant glass bubble. Sembado had never seen such an expansive view. The exterior water on the other side was masterfully illuminated, not like the harsh, utilitarian lighting around Sembado's home. The color of the light was softer too, attracting schools of beautiful fish. Several sharks could be spotted as well.

Sembado's eyes followed one particular hammerhead as it glided down the glass. As his eyes neared the floor, he realized there was a large desk with a chair behind it. The chair was facing the window, its high back to Sembado. The desk had little on it but a computer screen, mug, and an ornate metal nameplate with *J. L. Fabian* engraved across it. The chair slowly turned, revealing its owner. He was a blocky man with firm shoulders and a square jaw. His face looked tired except for his eyes. Sembado found his stare piercing and immobilizing. Fabian's gaze seemed to search Sembado inside and out. Finally the corners of his mouth turned up ever so slightly and he spoke.

"Have a seat, for goodness sake." He motioned to one of the two chairs across the desk from him. "Can we get you anything? Maybe some water?" He chuckled. His laugh was loud, but flat. The joke was lost on Sembado who was actually quite desperate for a drink. He nodded enthusiastically, painfully clearing his throat. The gravelly noise made Fabian wince. "Geez kid, what'd they do to ya?" he asked, pulling open a desk drawer and retrieving a small utensil. He rose and circled the desk, walking right up to Sembado. He held out the utensil and pointed it at Sembado's throat. The end emitted a green light in the shape of an orb and began to grow. The light looked just like the blue light from the death box, but this was a beautiful shade of green. Sembado pushed back in the chair, grimacing as he tried to distance himself from the device.

"Calm down, boy. I'm not gonna hurt you." Fabian made the orb grow larger, to about the size of a fist, and moved it closer to Sembado's neck. As the orb passed across his skin, the searing pain in his throat melted away. He held the device still so that the orb enveloped the damaged part of Sembado's throat, and it quickly eliminated the bruising and swelling, making breathing less of a chore and then altogether painless. In less than a minute, the man was back to his chair and staring at a dumfounded Sembado. "What? Do you think all we do is death and destruction around here? That may be our bread and butter, but we gotta take care of our guys too."

Sembado swallowed painlessly, rubbing his newly healed neck. "I'll take that water now."

Fabian smiled, pulled a water bottle out of his desk, and tossed it to Sembado. Sembado downed half the bottle as Fabian continued to speak.

"So, another Klisk in the Elephant's ranks? I was really hoping the idea of your little gang would have died off with your grandpa. Sorry about that by the way."

Sembado nearly choked on the remaining water. He swallowed the rest of it quickly, giving Fabian a confused and worried look. Fabian continued.

"You don't think I already knew he didn't survive that last run-in with Gerard? Took the little bastard long enough. We'd been after your gramps since I took over this role. I would have liked to see his body, but it seems your friends came back and took it away."

Sembado felt ill.

Grandfather? Dead?

Grief overcame him, but Fabian did not seem interested.

"Don't be so dramatic kid. That's old news. Now you think your gonna keep up his legacy? Your little band of hoodlums is going to avenge his death and kidnap Gerard? Well, you can have the little punk; no skin off my nose. I told his mother I wasn't putting up with his crap anymore."

Sembado became confused. It seemed Fabian had made some kind of mistake.

"Revenge? How could we kidnap him out of revenge if my grandfather died in the attack?"

"Don't play dumb with me kid. It doesn't suit you very well. I said I don't care about Hutch. He ain't my kid. Just tell me where gramps has his book."

"Book? You mean his old journ—" Sembado tried to stop himself, but he was too late. He could see in Fabian's eyes that he had confirmed a long suspicion.

"I told Gerard he hadn't gotten the whole thing. He had headed back to the apartment and could only find the old man's entries. That idiot. So where is it?"

"I don't know," Sembado said.

"Liar!" Fabian barked. "I don't have time for your damn games."

"I really don't know. I—"

"Shut up, kid. I'm not doing this. Not this late. You don't wanna play nice? Fine. I'll send some of my boys by your place. See how your parents and your little—" He looked on his screen to confirm details, "—brother will do with some extra attention."

"What? Why? I told you. I really don't know!" Now Sembado was the one yelling. "What do you want from me?"

"I want your stupid gang gone. I want them eliminated. I have an entire complex to control and keep in order. You and your grandpa's team are a big pain in my ass. You think we can't weed you out in this surface release? Why do you think we're even having it?"

"Isn't the radiation gone?"

"I told you I don't like being screwed with, kid. You know damn well there wasn't ever any radiation. Now, if your boys are going to try sneaking Gerard out the topside in a big crowd of people, what makes you think I'm not ready to waste the whole lot of ya? Gerard? My life would be easier without him."

"How about the crowd of innocents?" Sembado shot back, genuinely disgusted with the attitude displayed before him.

"Please. What would a couple hundred compare to the millions in the past? This is child's play compared to what we've done before."

Sembado's blood boiled. For the second time that night, his fears had been confirmed, but this was no panic attack. He stood up, slamming his hands on the desk. Fabian did not look worried, but slightly impressed. Sembado's curled lips let forth the culmination of his week's confusion and betrayal.

"I've known about the Elephants for a couple of days, and been a member for even less. Until tonight, I still wasn't sure I believed my grandfather, and had no idea that he died in the kidnapping, so how the hell am I supposed to plan revenge? So now, instead of playing it cool, you've gone and confirmed everything they've told me. All of the truths. All of the lies! All of the twisted power plays from greedy, greasy eels like you!" He finished with a well-aimed shot of spit right in Fabian's face.

Fabian howled, whipping his face to the side, and toppling sideways off his chair. He sprung to his feet to attack Sembado, but three penalty officers burst into the room. Two of them held Fabian back while the third grabbed Sembado by the neck and threw him to the ground, pinning him with one knee between the boy's shoulders.

"Who's given what away now, you little smear?" Fabian cried from behind the two officers. "I thought your grandpa was dead weeks ago, but now you tell me he was at the kidnapping? You little idiot; you gave it away! Now I'll hunt the old bastard down, and kill him myself!"

Sembado heard a continued mixture of gloating and laughter as he was hauled out of Fabian's quarters and back to the lift. His stomach boiled hot and cold as he felt the relief and realization that Grandfather was still alive. He also felt the agony of his situation, and the fate he had brought upon his family.

Chapter Fourteen
Castes of Captives

After a few distracting days had passed, no amount of talking with Mr. Feldman could help ease the hopelessness Sembado was feeling in his heart. As the days turned into a week and soon another, the dark and terrible reality of life in the penitentiary became his own. The long hours in their closet of a cell brought him and Mr. Feldman together in a way Sembado had never experienced. The typical priorities of privacy, decency, and comfort were abandoned the first time he had to use the toilet in front of Mr. Feldman, because it had no partition around it. The steel walls all around them were hard but thin, and all the disconcerting noises of the inmates on the other side were easily heard. These were by far the most desperate, terrifying circumstances Sembado had ever heard of, let alone experienced.

Sembado's heart sank more every day as the magnitude of his government's betrayal unfolded before his eyes. There had been very few crimes reported in the complex beside the so-called mutant attacks, and his entire life he had assumed the lack of crimes reported meant that crime was not happening. But many of the criminals Sembado had already seen in prison were real law-breaking felons. His world had always been presented to him as crimeless and safe, and now he was beginning to realize that the government was simply hiding the truth to keep the vast majority ignorant and content.

But even the monotony Sembado associated with the cell paled in comparison to the terror he felt every minute he spent in the common spaces of the prison. The commons were old, grimy, shadow-filled compartments. They were two levels high, so that a system of catwalks lined the second floor perimeter and crossed in a few places overhead. A few inches of ice-cold water continually covered the floor.

Sembado quickly took to following Mr. Feldman closely in these dark commons, and soon he learned the assumed rules and social constructs practiced by the prisoners. Many factions and allegiances existed in the prison; most of these were comprised of the common thugs and felons that accounted for a majority of the population. These men were dirty, foul, and evil. They swore, bit, spat, and not uncommonly fought with each other. Sembado had even seen an inmate strangle another to death in the short time he had already been there. For Mr. Feldman, it was the third murder that he had heard of, and his first and gravest piece of advice for Sembado was to avoid these characters at all costs. So Sembado spent his first few days in the commons darting in and out of the shadows with his trusted cellmate, and avoiding eye contact with everyone.

But despite his best efforts, on the tenth day of his entrapment, Sembado was caught in the path of one of these dangerous figures. The man was large and broad, and at their accidental collision Sembado was sent sideways into two others. Those two were even larger, and they held Sembado fast by the arms while the first man spat in his face. He stared closely at Sembado.

"Ya like getting close, boy?" the man growled inches from Sembado's face, while the other two laughed darkly in his ears. His face was jagged and scarred, and his breath was so rank that it made Sembado nauseous. Panic and desperation held him paralyzed, and his bladder released from fear.

"Oh look, boys. Little ginger here just pissed himself." The man grabbed a fistful of Sembado's auburn hair. Suddenly, the tension exploded as a number of shapes moved quickly behind the man and a closed fist chopped him in the throat. At the same time, the two men pulled back on Sembado's shoulders. Before he knew it, he was falling backward onto their chests. They landed with a great splash in the water on the floor. The crowd of prisoners around them was in an uproar, and then a hand reached for the collar of Sembado's shirt. He came out of his stupor as Mr. Feldman was ushering him away. He had just enough time to look back through the scattering prisoners to see the two men that had held him lying dead in a pool of their mixed blood. Their throats had been slit. Penitentiary guards were rushing to the center of the chaos, but by the time they got to the two bodies, Sembado, Mr.

Feldman, and a small group of others were well away and into the shadows of a second-level catwalk.

Sembado shook uncontrollably, and his legs were cold as his fresh urine began to lose its warmth. He was crouching with his back against a wall, and he was staring at a half circle of men: three strangers and Mr. Feldman. He tried not to vomit as his mind processed these most current of events. He had just seen two men murdered; he had been on top of them. This chaotic, hellish experience held Sembado in a sickened daze; he was barely cognizant of the conversation being whispered between the fellows in front of him. Mr. Feldman was desperately explaining his and Sembado's situation; his whisper was more of a hiss.

"I tell you, he is Hyron Klisk's grandson; he hasn't been here two weeks," he said exasperatedly, apparently for the second time.

One man shot back. "But what's he to you?"

"Yeah! You said you were ex-IFCG! How'd you end up in here, and with him," said another. "Funny you should befriend our little Elephant, here," he added skeptically, snatching quickly at Sembado's arm and turning it over for the others to see. "We've been watching you two since he got here; he follows you like a beaten dolphin calf. So what is he to you?"

"He's my son's best friend. He's only eighteen; how do you expect him to act in a place like this?" Mr. Feldman spat back. He was infuriated with the men's skepticism. "I was thrown in here for doing a little too good of a job in the Office of Internal Investigations," he added with a weak smirk. The humor seemed to be lost on the men. "Look, chance made the boy my cellmate, and he has filled me in on the Elephants' work. I want to help you; I want to join you."

The men looked gravely at each other and then at Sembado.

"Stop shaking like an anemone, boy! Are you really Klisk's grandson? Is he telling us lies?" demanded the first man.

Sembado tried to fight his shivering, but he grew increasingly colder from his urine-soaked pants and the water around his feet. He looked at the men, one face at a time, and tried to ignore the continuing discord behind them. He finally answered the man through chattering teeth.

"He speaks the truth. He is my best friend's father; I am Hyron Klisk's oldest grandson. Please, for my sake, trust this man."

The men's demeanor seemed to change immediately, and they were soon taking turns watching the developments behind them. Sembado soon realized there were other men watching them with interest. They seemed to be posted all around. The lead man must have seen Sembado's wandering eyes, for he presently addressed the boy's looks of concern.

"They are with us, brother. Our league numbers far into the dozens here, though I have never spoken with some of them. Most of them came here by mistake for spotting the falseness of a mutant attack or some other false imprisonment, and have been inducted with no mark of the Elephant. This is why it is important that the guards do not know who these unmarked are, though many of the prisoners have a good idea which of us are Elephants, and avoid us. We try hard to avoid confrontation, but I assure you, your three aggressors were not practitioners of reason."

The murder of his offenders had already been replaced in Sembado's thoughts by the conversation taking place, and he went pale and nauseous as the memory rushed back to his mind. The scene of chaos was dying down, and already the dead men had been carted away. The guards were angrily rounding up inmates and sending them back to their cells.

"We will keep in contact," hissed the man as he and his fellows disbanded quickly and scattered about to be herded separately by the guards. Sembado exchanged looks with a grim-faced Mr. Feldman. They stood and quickly joined the cattle-like throng as it was forced into ordered ranks.

Chapter Fifteen
A Call to Action

Meeting the Elephants brought Sembado and Mr. Feldman a sense of hope they did not think possible in their terrible residence. The incident moved the penitentiary administration to enforce stricter rules for ushering inmates from their cells to the commons or the feeding facility. He and Mr. Feldman could not even assume that they would always be able to walk together in the places outside their cell.

The limited interaction between inmates forced the other Elephants to begin communicating with Sembado and Mr. Feldman with small, scribbled notes. They were usually just messages of hope, but one day a note was forced into Sembado's hand as he was being ushered into a line to go back to his cell.

He quickly balled it up and stashed it in his waistband as he had been taught to do. He continued plodding along, careful to not dislodge it from its hiding place, but somewhere behind him, an inmate had tripped, and suddenly people were shuffling forward out of his way. One of these men bumped into Sembado and nearly knocked him down. While he regained his footing, he realized the secret note had slipped from his waistband and was sliding down the leg of his pants. Panic overwhelmed him as he felt the crumpled piece of paper move farther down his leg. Soon he was aware that his walking style and rhythm had become increasingly contorted to keep the note from exiting the cuff of his pants. His gait was so bizarre that one or two other prisoners were beginning to stare. Sembado held his breath.

What am I doing? I look like an idiot!

At that moment, another disturbance to his rear caused the inmate behind him to stumble and kick his heels. To his horror, he no longer felt the note. His stomach turned, and he felt like being sick. Soon another crash behind him shoved him forward even more, but his sudden despair was so overwhelming that he didn't notice. The group was mindlessly ushered forward like a herd of cattle.

Who knows what vital information that note might have held? Some use I am to this secret order. I'm not even a proper messenger.

Sembado continued the gloomy trek back to his cell. He was pushed and punched as he went. His disappointment in himself grew with every step. He wondered if anyone would be able to depend on him without worrying about his likely failures.

Before long, he was back in his cell. Soon Mr. Feldman would also enter, and the guilt Sembado felt would force him to confess his mistake. Until then, he sat with his head in his hands. His forehead felt oily and coarse from the little hygiene prison life allowed. Sembado's grief from dropping the message consumed him, and soon he started to feel as though his life and character were yielding to the will of this dark, troublesome place.

I have become just as dirty and careless as these animals around me. I'll never get out of here—

There was the familiar clicking of locks at the door, and Mr. Feldman was pushed inside. He wore an odd expression on his face. The door was jerked shut behind him, and as soon as it was closed, his odd expression broke into an enormous grin. He bent over, reached into his shoe, and pulled out Sembado's crumpled note.

Sembado's dark, desperate thoughts were transformed into an incredible high, and his heart danced as his hope was renewed. In his wildest dreams, he could not imagine what unbelievable luck had brought the note into Mr. Feldman's possession. He was nearly giddy waiting to hear an explanation. Mr. Feldman was just as anxious to oblige.

"My word, Sembado. Good thing I was only a few paces behind you, eh? A shoe might have been a better choice than your waistband, but I suppose it's only accessible when you've fallen over." He finished with a wink, and explained how he had seen the message exchange, and how the second commotion after Sembado had lost the note was a ploy to get the note off the ground before it was discovered by anyone else. He proudly displayed the bruise across his left cheek that the stunt had earned him.

At the end of Mr. Feldman's recount, their attention was brought back to the note as joy and excitement coursed through Sembado's veins; he was aquiver with anticipation. The two allies sat hunkered over the note, shoulder to shoulder. Sembado read the note quickly.

HYRON IN TROUBLE—MUST ESCAPE—WATCH FOR SIGNAL.

Sembado's heart raced. Emotions of excitement and fear and panic mixed uncontrollably inside him.

Fabian's found Grandfather, I know it! An escape? Yes! I need to get out of here and find him!

Mr. Feldman quickly folded the note and tore it into several small pieces. He divided the scraps between himself and Sembado, and the two of them swallowed them as quickly as possible. This kind of disposal had become commonplace. Sembado swallowed many of the emotions he was feeling with the small pieces of paper, and when they were all gone he felt alarmingly desensitized. This change would have been more unsettling to him if the lack of emotion were not so comforting. Sembado was finally beginning to feel the numbing effects of being part of a war, no matter how secret it was.

He and Mr. Feldman sat for a long while, getting the moisture back in their mouths. They quietly speculated what the signal could be, or when it would come.

It was late on a Saturday afternoon several days later when the door of the cell was unlocked. It was time for dinner, and once again Sembado and Mr. Feldman were shoved into line unceremoniously. Sembado hated that the long walk down to the feeding chamber had become so familiar, and the thought of eating another meal in that disgusting dining hall made him nauseous.

The prisoners were shuffled in and made to stand at chest-high troughs while various bits of vegetables, breads, and possibly meats were thrown down the troughs by the Pens. The first time Sembado experienced this, he had realized how darkly comical some of the IFCG's legislation was. As the other Elephants had explained, a law was passed that required the penitentiary system to allow the prisoners a choice in what they ate. By adopting the trough system, the inmates technically had the right to choose. The meat was always grabbed first, but that did not mean that the first man to touch it was going to eat it. Meat was usually stolen two or three times before the person holding it could get it to their mouth; Sembado had not eaten meat since he arrived.

Sembado was two corridors away from the feeding chamber and already the sweet funk of overripe fruit and yeast accosted his nose. He closed his eyes with disgust as he was prodded and ushered along, but opened them again when he bumped into the back of Mr. Feldman. They were some of the last dozen being moved into the feeding chamber.

The room was buzzing with the groveling of hungry inmates. The typical scuffles were breaking out; the more aggressive prisoners were throwing elbows and vying for the best position. Sembado and Mr. Feldman were directed to an opening big enough for only one of them. The two had developed a system of turn-taking in such a case. This time, Sembado stood by while Mr. Feldman took his place along the rail. Once all of the inmates were in position, the usual bell rang, and a small garrison of Pens marched in with buckets of various food stuffs. They marched along on a series of catwalks that ran down the center of each trough, kicking at any overly anxious hands.

Just before the dumping began, a commotion broke out across the chamber. Sembado turned to see three inmates hoisting a fourth up and onto the trough in front of them. The three Pens walking that catwalk tried to subdue him but the buckets they were carrying made keeping their balance difficult. As the first officer approached the inmate, the man dropped his shoulder and knocked the guard off the catwalk. The officer fell hard into the trough below, and he and his buckets were soon overwhelmed by hungry, frenzied inmates. The inmate on the catwalk began to shout before the second guard could reach him.

"Elephants—stampede!"

He lowered his shoulder on the second guard, but the third had already dropped his buckets and was drawing his weapon. The prisoner caught two rounds to the chest, and fell to the floor of the catwalk in a screaming heap. Small blue orbs could be seen forming on his chest. He was being eaten from the inside out.

A moment of silence passed before the chamber exploded with commotion. From all over, members of the Elephants' Guild could be seen moving toward the exit corridor. First it was only a half dozen, but they continued to gather numbers and momentum as they moved through the throng. Sembado and Mr. Feldman fought through the crowd of other prisoners to get closer. As Sembado took in the chaos around him, he saw that the non-Elephants were quickly gaining confidence. Several of the most brutish characters had crawled up onto the catwalks and were battling with the guards. One inmate was actually using another as a shield against the guards' dangerous bullets. He was soon close enough to knock the guard over the railing of the catwalk, and the weapon of that guard was soon in the hands of an angry inmate. Very quickly, his success was emulated all around the chamber.

Sembado stayed close behind Mr. Feldman, and in a moment they joined the group of rushing Elephants. Sembado soon realized that several of these allies had also apprehended the guards' weapons. His ears rang as hundreds of shots were fired by guards, inmates, and Elephants. All around him, men were grabbing at their chest or leg or face as the hideous blue orbs grew out of their bodies and then shrank back again, taking flesh and blood with them.

He could not believe the grotesque nature of the wounds left by the terrible ammunition. The fist-sized, spherical cavities broke at different depths below the surface of the victims' skin so that some were revealed as half-spheres, while others only showed small holes with the greater cavity existing deeper inside. The visible surfaces were cauterized; puffy, red, and swollen. The wounds existed wherever the bullets had hit the victims; some of them were missing their shoulder, a piece of their thigh, or large pieces of their face and head. Sembado assumed that the victims without visible wounds had experienced wholly internal loss.

Sembado's stomach turned, and he dropped his head and held tight to the back of Mr. Feldman's prison tunic.

Less than two minutes had gone by and the chamber was in total disarray. The crowd of Elephants had worked their way to the exit corridor while the other inmates mindlessly delighted in the torment of the guards and each other. The Elephants were now more than twenty strong, and someone in the lead had a gun to a guard's head. The guard was typing into a security keypad feverishly, while the other armed Elephants stood watch around the rest. They were firing at guards and other inmates without warning; they were taking no chances.

The door was soon opened, and the Elephants slipped out just as the chamber was taken over by the most vicious of inmates.

Chapter Sixteen
Back Through the Labyrinth

The quiet and calm of the corridor beyond was startlingly mismatched to the uproar in the feeding chamber. Their hostage was revealed to be an undercover defector, and the leaders of the Elephants had him lock out the door to the feeding chamber so that the riot inside would stay there. That done, the group moved on quickly. They traveled down three corridors before coming to an emergency stairway. They worked their way up two levels before meeting resistance. At that point, five Elephants were carrying guns and all five of them led the charge up the stairs against six guards. After a loud moment, all six guards lay dead, but so did three Elephants.

That said, the struggle offered by the guards was less than impressive, and the undercover defector explained that the training the guards went through was incredibly underfunded and inadequate. He had been more thoroughly trained in secret by the Elephants on the outside. Despite this encouraging development, it was obvious that some of the other escapees were wary of their accomplice.

Shouts were heard from the floors below, and the troop of Elephants moved to action. The leader began shouting orders immediately.

"We will split into two groups," he demanded. "The first group will stay here, and keep these stairs clear while the others go ahead. After twenty minutes, you get out of here. If you get outside, try and get connected with the members you know out there. And for God's sake, keep your heads down."

In response to these orders, five of the armed men returned to the landing below to keep watch. They removed the doors on the two lower levels from their hinges and created a makeshift barrier with them. Three unarmed men were given the weapons of the fallen Elephants, and they joined the blockade below. The other men, about fifteen, including Sembado and Mr. Feldman, followed the leader up three more floors to level A.

They cracked the door open carefully, and immediately shots were fired.

"Okay, they've got us covered hard," explained the leader of the group. "Let's grab the door from level B, and we will unhinge this one as well; they appear to be bullet proof."

In a moment, two men returned with the level B door.

"We will go in two groups; the first will be behind this level A door when we unhinge it and go. I want a single file line behind me or Rohn." He pointed to the defector. "We can get through this, but it's gonna be hot. Stay behind anyone with a gun until you can get your hands on

177

one yourself. The first group is going to go with me to meet up with Hyron Klisk. He and others are hiding with the refugees, and I was told they still have Gerard Hutch. The second group will go with Rohn. He knows what to do."

The men quickly organized as instructed, and they were soon preparing for their charge. One man held the door tight by its opening mechanism while another carefully tapped the pins out of the hinges, and it was soon free. The shots that were muffled a moment before were suddenly ear-piercing. Sembado's arms and legs shook from nervousness and apprehension. This was by far the most dangerous thing he had ever taken part in. Suddenly, the leader was calling their attention.

"Go on my mark, men. Three. Two. One—"

Sembado was pushed forward in a hurried shuffle, and his hearing was immediately taken by the explosion of gunfire ahead of him. He was fourth in a line of seven; Mr. Feldman was right behind him. Although Sembado was keeping his head down, the man in front of him was just short enough to see over. The first two men in Sembado's line were armed. As they moved, Sembado kept his head turned to one side and watched as the walls of the corridor were broken regularly by intersecting corridors; they were spaced approximately one hundred feet apart. Each time the group approached one of these intersections they would slow down slightly so that the lead men could take steadied shots, and the men in back could grab what weapons were available.

At the next intersection, more gunfire erupted, and once again the group slowed, this time to a complete halt. Sembado peered around the man in front of him just in time to see a guard taking aim at his face. The man fired right after Sembado retracted his head. The bullet struck the shoulder of the man ahead of him, and he began to panic; he clawed at his shoulder wildly. Sembado tried to console the man, but he was thrashing uncontrollably, and a rogue elbow caught Sembado in the nose. He lost his balance, and landed on his rear. His vision blurred, and two strong hands picked him up from behind. Mr. Feldman held his head down while he blinked repeatedly, trying in vain to regain his vision. His eyes refocused, and the first thing he saw was a steady drip of the blood from his nose hitting the floor.

His eyes were drawn up by the screaming in front of him, and he saw the man with the bullet in his shoulder as frenzied as ever as the blue orb of the bullet was just now reaching its maximum radius. It was about to start retracting, and soon the pitch of the man's cries revealed that the orb was beginning to shrink back into the bullet, and eat away as it went. The size of the spherical orb of energy was just large enough that the man's arm was completely severed soon after the melting process began. The detached arm and the chunk of meat being dissolved hit the floor at the same time. It landed with a pathetic flop, but the sphere bounced, and then rolled toward Sembado's foot. Before he could react, it bumped into his shoe. The devouring shell shuddered, and his shoe began to sizzle. He quickly pulled his foot away, and watched in disgust as the orb continued to shrink away, destroying its meaty contents and leaving nothing but a foul, stomach-turning smell behind.

The man's screams had subsided, but were replaced by whimpering. Sembado could not help staring at the perfectly round pit that was now where the man's shoulder had been. It was cauterized, and appeared puffy and tender; it was already starting to scar.

The gunfire at this intersection subsided, and as the group began to move again, a gun, along with an extra magazine, was forced into Sembado's hand. He held the weapon as though it were disease-ridden; he had no desire to inflict what he had just seen on any other person.

They were now making their first turn, and Sembado vaguely recognized the corridor they were on. They approached a heavy door, and the leader of the group dropped the door-shield and proceeded to furiously punch numbers into a keypad; they did not seem to be working. Suddenly gunfire could be heard from behind, and Sembado and the others turned around quickly to face their adversaries. The second group of men was a dozen yards away, seeking shelter on the other side of their door. They had been joined by the group that had guarded the stairwell, but they had sustained many losses and were still under heavy fire.

Three men from Sembado's group grabbed their door and marched it back down the corridor so that when the two doors were stood side to side they almost completely plugged the corridor. This afforded the men some relative peace to reload and regain composure. With the two doors secured, the three men returned. They were accompanied by eight men from the second group. One of these men was the man called Rohn. He was talking breathlessly to the leader of Sembado's group.

"Linx, we gotta' get outta' here, now! Here. Try seven-four-three-five-one-eight."

The doors slid open, and Linx called to the three men holding the barricade of doors. The men began shuffling quickly backward toward the exit; they were completely out of ammunition. The group Sembado was with was posted at the door; they took turns peering through it to see who was waiting on the other side, but no one was there. When the barricade men were twenty feet away, the attacking guards' gunfire stopped completely. The sudden silence was so awkward that it turned the heads of Sembado's group. The men with the barricade were so confused by the silence that they stopped dead in their tracks. A light, metallic noise could be heard from down the corridor. The three men had just enough time to look back at Sembado and the others before the explosion of a grenade consumed them. Sembado and the others shielded themselves from the blast, but they were all knocked down, and pieces of the doors and their comrades accompanied the heat that enveloped them. Sembado slipped from consciousness.

***

Sembado was flying through a great, open expanse. Above him there was no ceiling, but a white and gray sky, swirling with white powder. He rolled over to find that he was very high from a strange floor. It was an open expanse, and below him were small, green cones; the cones were covered in the same cold powder that swirled around his body. The floor below the trees could only be seen in small patches, but it too was covered in the substance. In the distance, he could see strange purple triangles rising out of the ground; their tips were frosted in the white powder. Sembado suddenly remembered that he had seen this landscape on a postcard from *Terranean Memories*. The postcard had the message *Greetings from Denver* rolling across its front in bright blue letters.

***

Sembado awoke to find himself being dragged across the floor on his back. His mouth was full of blood, and he quickly coughed it out on his chest and the floor. He continued to hack and spit until the majority of it was discharged, but when he snorted through his nose, more thick, salty liquid filled the back of his throat, and he gagged and vomited. He spat continuously for several moments before he remembered where he was.

He quickly looked around, and through his blurred vision he could see that those around him were also recovering. The others had dragged him through the doorway, and they were now in the room with the large glass window and posters of Elephants and other wanted criminals.

Sembado looked around and saw a few of the other men were behind the glass. Rohn was helping Linx to lock and secure the door, but he seemed to be having trouble. Half of the monitors on the wall behind them were destroyed; the other half revealed scenes of chaos. Sembado felt something hard and cold in his hand, and looked down to see that he was gripping the gun so tightly that his knuckles were white. He looked disgusted and tossed the gun to his side.

"You hold on to that thing, dammit!" said one of the other men.

Sembado tried not to glare at the man, and picked the gun back up begrudgingly. It had a formed grip so that he could grasp it tightly. The business end was blocky, but light. The man who had snapped at Sembado tossed a new magazine to him. The magazine was a flexible plastic strap the cartridges slid down into. The clip loaded sideways into the gun, just in front of the trigger group; as the bullets were used, the empty plastic strap fed out to the right so that it could be removed quickly. The plastic straps were perforated so that they could be torn to any length. Sembado imagined one, a continuous one, a hundred feet long.

As his regular thoughts came back to him, he looked around in a sudden panic; he had yet to see Mr. Feldman. A second later, he found him behind two other men. Mr.

Feldman was kneeling over the man who had lost his arm; the man was now dead.

"Okay!" shouted Linx. Rohn had finally jammed the door they came through. "That should give us enough time. Let's not have all of these losses be in vain. We are getting out of here!" It was more of an order than an encouragement.

Mr. Feldman helped Sembado up, and each man checked and reloaded his weapon. They approached the swinging doors at the other end of the surveillance corridor, and Rohn pushed the door open briskly. A single shot was fired, and he retracted his hand quickly, cradling it with the opposite forearm. Everybody gasped, but he gritted his teeth into a dark smile and revealed that the bullet had gone clean through. The men all cocked their guns, and prepared for the onslaught. Once more, Rohn opened the swinging doors, but this time he kicked them both so that they swung open wildly. He jumped back immediately, and the Elephants fired without regard.

Sembado hesitated for a moment, and several bullets whizzed past his face and arms before one grazed his shoulder. The sharp burn moved him to action, and he fired through the doorway as the doors swung back a second time. He gritted his teeth, squinted, and fired over and over. It was the first time he had ever shot a real gun, and the incredible amount of the frustration and confusion regarding the government and the Elephants flowed out of the weapon as he emptied the magazine. By the time it was empty, the shooting had stopped. Sembado joined the men as they reloaded their weapons.

As he was looking down at his gun, an arm crossed his chest and slammed him up against the wall out of sight of the door. He looked up to see the man who had yelled at him earlier glaring at him.

"If I ever see you shooting with your eyes closed again—especially with others in front of you—don't let me see that mud again!" He seemed very scared and upset, and Sembado took a moment to blush and feel incredibly ashamed.

Once again Rohn pushed the door open with his foot; the man to his left let out three quick shots.

"I think I got the last one," he said unsurely.

"Let's not take a chance," suggested Linx. He nodded to Rohn. Rohn took a deep breath, and pulled a plastic bag out of his pocket. It contained a small tube of beige putty. Everyone else backed away from him as he carefully broke the seal on the package, and started to knead the putty into a small ball. Sembado was not sure why they were being cautious, but he mimicked them.

Rohn nodded back to Linx, who cracked the door open with his elbow. Another shot came from the next room, but it ricocheted off the door. The shot startled Rohn, and he dropped the putty. Everyone, including Sembado, covered their faces with their arms and hands. A second passed, but nothing happened. Sembado peeked over his arms to see the others also stealing glances. Rohn was sweating and breathing heavily; he had caught the ball inches above the ground. Again he nodded to Linx, and the door was propped open. Rohn stood straight up, rolled his arm back, and swung it forward. The ball of putty flew out of his hand and sailed into the next room. As soon as Rohn released the ball Linx poked his gun through the cracked doors, took quick aim at the ball, and squeezed off one round. He immediately turned his face from the doorway, bracing the door with his foot. Rohn braced the other door.

The explosion was not very powerful, but it was shrill and loud. Sembado's ears rang painfully, and he soon realized why those around him had had their ears covered and their mouths open. The others looked like they were shaking some irritating water from their ears, but Sembado was more affected. His head swam with the aftershock of the blast. A muffled, tinny cry pulsed through his head.

Sembado was beginning to teeter on his heels, but Mr. Feldman grabbed him, and led him after the others. The next room was the processing room where the curt administrative receptionist had argued with Sembado's uncouth, original captors. It was in complete disarray. Computers and sheets of paper lay everywhere; some covering motionless bodies. Mr. Feldman led Sembado closely behind Linx and Rohn; the other Elephants spread out through the room. Two or three single shots were fired; victims were being put out of their misery. Sembado looked in horror at Linx for some consolation.

"They would have never showed us that kind of mercy," he said with a curled lip. His words muffled in Sembado's damaged ears, but the message was clear enough. They approached the center console that the haughty woman had been stationed at; it seemed to have taken the brunt of the explosion from the putty ball. A dead guard had taken the woman's place. Rohn worked around the body as he searched for the button for the exit door. In a moment, the door was open and the Elephants were massing near the exit. Sembado, Mr. Feldman, and three others went with Linx. The remaining eight followed Rohn.

Moments later, the team of Pens that had been chasing the Elephants broke through to the surveillance corridor. They rushed through the swinging doors, and charged across the processing office, but the corridor beyond was empty. The Elephants were gone.

Chapter Seventeen
Shocking

After two weeks of life in prison, Sembado had to fight to assure himself that the unreal freedom he was suddenly experiencing was, in fact, real. He moved along with his five companions swiftly. The other nine had broken off shortly after escaping the penitentiary office; they had obligations elsewhere. The group's immediate goal was to find regular clothes to replace their prison pants and tunics. Linx led them along, explaining the plan as they went. Sembado noticed for the first time how Linx's soft blond hair and blue eyes combined for an unintended feminine look.

"First, we are headed to the safe house behind *Terranean Memories*. We need to stop there for clothes, supplies, and an update. After that, we'll head to the refugee chambers." He paused at the next corridor intersection; penalty officers would surely be out in force looking for the escapees. The way was clear, and they continued onward. "Hyron will be waiting for us there. We need to get to him."

Sembado's thoughts were of his grandfather's safety.

Forget these prison tunics! We need to get to Grandfather!

Despite his exasperation, Sembado had to admit that they were making good time through the complex. They had only seen six citizens so far, but had attracted no attention. Although their prison clothes would seem eccentric to most, the average citizen had no idea what the penitentiary garb actually looked like.

They were now in a section of the complex that was familiar to Sembado; they were making their way through the corridors that he would use if he were traveling from Mr. Fenguino's shop to the Civillion. In two more corridors they would be entering the Civillion through the southwest entrance. As they approached, there was a dull roar coming from inside. Sembado was suddenly reminded of his regular life on the outside, and how busy the Civillion could be.

I wonder what all of the excitement is about. Maybe gossip about the prison break? Would the public even know yet? We will have to stay low to avoid attention.

This thought seemed to have occurred to the others as well, because Linx stopped them just short of the entrance. He grabbed Sembado and instructed the others to enter in pairs, spaced a couple minutes apart. He led Sembado out into the crowd. *Terranean Memories* was on the southern side of the Civillion; they only had to go about fifty feet.

Most of the people were too busy chatting, buying, and selling to notice Sembado and Linx's odd clothes, but a few scoffed at their ragged appearance. Sembado and Linx were more concerned about any Pens that might be around than their current fashion sense. The coast seemed clear enough, and the two made their way to *Terranean Memories* hastily. They pretended to look at the window while Linx gave quick directions.

"If M'Gereg is in, let me do the talking."

Sembado nodded, and they entered quickly while a crowd of energetic youths paced loudly outside. M'Gereg was nowhere to be seen, but a man, a little older than Linx, was standing behind the counter. When he saw them and their prison clothes, he quickly checked the shop for customers; there was one older woman looking at the interior side of the window display. He motioned for Sembado and Linx to bring their heads in close.

"You got marks?" he asked quickly, giving them both a piercing stare. Linx nodded to Sembado, and he quickly revealed his Elephant tattoo. The man looked at it carefully and then looked at Linx.

"And you?" He looked at Linx very seriously. Linx gave the man an equally serious look and pulled up his sleeve begrudgingly. Sembado looked down in time to see that Linx's mark was more of a scar, as if it had been carved into his skin with a knife.

"Got any trust left, Reece?" he asked of the man; it was more of an accusation than a question.

"M'Gereg's orders, Linx," the man replied coldly. "He's in the back with Bowers," he added, nodding to the back end of the shop. Sembado watched Linx give Reece one last nod; the two seemed less than friendly toward each other.

"What was that about?" Sembado asked. The look Linx gave him made Sembado regret the question as soon as he asked it.

"He's my brother."

Sembado couldn't imagine behaving like that toward Herbert. He suddenly remembered that apart from not seeing Grandfather, he had not seen his family in two weeks. A wave of emotional realization crashed over him, and something tugged hard at the back of his stomach. He suddenly had a good reason not to go immediately to Grandfather—maybe not reason enough, but a reason just the same. Before he could ponder much longer, he and Linx were at the back wall of the shop. The secret shelf-door was open, and the two were soon closing it behind themselves.

A low conversation in the adjacent room stopped abruptly when they entered the connecting hallway. The intricate, old gate was wide open. A head popped out from the room beyond; it was the stuttering old man from the Elephants' secret meeting.

"H-holy sht-shtar fisch! It'sh Hyron'sh g-grand b-b-boy and L-l-linxsh!"

"Would you keep it down, dammit!" replied another familiar, old voice. "Well, tell them to come in, and keep quiet!"

Sure enough, Sembado passed through the high, iron gate to see old M'Gereg sitting at the long table; it was still a mess with scattered papers. M'Gereg's face wore an odd combination of surprise and respect.

"I heard there was a jailbreak, but I can't believe both of you got out. You are headed to see Hyron, yeah? Don't say anything! Grab them some regular complex clothes and a couple fresh shock sticks."

The man named Bowers went out the iron gate and back into the main store. He returned moments later with a heap of clothes, Mr. Feldman, and the other three Elephants.

"I told you to come in pairs!" growled Linx.

"Oh, keep it down, son," snapped M'Gereg. "Ya'll didn't trail any stinkin' Pens in my store did ya?" The new group shook their heads. It was then that M'Gereg caught sight of Mr. Feldman; he recognized him immediately.

"What the hell is he doin' here?" he shouted, ignoring his own priority of hushed conversation. It took several minutes for Linx and Mr. Feldman to hurriedly explain the events in the penitentiary, but even after Gen Bowers seemed satisfied, M'Gereg remained skeptical. Sembado finally decided to risk a scolding, and offered his piece of assurance.

"Mr. M'Gereg." Everyone but Mr. Feldman glared at him. "This man is my best friend's father." There was a pause, and Sembado took the chance to continue before anyone interrupted him. "I have spent the past two weeks in a government penitentiary cell with him, and he spent the majority of that time guarding me with his life. He was thrown in there for nearly exposing what we are fighting so desperately to expose. He is a father and a husband. Please trust him." All of the men were surprised that old M'Gereg seemed satisfied with the young man's plea, but Sembado was more taken aback at himself for referring to himself and the Elephants as "we." He no longer doubted the Elephants' cause or the truth, but this was the first time since his incarceration that he had the chance to put his new, solidified opinion into perspective. Being a part of this truth-seeking movement was no longer disturbing to Sembado, but galvanizing.

It was not until the dispute was resolved, and the fugitives had changed clothes, that Sembado was reminded of his curiosity at the mention of a "shock stick," an item that M'Gereg had instructed Gen Bowers to retrieve for the escapees. He had never heard of such a thing. Old Gen revealed a small tool bag with several handheld metal wands inside. Each of the six escapees took one.

Sembado turned it over in his hand. The majority of the stick was black, but the tip was red, and had three wire coils around it. The handled end had a silver pivoting disc. M'Gereg was holding one as well; the others watched as he demonstrated the use and explained their origin.

"The IFCG developed these little buddies for their elite strike teams. They can be lethal to wet skin, but mostly they are for subduing a target without the drawing attention like gunfire." As he said this, he rotated the pivoting disc out of the way to reveal a yellow button. He pushed the button in an exaggerated way so that everyone could see what he was doing. The wire coils around the red tip glowed bright blue immediately and emitted a steady hum. He continued his explanation.

"This is the shock setting. This will get someone's attention, but don't expect to knock them over." He carefully clicked the button a second time, and the coils made a sharp zapping noise while their color quickly changed to a bright, hot red. M'Gereg purposefully showed that he was holding it well away from himself and others.

"This is business mode," he said through a cracked smile. "This," he continued, sparking it across the table and smoldering some papers, "will ruin your day. This setting will knock a man clean out, and give him a real nasty burn to remember. If you hit someone while they are wet, you could kill them."

He seemed to notice some of the younger men's grins, and he did not seem to like it.

"If you hit someone while you are wet, you could kill yourself. Don't screw around with it. It's not a twirling baton!"

The fugitives all packed their shock sticks carefully into their jackets, vests, or waistbands until M'Gereg was satisfied with their concealment. They continued preparing for their departure, and M'Gereg offered a last few gruff encouragements.

"We nearly lost an Elephant getting those damn sticks, so don't go losin' 'em! Now, you six are headed to rendezvous with Hyron and see to his condition." The old man was careful to avoid Sembado's eyes. This made Sembado's stomach incredibly uneasy, but he pushed the feeling away so that he could concentrate on the task at hand. His stay in prison had afforded him the ability to deal with discomforts that he would have never thought he could.

"Linx and Sembado are going to see to Hyron's health," M'Gereg ordered. "But the rest of you will meet back up with Rohn; he contacted me shortly before you arrived. You will deliver some information and supplies to him before going to see Hyron yourselves."

The group of men packed up their supplies and started leaving in the same order they came in. Sembado and Linx left first. Sembado trailed right behind Linx as they started to weave their way out of the Civillion, but Sembado's mind started to drift under all his preoccupying stresses. His thoughts wandered to his parents, his brother, and of course his grandfather. He wanted them all to know he was okay, but he mostly wanted to know they were okay. His run-in with Fabian made him very uneasy about how much information the government had on him and his family, and more importantly, how Fabian was willing to use that information.

In addition to his family Sembado added his friends to the jumble of worries growing inside. He wondered what might happen if the IFCG was not satisfied with Mr.

Feldman's capture, and moved on to pursue Meligose and the rest of the family.

"Hey, watch it!"

Sembado suddenly stood face-to-face with a penalty officer. His face flushed, and his blood ran cold, but then he realized that this penalty officer could not be more than a year older than him. The boy seemed just as flustered, and Sembado quickly apologized and stepped aside. He quickened his pace to catch up with Linx, who was half hidden around the corner of a nearby vendor's cart. He looked completely flummoxed. They did not speak right away, but instead continued their quick trot all the way out of the Civillion.

Once in a vacant corridor, their pace became a near sprint as they put as much distance between themselves and the officer in Civillion as they could. The two companions rounded one last corner and slowed to a walk. They looked both ways before collapsing against the walls and handrails to catch their breath. It was several minutes before either could speak, but words came to Linx first. He spoke between gulps of air.

"I can't believe—that Pen—just walked away. What the hell were you doing?"

Sembado took a moment to slow his breathing a little more before answering.

"I don't know. That's the first time I've had a chance to think in weeks. I guess my mind started to wander."

Linx was not satisfied.

"Don't get me wrong, brother. We got out clean, but you can't be doing that. You gotta go without thinkin' for a few more days at least." His expression changed as his temper eased. "I can't believe the look on that Pen's face. He looked more scared than you! You think he even knew who you were?"

Sembado's face broke into a smile for the first time in weeks.

"Not a chance. But yeah, he was barely older than me; I think his voice cracked when I bumped into him. I didn't know they could be that young."

Linx looked more pensive than before as he mulled Sembado's point over in his mind. He answered in a more somber tone than before. He motioned to Sembado to follow him as they started on their trek again.

"They weren't always. They used to have a minimum age of twenty-one."

"Yea. That's what I thought."

"They must have lowered the age to get more new recruits signed on quickly. Probably uppin' enlistment for the surface release."

They were both quiet for the remainder of the corridor, and at the next turn they quickened their pace to a trot once more. They continued on in silence for some time, and soon Sembado found himself less familiar with the corridors they were traveling down as they worked their way closer to the refugees' territory.

Sembado was struck by the state of the corridors as they traveled through them. These corridors should have appeared old and derelict, but instead seemed careworn, and humbly yet meticulously maintained. The patchwork on the walls and pipes looked rudimentary, but neither a puddle of water nor a spot of rust could be seen.

Linx had slowed to a defensive gait with Sembado at his side. The side corridors they passed started to contain people; each one they passed held more. Sembado looked to Linx for direction.

"Just keep your head up, but avoid eye contact. Act like you mean to be here, but that you are a visitor. They aren't an aggressive people, but the young men can be overly defensive. Hyron's only brought me here twice, and the first time didn't go so well. So keep your mouth shut and hope that I can do the talkin'."

Sembado could now smell foods and spices he had never smelled before. He focused so that he would not be distracted like he was in the Civillion. They made one last turn, and found themselves at a dead-end corridor with a heavy door at the back. There was a government sign across the door:

IMPLODED CHAMBERS: DO NOT ENTER
BY ORDER OF THE IFCG SECURITY BOARD

Three dark, heavy, glaring men stood with arms crossed in front of the portal. They stared even more dubiously when they saw Sembado and Linx. Sembado's eyes darted everywhere but at the faces of the three towering sentinels. It seemed like ages before Linx and the men engaged in conversation, and it was the man on the right that spoke first. His English was deep and booming.

"Whatta ya want?"

"We are here to see Hyron Klisk. This is his grandson."

All three men immediately eased their stances, although they maintained their abominable grimaces. The man on the right spoke again.

"Deeka'll take you to see Mr. Hyron, but be warned: Mr. Hyron is in a bad way."

The other two guards looked on somberly as the man called Deeka expressed his remorse over Grandfather's seemingly poor health; Sembado did a poor job of hiding his distress. For the first time since the beginning of the interaction, the three men dropped their formidable front. Deeka reached out and dropped a giant, gnarly hand on Sembado's sagging shoulder. The massive palm weighed down on Sembado.

"Come on, kid."

He then spoke to his two friends in their own language. The other two men nodded solemnly, and Deeka turned to open the heavy door. The other two stepped forward and out of the way. Sembado, Lynx, and Deeka stepped through. The other men called a farewell in unison through the doorway as it shut with a deep, heavy thud. Deeka echoed the phrase to himself quietly as the door sealed with a hiss.

Chapter Eighteen
Reunited

The corridor on the other side of the door held a world that Sembado could have never dreamed of. It was nearly impossible for him to tell that he was walking down an actual corridor. The walls had been knocked down all along one side so that the living chambers on that side created one large, continuous space through which children were running and shouting. Sharp, lively music could be heard drifting in and out. Strings and flutes made the melody, while a light, soft drum called the tempo.

To add to the mystique, the vast majority of the floor and walls was covered in a variety of potted plants and vines. Tremendous, vibrant blooms hung from every corner and crevasse with overwhelming scents to match. Along with the flowery fragrance was an even stronger version of the tangy food odors from the previous corridor. Natural materials were woven and thatched to cover the remaining metal surfaces.

Hammered metal containers, chimes, and other trinkets hung at the entrance of every living chamber. The refugees had devised all sorts of interesting ways to modify their corridors and chambers, keep suitable light on their plants, and keep their quarters fresh and well ventilated. The most impressive aspect of their accomplishments was that they had been achieved with a combination of the most basic technologies and natural phenomena.

Sembado was so captivated by this enchanting place that he had nearly forgotten about Grandfather, that is until Deeka made a quick left, and led them to the door of a nearby living chamber. Next to the door sat an old, frail man in a rocking chair. He looked into Deeka's eyes and spoke his language in a soft, hoarse voice.

Deeka responded with a submissive nod and led Linx into the chamber; Sembado followed closely, and as he passed the old man, he glanced at his face. The grizzled elder caught Sembado with a piercing stare, and their eyes locked. Despite his dark, weathered appearance, he had the most vibrantly blue eyes Sembado had ever seen. He gave Sembado a solemn nod of approval, and Sembado instinctively returned it as he stepped out of sight.

The inside of the chamber was crowded with furniture, knickknacks, and a makeshift bed that was too large for the space. Sembado scanned the bed in disbelief as he saw his tired grandfather. The old man was propped up on pillows of various colors and shapes; his right arm was in a sling. He smiled weakly as Linx and Sembado shuffled in. His first question proved his stony resolve.

"Did you two meet with M'Gereg?"

Sembado nearly smirked at his grandfather's hard persistence. The two young men quickly explained every detail of their experiences over the past few weeks. Each one started with his own separate story and told it to the point when their paths crossed. Sembado was careful to explain every detail about Mr. Feldman's predicament. Grandfather listened intently as if he were a small child listening to a bedtime story. When the two young men had finished their stories and repeated all the details Grandfather asked of them, he spoke.

"Well I gotta say, boy, I'm glad to see you're okay. And let me tell you, I was very worried about you. You were never supposed to be caught up in this, and I can't imagine what your parents are thinking. I haven't had a chance to talk to them since this thing blew up. Have you?"

Sembado was overwhelmed with anxiety as the thoughts of his family poured over the hardened defenses he had built up in prison. His expression sufficed as an answer as it changed to absolute desperation. Sembado's mind raced as he finally gave thought to the well-being of his family. He wondered how far Fabian had gone with his threat.

Would he have them on lock down or just followed?

He voiced his concerns aloud, informing his grandfather of his interview with Fabian. "Fabian. He knows who I am. He thought you had died in your apartment attack, but I—I accidently told him you were still alive. He's personally after you now, and he—he threatened the family. I don't know what he's going to do, but he knows where they live, and he isn't playing by the rules anymore."

The old man looked away at the ceiling while he thought about what he would say. The silence was deafening in Sembado's ears. Grandfather finally spoke.

"I've thought about that for a while, Sem. They've known where you live for quite some time, but they also know that your mother and father's allegiance to the government is genuine, and that it has caused a rift between us. But understand this: Fabian has never played nice, he's just turning up the heat now. Haven't you guys heard how hectic it's been? They're doin' everything they can just to keep the lid on this place."

Sembado and Linx exchanged curious looks. Linx responded first.

"We had no idea, sir. We've only been out a day, and we hadn't heard anything on the inside. The Civillion seemed fairly orderly. Are you sure?"

Grandfather responded with confidence.

"Listen up. We have had a more sympathetic response to our cause in the past weeks than ever before. All over the complex, people are whispering about the kidnappin' of that little Hutch bastard, and they're starting to get fed up with the IFCG's terrible cover-ups. There was another bogus mutant attack three days ago, and even without an Elephant intervention it was a total blunder. They've barely been able to keep it out of the news for God's sake."

Sembado could not contain himself. He began to blurt excitedly.

"So if we go public, we'll get more support, right? What's happened to Hutch anyway? Do you still have him?" Grandfather did what he could to satisfy the two younger Elephant's enthusiasm, but they grew more eager by the minute.

"No, we cannot go public. I've spoken with the other leaders, and we've decided that if we go public with who we are it will become about us, and that's not what we need. We need for the IFCG corruption to blow open by itself so that it becomes about who they really are. Now, as far as Hutch, we've got'm held up tight here with Mahana's boys. We already dropped a message to Madam Fabian sayin' that her little boy's going right to the surface if they come lookin' for him. What they don't know is that we will be heading to the surface in a couple days whether they come after us or not. We are leaving Hutch here for now, but a couple of Elephants will stay behind and bring him when they can. We are to meet up with some of Mahana's family on one of the islands. They have a compound there that they have kept guarded from the government for years now. We will need a guide, which brings me to my next point."

The old man paused as the door to the room swung open. Standing in the doorway, flanked by two large men, was a dark young woman with bright green eyes. Her dark, choppy hair fell around her neck to one side, but was tied up in an intricate braid on the other. Her brown skin appeared to be honey-colored silk. Her baggy, simple clothing did little to hide her delicate, demure frame, and despite the careful purpose with which her figure had been minimized, she was undeniably feminine. Sembado was careful to make these observations quickly and discreetly, but he was just recognizing how her green eyes seemed to glow against her brown skin when he realized she was glaring at him stoically. It was not a look of contempt or disapproval; it was more like the disinterested look a cat gives a curious young dog. Sembado quickly averted his gaze, suddenly taking an interest in his shoes. The two young men that escorted her in disappeared by the time Sembado looked up. The green-eyed girl was speaking quickly, but quietly, with Grandfather. He smiled kindly at her as he continued his briefing with the young men.

"Boys, this is Kaluna. She is Mahana's niece, and she'll be our guide to the island. She was born on the surface, but was brought down here when she was still very young." These kinds of surprising details still caught Sembado off guard. Despite his time in the detention center, he still had trouble accepting facts that conflicted with his previous reality. Just weeks ago, he would have sworn on his life that no one had been born on the surface since before the catastrophe, and now here was a young woman, possibly younger than him, that had only come to the complex a decade ago. Grandfather continued.

"We will be leaving two days from now, but first we will rendezvous with the other Elephants. Until then we will continue to prepare for the escape. We are supposed to have a large group of subs lined up—Sembado, I want you with me and Kaluna, and whoever else can fit will join us. You will need to use tomorrow to reconcile with your parents before returning straight here." The pang of guilt

205

suddenly returned to Sembado's chest as he remembered how long it had been since he had seen his family.

Linx and Sembado were introduced to Kaluna more formally, but she acknowledged Sembado even less the second time. After catching a fleeting smirk on his grandfather's face, Sembado got the distinct feeling that his awkward encounter amused the old man.

Chapter Nineteen
Fabian's Watch

Sembado slept easy for the first time in weeks that night. Despite being in such strange surroundings, the company of his grandfather, the rocking motion of the hammock the refugees had provided him, and the calming effect of their home-made fruit liquor gave him an incredibly peaceful and drowsy evening. He fell asleep just after a heavy, colorful meal, and woke early the next morning.

Sembado and Linx left the refugee's village a little too early, and soon found themselves traveling though very empty hallways. Grandfather had asked Linx to accompany Sembado for protection, but it was Saturday, and it seemed that many in the complex were still in their personal living chambers. They passed several penalty officers carefully, and their travels went on uneventfully. They took their time moving from corridor to corridor, stretching what would have been an hour's journey into a nearly ninety-minute trek.

Sembado was glad he had Linx as a guide, because as they moved along, his mind was distracted with what he was going to say to his parents. He and his grandfather had decided it was right to tell the truth, agreeing that it could do little more damage at this point. They also came to the conclusion that Sembado's father would be the biggest skeptic of the Elephants' movement, as he had always been far more confident in the government than anyone else in the family. In fact, Grandfather would frequently express his disappointment in how ready his son-in-law was to conform to any of the newer, stricter laws that the government would come out with from time to time. He never questioned the government's motives, and this seemed to be a continuing point of contention between the two men. Sembado hoped that the story of his stint in prison and rooming with Mr. Feldman would be enough to convince his family that the Elephants' cause was a righteous one, but he did not want to get his hopes up.

The minnows in his stomach increased in numbers and potency as he and Linx entered the second-to-last corridor off of which his family's chamber branched. He had not been home in weeks, and this familiar place was not bringing him the sense of comfort he had hoped for; on the contrary, he felt extremely vulnerable and on edge. Sembado was now leading the way, walking down the hall.

As they turned the next corner, Sembado stopped cold, jumping back around and dragging Linx with him. He held his hand up to Linx's mouth and signaled to look around the corner. They took carefully took turns peering. Halfway down the corridor, flanked on either side of Sembado's front door, were two very serious looking penalty officers.

They were unlike the young man Sembado ran into in the Civillion. These were large, hardened soldiers.

"See anything you like?" a voice behind Sembado and Linx asked.

They whipped around to see a third penalty officer with his weapon drawn at his hip. As the officer took a step forward, Linx slipped his hand inside his shirt and revealed his shock stick. The officer began shouting orders as he raised his weapon to chest level. Sembado dove to push the gun upward as Linx activated the shock stick and joined the struggle. As Linx made contact with the officer's neck he collapsed, freeing the gun into Sembado's hands. They both recovered their footing and took off in a dead sprint as the other two officers rounded the corner, drawn by the commotion.

The officers shouted for Sembado by name; he responded by turning in stride and brandishing the confiscated weapon. The officers ducked for cover, and fired shots after Sembado and Linx. The two continued to run, putting as many turns and as much distance between themselves and the officers as possible.

Thirty minutes later, Sembado and Linx were back to the refugees' end of the complex. The refugee guards allowed them by when they approached, but not without sufficient glowering. They were ushered inside, and immediately brought to Grandfather, to whom they explained the entire run-in. His resolve was as steadfast as usual.

"The family will be fine. Just try to keep this thing under wraps. These folks don't like the idea of us outsiders bringing the government's attention into their midst. It is their least favorite thing. Keep your heads down. And Semmy, try not to worry. Your dad and I may not see eye to eye on much, but he's a smart guy, and he knows how to take care of your mom and brother."

Linx pulled Sembado away to give Grandfather more time to work logistics with Mahana. Fortunately, there was plenty of distraction in this foreign place.

Chapter Twenty
Olahi the Curious

That afternoon found Sembado and Linx lost in the refugee's chambers for some time before they finally caught sight of Mahana's niece, Kaluna. She had spotted them first and was already marching toward them. Their very presence seemed to exasperate those around them, but Kaluna could not seem less perturbed. She acted as if she were corralling a couple of children. She did not speak, but merely motioned for them to follow. Sembado took in the strong odors of smoke, charcoal, and pineapple as he weaved in and out of the throng. The smells were intoxicating and paired well with the bright flowering plants all about, and the soft din coming from the people as they seemed to hum the same ancient melody as one. This place continued to defy his understanding of the world. The people acted as one single entity, and the transformation of the cold, hard complex into this bright oasis was unbelievable. He continued to bump into people as he focused on a new distraction. Linx avoided collisions carefully as he followed Kaluna, who seemed to shoot through the crowd effortlessly. Sembado got the feeling that no one noticed her passing. Despite her exotic looks, her personality seemed less colorful than those around her. She was just as rich of character as her people, but she was unmistakably subdued compared to the others. Sembado was concentrating on her asymmetrical braid, which bounced lightly off of her honey-colored shoulder blade. He ran into yet another bystander. Just as tempers started to flare, Linx pulled Sembado through a doorway.

It was not actually a doorway, but a beaded archway. It created the entrance to a small covered porch that had many open windows that passed into the communal space outside. The disgruntled residents Sembado had just left behind would have been able to see inside if it were not for the piles of small trinkets and artwork that blocked out everything but a few determined rays of light. Sembado followed the thick, matted decorations around the space to where Grandfather and Mahana sat shoulder to shoulder on an old bench made of natural materials. Kaluna continued on into the living quarters beyond the entry patio, giving a barely audible greeting to her uncle and Grandfather. Sembado caught himself staring after her. He realized at that point that his interest in the girl was little more than curiosity. He would admit right away that she was incredibly beautiful, but his interest was more basic. She had lived a very different life than he had, and he wondered about her habits and what made their two lives so different. His thoughts came back to the room when Mahana started talking. His first few words were undecipherable to Sembado. The man was speaking English, but Sembado was not yet accustomed to his accent and husky baritone voice. His words made more and more sense as Sembado became familiar with the cadence of his voice and the quirks of his vocabulary. He was joyous like most of his people, laughing between every other sentence.

"She's the strong, silent type, Kaluna, just like her momma," he chuckled. "But fiery too, like her daddy. That ol'—" He now seemed to only be speaking to Grandfather. "Did I tell ya they found his body out a driftin'? Damn fool went to see Narall after all these years, and she cut him loose." This last detail seemed to warrant more laughter. He finished visiting with Grandfather before stepping outside. A burst of shouts, laughter, and singing erupted at his appearance, and it took several minutes for the din to die down enough for Grandfather to be heard. He first addressed the curious look Sembado wore. Linx sat patiently, fiddling with some of the closer trinkets.

"He was talking about Kaluna's parents," he started. "Her mother is up on the surface; she's on the island Kaluna will lead us to. Apparently, her father has recently reconnected with her mother, but only for money."

Why would her parents need to reconnect? When were they separated?

Sembado's face gave away his confusion. Grandfather provided a retort right away, as if he had read Sembado's mind.

"Her father left her and her mother when she was a baby. He was a very selfish and unreliable man and refused

213

to come live in the complex. Kaluna's mother knew that she would be safer with the people here than on the surface, but could not stand living down here herself, so she returned to the surface after a couple months. Kaluna has lived here with Mahana ever since." By the time he finished, even Linx was listening intently. Sembado struggled to wrap his mind around the story. Broken homes were discouraged through the IFCG's family registry programs. Very rarely were families separated and even then, there were punishments involved. He could not imagine the feelings of loss associated with growing up without a parent around, let alone two. A soft rustling to his side startled him, and the three of them turned to see Kaluna standing with a tray of small baked food items. Her hands gripped the tray so hard that her knuckles were white, and although her expression remained cold, her shocking green eyes where distinctly moist. And for the first time, she was staring at Sembado, not past him, but right in his eyes. For a fleeting moment, he saw how very delicate and vulnerable she could be. In a second it had passed, and she quietly set the tray down and returned to the room she had come from.

The look Grandfather gave Sembado and Linx sufficiently summed up the awkward embarrassment they all felt about the situation. He stood slowly with an ache-filled groan and led them outside to continue coordinating with Mahana.

Sembado followed closely as he was led through the refugee marketplace for a second time. He had to listen carefully so that he would not lose the conversation in the dull roar of the bartering around them. Grandfather and Mahana even had to pause when a small scuffle broke out between two traders who could not agree on a price. Mahana stepped in and eased the tension with his booming laugh, but Sembado had the feeling that the men had backed off for more than just respect. They seemed slightly nervous when confronted by Mahana. He was a prominent leader with these people, and Sembado began to feel more confident about their odds in escaping to the surface. The commotion had now subsided, and the market was back to its soulful hum.

"Our second group is arriving tonight," Grandfather said. He was talking to Mahana, but intended for Sembado and Linx to follow along. "They'll be bringing some important supplies and information. I'm also interested in hearin' what Feldman knows about the IFCG that we might've missed."

Sembado spent the rest of the afternoon following Mahana and Grandfather around. He met many people through Mahana's introductions; some seemed very friendly, but most acted guarded to Sembado. He noticed that everyone seemed to treat Grandfather with a similar respect that Mahana received. The old man finally shed some more light on his history with these strangers over an early dinner.

They sat around a large square table to dine on what Sembado could only describe as a feast. The table was piled with fresh fruits, typically a pricey commodity, and lots of variations of the same, oddly shaped meat that Sembado was certain he had seen emptied from a metal can of some kind. It was all overwhelmingly sweet and delicious, and they soon sat back, breathing lethargically, as Grandfather told stories of how he first came to this part of the complex. Sembado, Linx, Mahana, Kaluna, and two of her kin sat peacefully as the old man set the stage.

"Many years ago, when I first started getting around the complex, these chambers were part of an industrial center. The IFCG had large, multistoried chambers that were big enough to fabricate all kinds of things. They would preassemble new living chambers and build and repair government submarines. That's why some of these chambers are opened up to each other like they are. This used to be a very crucial manufacturing wing. It started losing its purpose as the population growth slowed from government birth control, and it became completely obsolete with the newer robotics technology. They didn't need to preassemble these components with human hands when robots could assemble them in place around the clock. Around this same time, Mahana's father, Olahi, had started making regular trips to the surface. He and his men knew of the government's secrets, and they had found ways of circumventing the surface controls. The Office of Security tried threatening them into submission, but Olahi had become very proficient at calling the complex government's bluffs. He instead made a deal in which his people would take over and maintain the aging manufacturing facilities in exchange for their silence. As long as the government stayed out of their affairs, they would stay quiet about the truth and all that had happened. They had been settled here for many years before I finally met them. That day, M'Gereg and I were conducting some Elephant espionage with our partners."

"The other two boys that discovered those files with you?" Despite Sembado's excitement, his stomach was still too full to say much more. His grandfather chuckled at the interjection as he continued.

"Well yes, those were the two others, but we were grown men at this point; a few years older than you are now. In fact, your mother wasn't even walking yet. We had to split up as we finished our mission that night because of a security scare. One of the other men, Claude, had joined me to run back to my house at the time. We were nearly there when we realized that some government agents were still following us. I didn't want to lead them right to your mother and grandma, so we made a big loop away from our house. They chased us here. Mahana's father, Olahi, had his people grab us and bring us in, closing their doors quickly to cut off the agents. Their system of lookouts had seen that we were being pursued, but recognized that we weren't typical criminals. Olahi was curious like that."

This solicited a soft chuckle from Mahana, who was listening as intently as Sembado, but had now closed his eyes peacefully as the story led on.

"He found out who we were and what we knew, and it humored him that some of the 'little sheepies,' as he put it, were clever enough to figure it out. He offered us protection, and an untraceable way to communicate with your grandmother so that we didn't have to leave right away. If it weren't for Olahi, Mahana, and their people, the Elephants wouldn't be what they are today; we probably wouldn't be at all. But Claude was extremely nervous about the whole situation. He didn't trust Olahi anymore than the IFCG. He ended up sneaking out without me."

Sembado now had his eyes closed too; it made imagining the story much easier and more vivid. He opened them when Grandfather had paused for much longer than normal. Everyone around the table waited patiently as Grandfather was clearly struggling emotionally with the conclusion of this particular tale. After many drinks from his glass, he finished.

"We never saw Claude again. Word was he got snatched by the Pens, but he must have kept his mouth shut because we were never found out."

The whole table sat quietly for a long while, especially Grandfather. After nearly a half hour, Kaluna rose silently and began clearing the table. Sembado stood to help, but she blocked him from grabbing plates with her shoulder, and he sat back down quietly. Mahana, despite his eyes remaining closed, let out another soft chuckle. Sembado tried to fight off the hot feeling that was flushing through his face, when the sentinel that had led him and Linx in popped his head in the door, summoning Mahana and Grandfather. Sembado, Linx, and the other two young men that remained at the table exchanged curious looks before rushing out after their leaders.

Chapter Twenty-One
Snake in the Sea Grass

The other Elephants had finally arrived. They told their waiting friends how the last few hours had proved most interesting. Word had apparently spread quickly about the IFCG, and although a good portion of the population was skeptical, dozens of open riots had broken out, an absolute first. When enough citizens had started to openly demand answers, Fabian's only response was penalty officer crackdowns. Protesting, violent government responses, and citizen self-defense were sweeping the entire complex in waves.

Grandfather and Mahana wasted no time in leading the group farther into the refugees' village. The entire guild was not there, but all of the Elephant escapees were soon shuffling into one of Mahana's meeting spaces; Mr. Feldman was with them. Sembado stepped into the room to see the ceiling rise up above him. He was amazed to see they were in a very tall cylindrical space with a ceiling nearly thirty feet high. This was one of the old manufacturing centers Grandfather had spoken of. He nearly tripped on the rough floor, and looked down to find that the room had metal grating underneath. The space continued down below the grating as far as the ceiling rose above. Through the dim light below, he could make out the profile of several large submarines.

Sembado moved to the center of the room as the remaining men shuffled in. He was humored to see all of the recent escapees eyeing Kaluna as she was the only female present. He and Linx even shared a subdued snicker as the girl noticed the new men's interest and returned their stares with her most intense glare. It was quite amusing to see a pack of such potentially dangerous men be completely intimidated by the one-hundred-and-twenty-pound refugee girl. Mahana released another booming chuckle at the entire exchange, bringing all of their attention back to the task at hand.

As Grandfather and Mahana brought their respective men up to speed, Sembado looked around absentmindedly and noticed that one of the only bodies moving about belonged to Mr. Feldman. He was now within arm's reach of Sembado and only just seemed to recognize that Sembado was there. He looked incredibly nervous: very pale and sweating. With a hushed voice Sembado offered a reassuring greeting.

"Don't worry, Mr. Feldman," he whispered. "This is a good group of guys; they'll take care of you." Mr. Feldman acknowledged Sembado's statement with a wild sideways glance, but nothing else. He looked upset, almost angry, a look Sembado had never seen on his usually compassionate face. Sembado was concerned, but the words his grandfather was speaking were suddenly more compelling.

"We go to the surface tonight," the old man finished solemnly. "Groups of ten or less with at least two of Mahana's men per group. They know the way through the net and where to go once you're through."

Sembado felt a swell of excitement, anxiety, and fear, and he was quickly muttering with the others about the sudden news. He turned to console Mr. Feldman further, but found that he had backed away from the group; he was nearly against the wall. Even stranger, he held the cuff of his shirt to his mouth and was speaking softly, but quickly. His eyes darted around the group of men and he started to inch his way toward the door through which they came.

"Mr. Feldman? Are you okay—"

Before Sembado could finish, a growing commotion rushed passed him as half a dozen angry Elephants, shouting insults and protests, converged on the man.

"He's a rat, I told you!"

"He's phonin' his IFCG friends!"

"He's wired! Get'm!"

"Kill'm!"

Mr. Feldman now broke into a sprint as he made for the door. He barely got through and was gone, a small mob of angry Elephants racing after him. The scene they left was utter chaos. The younger men were trying to talk over each other, and soon turned to arguing as they searched for their next step. The commotion turned to a dull roar before they were interrupted.

"Quiet!" A deep voice bellowed.

They all turned, silent, to see Mahana holding up his hands. His aged, brown face was tight and severe; his normally soft eyes were black lights.

"This changes nothing," Grandfather demanded. "We leave now, as planned. Let those bastards try and stop us!" There was a cheer, and Sembado knew that this uncharacteristically brash attitude was his grandfather's way of distracting his men from a very dangerous turn of events. "Follow Mahana's men. They know what to do!"

Mahana's young brethren were quickly shouting orders to the Elephants around them. Their English was cleaner, and less encumbered, but Sembado still got the feeling they preferred their native tongue. Soon, there were groups of eight, nine, or ten rushing to three ladders at the edge of the room. Some went up; some went down, and soon Sembado was being led by the hand to start down one of the ladders. He looked from his hand then up the arm to the one holding it, to find Kaluna forcibly pulling him to one of the ladders.

"Keep up," was all she said in a stern whisper.

Just as he got his feet planted and began his descent, Sembado heard a commotion from the main door, and the Elephants who had chased Mr. Feldman out came running back in with dozens of refugees behind them. One of them shouted an update as a refugee led him to a ladder.

"The refugees are fighting off Pens! Hundreds of them! Feldman led them here for an ambush! They're shooting on sight! They know we're headed to the surface!"

Linx forced Sembado down the ladder and was climbing down just above him; Kaluna was just below. Sembado hurried down as quickly as his feet would allow, and although he slipped multiple times, he was very careful not to kick or step on the young lady's hands and head. They hit the landing below with a splash. There was a foot of sea water already flooding the chamber, and it was climbing quickly. Sembado was relieved to see that Kaluna was leading him and Linx to a larger submarine that already held Grandfather and Mahana. Sembado and Linx shuffled in with two more Elephants and lastly a refugee shoving them in. The young ethnic pushed them aside so that he could assume control of the pilot's seat. Water was now rolling up the front of the submarine and the small waves were breaking on the front viewing guard. Kaluna was still outside, wading in water up to her waist. Penalty officers were climbing down the ladders in dozens, the ladders swaying under their weight. Kaluna was nearly to the submarine when the officers landed, drawing their weapons. A recently escaped Elephant in a nearby submarine popped out of a top hatch, holding a shock stick in one hand. His face was twisted in bitter hatred. He quickly fixed the stick to its highest setting and tossed it toward the water without hesitating.

Ignoring the imminent danger, Sembado quickly leaned out of the hatch and grabbed Kaluna under the arms as she struggled inside. He pulled her backward on top of him. Kaluna quickly pushed off of Sembado and rolled over to see the horror outside as it was framed neatly in the hatchway. The shock stick had turned the open water to a death trap. More Elephants copied their angry brother and soon every officer was being violently electrocuted by the powerful weapons. Even the officers still on the ladders were being zapped as the metal rungs conducted the electric shock. Some fell to the water as their agony continued.

Kaluna, still leaning against Sembado, kicked the hatch shut, stood up, and leaned over the pilot's shoulder, muttering to him in their language. He responded sarcastically, and she smacked the back of his head. Mahana released a chuckle and quickly returned to the hurried conversation he was having with Grandfather.

From below them came an immense creaking noise, followed by a strong shuddering. The shuddering stopped, but the creaking continued for a little longer, and was finished with a dull and heavy bang.

Suddenly the bottom of the sub seemed to fall out from under Sembado, and he looked out a side window to see the other submarines around them descending nose first. The refugee pilot barked something at Kaluna, and she reluctantly took her seat next to him, strapping in. He brought the front of the sub down, and soon all the submarines, eight in all, were falling out of the giant hatches that had just opened at the bottom of the manufacturing facility. Sembado dared one last peek out the window and saw the refugees' mismatched and dated submarines taking off in every direction. His eyes widened as he saw three penalty officers' standard subs appear through the murky depths. Three subs had just become five when his head was jerked away from the window by the pilot's quick maneuvers. Sembado looked through the front glass guard to see that the refugee was breaking every traffic rule in existence. He had just cut across a busy submarine express lane before cutting up sixty feet without warning. Kaluna yelled at him as she flipped switches on the main console. A poorly rigged monitor screen between them showed a camera's view that was attached to the rear of the sub. Two Pen subs had just swung into view. Their lights were flashing chaotically as they started to hit the escaping sub with blasts of concentrated water pressure and sound energy. The ear-ringing noise made Sembado's head hurt. He could barely hear Mahana giving orders to his niece. She quickly pushed buttons and pulled switches as he talked. Soon the monitor showed a black orb trailing behind them. The orb continued to grow, and soon the Pen subs and the noise were gone. Mahana continued to give orders, and the pilot took the sub into another sharp climb. Sembado leaned over to Linx to ask him what had just happened, but Linx met him with the answer first.

"Raw crude oil," he whispered. "They released about half a barrel, but that's more than enough to cover those Pens' viewing shields. It'll take hours of dry scraping to get it off," he finished with a grin.

Sembado pressed his body back into his seat and closed his eyes, inadvertently holding his breath. He tried to concentrate on his thoughts, but could not get, of all things, the sound of Kaluna's voice out of his head.

Chapter Twenty-Two
No Rest for the Weary

Sembado opened his eyes over two hours later and realize that he had been unconscious. They were in territory much farther away from the complex than he had ever been. They were higher too. They were racing just feet below the containment net. At this depth, the sunlight above was actually helping increase visibility. In the distance, a resting chamber sat two hundred feet below the containment net. It was a large, round dome whose tethers disappeared to the ocean floor below. Sembado had learned about them in his sub-piloting class, but he had never been to one. It held parking stalls for multiple subs and provided fuel and sleeping quarters for those needing rest. Few people ever ventured this far away from the complex. Kaluna murmured a routine command to the pilot; his response was brisk. She adjusted a control to pan the rear video down. She started talking faster and louder; a group of penalty officer subs had been trailing them down below the view of the camera. Kaluna gave more orders in a dry, flat tone. Sembado noticed that despite his snippy responses, the pilot responded to her every command. Mahana was not even paying attention at this point; he had given her full control as he was engrossed in a conversation on logistics with Grandfather.

They maintained their course, not wanting the Pens to know they were aware of their pursuers' presence. They were quickly approaching the resting chamber, and it grew larger and larger. Sembado had not realized until now that the structure was nearly two hundred feet in diameter. Just as they were starting to pass it, a loud alarm sounded in the cockpit, and a flashing light highlighting the side of Kaluna's face as she turned back and shouted, "'Cuda!"

The passengers all snapped their eyes to the monitor, which showed a quickly approaching metal tube. Barracudas were a very rarely used sub-to-sub weapon that had gained a deadly reputation over the past few decades, despite the fact that they had only been used in six recorded incidents. The crew braced for impact as the pilot tried what feeble attempts at evasion that he could. After two slow rolls to the left and a nearly vertical dive, he leveled out again just in time for the torpedo to pass the camera's point of view. With a horrible screech, the barracuda ripped through the right wing of the submarine with its sharpened, gear-like implements. Barracudas were intended to be nonlethal and only disable a vehicle, but the stories about them always ended in a drowning or crash. The force of their momentum and the drag of the water pulling on the wing were enough to shear it off completely before the barracuda could even finish the job. The terrible sound of tearing metal accompanied the jerking motion of the submarine, as the pilot not only lost the wing stabilizer but the engine attached to it as well. He leaned with all his weight against the direction-control paddles, but the loss of the maneuvering equipment was too severe, and the submarine started to spin and twist. The view out of the front was nauseating as the surface came into view, then the murky depths, next the pursuing submarines, and finally a very close resting chamber. The pilot and Kaluna slapped buttons frantically, but it was too late. The submarine ricocheted off one of the connections where the large tethering cable attached to the structure, and then corkscrewed once more into another tethering joint head on.

Part Three
Breaking the Surface

Chapter Twenty-Three
Going Up!

The lights in the submarine had gone out as it lost power, but soon the emergency lights from inside the facility came on. Sembado saw that they had all been encapsulated from the jaw down in safety foam; having served its purpose, it was dissolving quickly. They had come up through the floor of a docking bay, and the emergency robotics system had already sealed up the leak with inflatable bladders and plastic welds.

The occupants of the submarine slowly came out of their daze as the safety foam melted off and evaporated. Sembado could hear nothing; his ears were covered in the stuff. It smelled strongly of overly processed plastic. Even after he cleared it away, there was a loud, persistent ringing in his ears that blocked out everything else. He looked around to find Linx and one of the other Elephants trying to resuscitate their third comrade. The pilot, Kaluna, and Mahana each had one of Grandfather's limbs and were trying to lift him out through the broken viewing shield in the front of the sub. Grandfather's eyes were closed, but his chest was heaving. Blood was starting to trickle out from under his thinning hairline. Sembado rushed forward to help, and as the unconscious Elephant was helped to his feet, the entire crew was now out in the docking bay and standing in several inches of water. The emergency system soon began pumping the water out, and they moved through the docking bay, which had very few vehicles in it. What they could find were either government submarines or very small and expensive personal cruisers. The Pens had not arrived yet, so Sembado and his companions quickly continued to search for an alternate ride. As they plodded through the docking level, the facility continued the steady series of creaking and moaning and popping it had started moments after the crash. They rounded a corner and found a large government personnel carrier, just as a low, deep pop sounded from far off, followed by a lurching in the floor that sent them all to their knees. Those carrying Grandfather lost their grip, and the old man fell hard on his back. He emitted his first painful moan since the crash. The floor was now slightly off level and, as Sembado gained his bearings, a second pop sounded, and he fell once more. After three more pops, the floor was at an uncomfortably steep slope, and the group had to work hard to get Grandfather's limp frame toward the new submarine. Before they could make much headway, a nearby door was kicked open, and a small crowd of penalty officers tried to enter the room. The first two pulled and aimed their weapons, but before they could fire, a final, resounding pop sounded, and everyone hit the floor as the structure started to rock and spin freely.

The damage that the refugees' out-of-control submarine had caused to the substructure had been fatal, and the tethering cables had given way. As each one was lost, the remaining cables were put under too much stress. The entire structure was now completely free from its anchors.

As the resting facility rocked in the ocean current, it started to move slowly upward with a million pounds of buoyancy force lifting it cavalierly toward the containment net and the surface beyond. Inside, the fleeing rebels and their government pursuers had abandoned attempts to stand up, as the room they were in was rolling nearly end over end. Sembado and his companions had at least worked their way around the large submarine they were after, so that the penalty officers did not have a clear shot.

The giant metal dome continued to rise toward the surface and slowed only slightly when it encountered the containment net. The metal grid was not designed for such a magnitude of impact, and after being lifted several stories, the containment net finally gave way and ripped. The surfacing structure left a three-hundred-foot gash across the net, and dozens of penalty officer submarines were now racing after the ascending dome as it quickly approached the surface.

Sembado and his accomplices had worked their way into the armored personnel sub, and Linx and the young pilot were working on splicing multicolored wires to try and jumpstart it. The penalty officers that had been assaulting them were nowhere to be seen. Grandfather was now sitting upright without assistance, and Sembado and

Mahana were working to reorient him. As they spoke to the old man, Sembado felt an uncomfortable dull feeling growing in his ears; the facility continued to rock and sway, and he felt heavier than normal, like going up in an express lift.

Several of the pursuing government submarines had already raced past the rising structure, surfaced, and were preparing for the impending breach. More and more submarines surfaced, each choosing a position away from another until two dozen of them formed a large ring, three hundred feet across.

Despite their preparation, none of the penalty officers anticipated the immensity of the situation, and they were overwhelmed as the large metal dome broke the surface and continued to rise. The force from the structure's momentum lifted it almost completely out of the water. The observing Pens sat, dumbfounded, as the dome began its descent back into the ocean.

Those inside the facility were just as unprepared. Many of Sembado's friends were gripping their painful ears like he was, failing to strap themselves into the two opposing benches that ran down the middle of the submarine. The refugee who had piloted the previous submarine was back at the controls, while Kaluna, despite trying to maintain her poise, was now highly aggravated as she gripped one ear with her left hand and pointed at the depth gauge with her right. Sembado had yet to buckle in as he struggled to get his ears to pop, and he just caught sight of the gauge she was pointing at. He gave it a stupefied stare as he watched

235

it pass the "surface" mark. Suddenly, he was not sitting in his bench anymore, and for a fleeting moment, he was floating weightlessly over the center walkway. He watched the floor race toward his face and put his hands up just in time to cushion the blow to his forehead. The submarine soon settled, as the giant structure that housed it found its equilibrium on the ocean waves.

The result of the massive facility crashing into the water on its return descent was a circle of giant waves that raced out in all directions. The pilots of the various government submarines that surrounded the structure barely had time to brace for impact before forty-foot swells tossed their vehicles carelessly. The waves coupled with the natural rhythmic peaks of the ocean, pitching and tossing some of the subs high into the air. They turned end over end before they crashed back into the surface.

The giant structure had a port on the bottom side in the direct center. In its intended configuration, the hole allowed small submarines and free swimmers to come up through the bottom in emergency situations. It was always open, but the air pressure inside, combined with the level positioning the tethering cables kept water from leaking up into the interior space. The structure, however, had settled into a new position that was not remotely similar to the way it was designed. The required levelness had been lost, and at the surface, the air pressure inside released violently. Massive, percolating bubbles billowed out of the bottom port as the air inside was replaced by clear seawater. Just as the dome had settled on the surface, it began a slow, steady march down toward the sea floor.

Chapter Twenty-Four
Going Down!

The docking chamber that Sembado and his team were in was very close to the emergency evacuation port that now sent cold seawater blowing in by hundreds of gallons each second.

Kaluna and the pilot were back at their bickering as they tried to acquaint themselves with the controls of the government sub. Kaluna had found the navigational system, which was now showing them how to maneuver to the nearest escape port. The chamber around them was filling with water quickly, and soon the weight of the submarine was being supported completely by its own buoyancy. As the water picked the submarine off of the floor, the passengers were rocked back and forth gently.

The level they were on was almost full of water as they started to shift and move through a tunnel and toward the exit. The pilot took it slow, and for once, Kaluna was not criticizing his every move. He was not used to the control system, and his first few turns were wide and into the tunnel walls. Each time he swore under his breath and carefully backed up to correct his turn. Kaluna was now becoming aggravated with him as she realized that the depth gauge was falling again. He used the utmost care to maneuver them the rest of the way out of the structure. The nose of the submarine was just creeping out of the escape port when the crew caught a glimpse of where their current course was taking them. The containment net was straight ahead, and in seconds, the sinking structure was going to pin their exit hatch against the steel grid. The pilot wasted no time and slammed the accelerator as hard as it would go, rocketing them out of the exit port and toward the net. Still new to the controls, he did his best in performing a large swooping arc maneuver out from under the structure, coming within feet of the net as he brought the nose back up toward the surface. They had made it out from under the sinking behemoth and were just passing it, when the submarine began to stall and slow to a sluggish, jerky pace.

Kaluna barked questions at the pilot as she started to troubleshoot their acceleration problem. He snapped back, pointing to a full fuel gauge.

"It's the cavitation from the sinking dome," Grandfather said, barely whispering in his current state. "We have to get farther away from it."

Sembado climbed vertically toward the control seats as the submarine was now climbing straight up. He repeated his grandfather's explanation and orders to Kaluna. She did not look at him, but acknowledged him with a nod and started to give the pilot a series of maneuvering instructions. He pulled away from the sinking dome and leveled out. They started to descend again as the cavitation pulled them, but as they fought to gain horizontal distance, they recovered more and more power, and soon they were making good progress. They reached a point just yards beneath the surface, and Kaluna used the navigation system to apply the coordinates of their destination. The pilot reoriented the craft, and soon the commandeered submarine was speeding toward the horizon and the Hawaiian Islands beyond.

Chapter Twenty-Five
The Surface

They went on for several hours, stopping at sunset to tend to bodily functions. Sembado felt the swell of excitement inside the submarine as it breached the surface. The water poured off of the front viewing shield to reveal an endless stretch of ocean. First they were in the pit of the swells, and then on the peaks. Being raised this high had afforded them a view into the distance, but it was all ocean, for miles and miles. He felt a light grip on his wrist and turned to see his grandfather's tear-filled eyes looking back at him. The old man's feeble grasp was completely foreign compared to the painful, viselike grip he had held Sembado's arm with weeks earlier in his recently ransacked home. His eyes were different too; they were tired and weak. The past few weeks' physical and mental loads had taken their toll on the old man, and his spirit seemed nearly broken.

The rest of the crew agreed to allow Grandfather to exit first, and they waited patiently as Sembado escorted him toward the escape hatch over the left wing of the submarine. The pilot was helping Linx break the seal on the door, and as they did so, the pressure in Sembado's ear made one final, resounding pop. After a brief moment of pain, he experienced an overwhelming clarity in his hearing that he had never felt before. The ambient noises in the submarine now sounded sharp and loud. Not painful, simply fuller.

The two young men slowly pushed the hatch out, and Sembado's senses were immediately assaulted. First, the familiar smell of salty seawater, so thick he could taste it on his tongue. With his newly liberated ears, he could hear the rolling splash and sloshing of the ocean swells outside. Most overpowering was the light. The slowly opened hatch started revealing a sliver of white fire, but soon it was completely opened, and the blinding light was too much. With one arm firmly supporting Grandfather, Sembado brought the other up to shield his eyes. On the back of his arm, he could feel the warmth of the sunlight slowly growing stronger as it worked its way deeper into his skin. It was satisfying and real. Kaluna called out to the others, and the hatch was closed. It took Sembado a few minutes to blink the light away, but even then, bright spots danced in front of his eyes.

The front viewing shield had automatically transitioned to a dark tint, and the true, unfiltered sunlight was waiting just on the other side. Linx and another Elephant had found a supply case while rummaging around in the back of the vehicle. Inside were a number of light medical supplies and, among other things, several pairs of protective sunglasses. They were passed around to everyone, and soon

Sembado and Grandfather were preparing to go out a second time.

With the glasses squarely on his face, Sembado lost a great deal of the dark details inside the submarine. Even the view through the front shield seemed darker. As the exit hatch was cracked open again, the same smells and sounds from before made a fresh appearance. This time the sunlight was not as harsh, and Sembado and his grandfather slowly stepped out onto the wet, shining wing of the submarine. A strip of the surface had been treated with a treading material that offered their shoes better grip and footing. As Sembado breathed in, his lungs were filled with the fresh, salty spray of the sea. His first breath of unfiltered, natural air was a personal renaissance. This air felt intuitive and honest. He immediately started to contrast this new experience with his lifetime of filtered, purified, oxygen-rich air. He felt light-headed from the exhilarating breaths, and it took a few moments for him to realize that his grandfather's sunglasses were off. The old man had his eyes closed, his head back, and a deep and satisfied grin on his face. He had turned his face toward the sun and was presently pulling off his shirt. When the shirt caught around his head, he reluctantly accepted Sembado's help in pulling the garment over his head. It hung on his slinged arm.

The two quietly stood together until they heard the splashing noise of the others' footsteps on the wet wing's surface. Sembado and his grandfather shuffled to the end of the wing and helped each other sit down on the edge to make room for the others. Mahana, Kaluna, and the pilot had been to the surface before and looked as if they were greeting an old friend, each taking off their glasses after a short while. Linx and the other Elephants looked as overwhelmed as Sembado as they took their first lungfuls of misty ocean air. Soon the others had their feet dangling off the side of the wing as well; the rocking motion of the submarine dipped their feet and legs into the warm sea. They sat for a long time, and let the sun soak into their skin, down to their bones. After a while, the glasses seemed to have become darker, and Sembado could no longer fight the urge to remove them. With his eyes clenched shut, he slowly slid the glasses away, immediately seeing the blinding sun through his eyelids. He experimented with how quickly he could open his eyes; his first try was too sudden, and his lids slammed shut in response. He very carefully tried again, this time slowly and with intermittent breaks. Soon the bright light started taking on a color, and before long Sembado was squinting at the most remarkable blue sky. It was as full and rich of color as anything he had ever seen, and as his eyes opened more, he took in the light, weightless clouds that dotted the sky. Tears swelled in his eyes as he let out an emotional laugh that brought more tears with it. His grandfather reached over to hold his hand and then pulled him into an embrace. The two held each other and laughed as the rest of the crew shared similar experiences. Soon the laughter turned to song, and the young men were now diving and flipping off the wing into the water. Sembado even caught a glimpse of Kaluna smiling and clapping for the first time since they had met.

Grandfather and Mahana were now embraced. The other young men were floating in the water, taking turns relieving themselves under the water as the practicality of the stop returned to them.

Sembado found himself now sitting next to Kaluna as their older relatives rejoiced.

"It's so beautiful," Sembado said, addressing her directly for the first time. She did not look at him, but acknowledged the statement with a clear nod, taking in the sky, the clouds, and the sun.

The sun was high in the west; it was midafternoon. Sembado's eyes were now completely open, and he continued to stare in awe at the engrossing azure hue above. His eyes followed it down to the horizon where the sky met the endless expanse below. He took in the glint and glitter of the sun as it danced off the caps. The sparkles became smaller and smaller in the distance. His view of the horizon was cut off regularly as the submarine dipped down into the valleys of the swells. His sight would then be elevated back up to see the distant glimmers again. Some of the shimmering lights seemed bigger than others. Sembado tried to relocate them each time he could see above the waves, but by the time he could find them and concentrate, he was dipping back below another swell. Finally, they had drifted to a position where he could see the glimmering lights more consistently, and he noticed that unlike the shimmering sunlit water around them, these reflections were constant. These lights also seemed to be moving inconsistently with their surroundings. Sembado's curious stare seemed to attract a few of the others' attention. Soon Linx and the other Elephant were looking too. The young men were just about to call to their older counterparts when the glimmering lights finally took shape. They stood dumb as several speeding submarines raced into focus.

Chapter Twenty-Six
Losses

Sembado was just turning to Grandfather to see the old man focusing on the submarines as well, when a distant crack sounded, and a racing bullet shot through the old man's shoulder, a small spray of blood chasing it out through his back. Grandfather brought a hand to his fresh wound before wavering. Sembado jumped forward to catch him, but the old man fell backward into the water with a splash. Just before jumping in the water, Sembado caught sight of the Elephant next to Linx catch a projectile in the chest. Suddenly, the wing erupted in loud sounds as a spray of bullets peppered it from a distance. The pilot and the other Elephant were hit before the remaining crew could dive to safety. Kaluna was able to fall back into the submarine. Sembado had already made his move into the water and was swimming down a few feet to collect his unconscious grandfather. The old man floated near the surface, but was not making an effort to swim. A light trickle of blood floated out from both ends of his gunshot wound. Sembado grabbed him around the chest and started to make his way back to the submarine, only to find that it was moving. Kaluna was bringing it around to shield the entry side of the submarine from their attackers as the heavy armor was enough to guard from the bullets. As Sembado surfaced, he could see Linx helping the other Elephant out of the water. Just before Sembado came up for air, he caught a glint of blue light that seemed strange in contrast to the sky above. He worked his way over to the submarine and was relieved to see Grandfather hacking up water on his own before they even reached the door. Kaluna was now lying down out of the door to help hoist the old man inside. Mahana appeared next to Sembado to help push from below. As they heaved Grandfather in, Sembado's ear caught the sound of a blood-curdling scream from behind him. He turned in the water to see Linx trying to help the other Elephant up onto the wing. The young man was flailing about and beating and clawing at his chest, which had only a portion of an electric blue sphere protruding from it. It was just growing to the size of a small melon when it stopped. Linx continued his efforts in vain as his friend's panic escalated. With Mahana's help, Sembado worked his way up onto the wing. He kept his head low to avoid exposing it over the top of the sub, and he quickly worked his way to the part of the wing the young Elephant was near. He grabbed one of the young man's arms and pulled as Linx pushed from below. The young man did nothing to help as he was using his other arm to claw at his bare chest, which was now covered in blood from his bullet wound. His entire left pectoral was engulfed by the blue hemisphere so that the blood under the blue light looked black. Suddenly, the light energized within his chest. Not thinking it possible, Sembado grimaced as the screams became worse. He and Linx struggled frantically as the young man started coughing up blood. Sembado watched in horror as the orb began to retract and dissolve through the chest. The arm he was holding gave way as it was severed and came off, and the struggle ended as the man died in Linx's arms. Sembado gripped the disembodied arm and dry-heaved as the overwhelming experience continued in the water. The other Elephant and the pilot were both thrashing violently in the water as well, but soon shed their mortal coils as the orb cut off vital blood circulation and their hearts failed. Mahana sobbed deeply as he forced Sembado inside, taking the arm from him and saying a muffled prayer as he cast it into the ocean. Linx had only just abandoned the corpse, and was now on the wing. He had to push Sembado to get him all the way in as Mahana pulled the hatch shut behind them.

Kaluna wiped her tear-filled eyes as she sped away toward the islands. Every few minutes, she looked back over her shoulder, pale-faced, to see the progress with Grandfather's shoulder. They had made an earnest attempt at a tourniquet and, although the bleeding had slowed to an ooze, Sembado continued to apply pressure; he refused to let his guard down. The old man was now conscious again, and after twenty minutes of whispered reasoning, he was able to get his grandson to relent in his efforts.

Their pursuers were now behind them, firing every so often. Each shot rattled the back of the submarine.

***

Despite the noise, Linx was now sleeping in the back; the sun was just setting, and Mahana was at the copilot seat next to his niece. He got up and offered to tend to Grandfather so that Sembado could have a chance to get some much needed sleep, but the stress of the recent events was still coursing through Sembado's veins. Instead of sleeping, he crawled into the copilot's seat Mahana had just vacated. He settled in and took a look around. The sunset was straight ahead, and as it lost its intensity, the auto tinting on the front viewing shield softened so that all of the richness of the sunset's beauty could shine through. Sembado and Kaluna sat quietly for a long time, listening to the soft humming of Mahana's prayers as he bowed his head over Grandfather. Sembado finally broke the silence.

"How much farther?" he asked flatly. Just days ago, even talking to Kaluna would have been awkward and difficult, but these dire circumstances made those trivial challenges truly inconsequential.

"Not far," she responded. "I am afraid of getting too close and leading them to my island, but something tells me they know where we are headed."

They continued on until darkness had set in completely.

Chapter Twenty-Seven
Trapped

According to Kaluna, they were just a couple hours away from the islands. Sembado watched two ever-changing numbers on the display as they slowly blinked past seventeen and negative one hundred fifty-two.

"How will they know when we've arrived?" Sembado asked quietly. He and Kaluna were the only ones awake.

"We could have called them on our own radio system, but it was left in the other submarine," she responded. "But they are always watching. I only hope they don't think we are actual Pens. They tend to shoot first."

How can we communicate to the islanders that we are not actually IFCG? Perhaps if we marked the front of the submarine in the refugee language they would at least be curious enough to board.

Without warning, a hole exploded in the back of the submarine, and a large metal rod with a cable attached shot through the cabin. It slammed into the console between Sembado and Kaluna. Just as it rattled to a stop, three hook-like fins shot out from the head. The cable started to lose slack as it was yanked back through the hole that that the harpoon had blown through the back of the sub.

The remaining passengers were now awake, and Mahana was just able to jerk his head to the side before one of the hooks caught his face. It was still able to leave a small gash in his shoulder as it flew by. Before they could get up, the hooks had seated themselves on the rear wall of the sub, slowing its progress with a jarring crack. Kaluna tried to increase the throttle, but the submarine continued to slow. Sembado was slowly working his way to the back where Linx was already beating on the head of the harpoon with a large wrench. Sembado picked up a similar tool and together they started beating on the hooks at a regular pace. They had nearly mangled one completely apart already. The joint on which it pivoted had nearly given way, when the tip of the harpoon suddenly started glowing an all-too-familiar blue. Sembado and Linx both jumped back with a shout, and soon the others were aware. The submarine exploded in confusion.

"What do we do?"

"We have to abandon ship!"

"They'll shoot us anyway!"

"Maybe 'del take us prisoner."

"That's no better!"

"We have no choice! It's starting to grow!"

Sembado looked to see an orb growing off the blue harpoon tip as if someone were blowing a beautiful and deadly bubble. Soon it had expanded past the back wall of the sub, and the surface nearest them continued expanding.

Sembado had Grandfather in hand and was propping the old man up with one side of his body, while he helped Linx shoulder the door open.

The door broke open into a flood of light. Several submarines' spotlights were trained on the hatch, and Sembado could do nothing but squint and grimace, not knowing what awaited them next. He moved Grandfather farther down the wing as the others were still in a hurry to get out of the submarine-turned-deathtrap. The blue orb could now be seen almost completely outside the sub slowed to a stop. Its current size had forced Sembado and the others to move out on the end of the wing, and their combined weight was now making the submarine list and tilt.

Before the sphere was energized, three smaller crafts appeared from between the larger ones that surrounded the captured sub. They were open-cockpit surface crafts that held two men apiece with room for two more. The captors maintained their weapons' aim on Sembado and his friends as they pulled up alongside the wing. Without speaking, they started to load the captives into the vessels. Sembado and Mahana were put in the first boat despite Sembado's protest. Grandfather and Linx were loaded in the second craft, and Kaluna was forced onto the third by a noticeably more aggressive assailant. He held her close and laughed while the others struggled on their separate boats. The man's contorted grin was made even more menacing by the flood lights on the boats. They just started to pull the boats away from the submarine as the sphere started to complex.

Mahana struggled the hardest at the sight of his niece being accosted by the attacker. He jerked from side to side with all his weight and girth. The pilot of the boat had to stop to assist his partner, ultimately resorting to threatening Mahana's life by pressing his weapon to the old islander's temple.

Sembado suddenly dropped his shoulder into his guard's stomach and had skipped across the bow of two boats before the man could react. He landed next to Kaluna, preparing to punch her tormentor in the face, but his landing found him sliding across the deck. Just as he gained his footing, Kaluna's captor backhanded him in the face with his gun, knocking Sembado on his back. The man continued to laugh as he groped her more aggressively; her efforts to fight back were powerless against the armored aggressor.

Chapter Twenty-Eight
Shots Fired

Suddenly the man stopped laughing, and for a moment there was only the roar of the sea. Sembado looked up to see a stream of blood trickling from the man's forehead. Kaluna shook off his hold, and the man slumped backward on the deck of the small boat. Captors and captives alike had only moments to exchange the beginnings of bewilderment when the floodlights on all the larger ships cut out.

There was one shout for orders, and then the surrounding ships erupted in gunfire. The profiles of defeated penalty officers were silhouetted everywhere. The thunderous roar of battle nearly drowned out the ocean as it reached a painful level. And then there was silence. After the spectacular clamor, even the ocean spray sounded muffled and distant. The lights came back on and the penalty officers had been replaced by a great number of refugee fighters. Kaluna gave Mahana a reassuring nod that she was okay and helped Sembado up off the wet boat deck. The refugee leader let out a booming cry, and it was echoed a hundred times by his surrounding comrades.

The cheers continued on for several minutes as the refugees helped their newly freed comrades into a variety of pieced-together crafts and the freshly commandeered government boats. Even the armored personnel carrier that Sembado and his friends had escaped in was taken away as soon as the harpoon was dislodged and discarded. As the rebels scurried to the various boats to prepare to depart, Sembado made sure to stay close to his grandfather so that they would not be separated again. He nestled down next to the old man as he was delicately placed in one of the larger boats. Mahana sat at his other side; Kaluna was at his feet. Their progress was slow and steady as they moved away from the scene of the rescue and shifted into a cruising formation. Once everyone was moving in the same direction, the boats picked up a faster pace. The pilot of Sembado's boat was careful not to cut into any waves that would jostle the wounded old man.

***

After several hours Sembado opened his eyes, and looked in awe to the rear of the boat as a dull glow started to creep across the horizon behind them. Suddenly, a fiery blaze broke over the edge of the world and the sky exploded into life and its various details were highlighted during Sembado's first sunrise. He stared, eyes full of tears, and took in colors whose vividness he had never seen, not even in a 4D visor. His heart pounded in his chest as the beautiful vista stretched past the boundaries of his peripheral vision. The orange orb made a yellow sky that slowly morphed to green, and blue, and then violet. As he followed the transition up and over his head, he watched the violet sky fade back into night. He saw the moon and then the stars ahead of them in the sky to the west. His gaze drifted down so that he was staring at an odd break in the reflections of dawn in the water. As they moved closer, and the sun moved higher in the morning sky behind them, he could now see a line in the water that was well ahead of the western horizon beyond it. He also noticed what looked like clouds ahead, but they were too low to the ocean, and there was no other fog or haze around. As the sun rose higher, the low lying clouds took on shadowed hues of green and yellow and brown. Sharp, jagged lines were cut vertically in the masses that now appeared clearly to him for the first time.

"They are mountains," Kaluna whispered in his ear. "The mountain islands of Hawaii," she said with honor, as if she were introducing him to an honored and respected elder.

The mountainous mass of land continued to rise in front of them as the growing sunlight and closer vantage point offered sharper details. Mahana let out a shout and started singing a song, and even over the crash of the various skiffs' bows through the surf, Sembado could hear the islanders chanting along from the nearby vessels. Kaluna too had shamelessly joined in the poetic prayer. The smaller, more agile submarines were being made to jump out of the water, even to roll and flip, before crashing back under the waves. Sembado had never seen such fast-paced acrobatics.

In a short time, the boats had slowed as they approached the island shore. All of the recently captured boats and several of the islanders' own crafts broke off the formation and disappeared behind a point to the south. Sembado noticed an outpost on the point made of steel and concrete. Behind it was another. The small watchtowers traced the bay that his boat was now headed straight into. They continued on as a small group of people came out of the surrounding battlements and then the trees beyond. Sembado's eyes drifted from this tree line upward, as the foot of the mountain gave way to a white-tipped summit. He blinked, mouth agape, only looking away when the sounds of the islanders calling from the shore brought his attention back down. In the time it took him to observe the island's peaks, the small group had exploded to over a hundred. They cheered and laughed and sang as they recognized Mahana and Kaluna on one of the incoming vessels.

Word of Grandfather's injured state must have been radioed ahead, because a small medical troop was ready and waiting when the boat touched the sand. Sembado stayed aboard to help load his grandfather out from the inside. Once the old man was settled into a gurney on the beach, Kaluna hopped out and turned to give a hand to Sembado. He made an awkward jump out of the boat and splashed into a foot of water. He could feel the tide washing the sand out from under his feet as the rushing water created little eddies. He sank a couple of inches, but was still much taller than the girl. She let go of his hand and trotted up to the group of people, dozens of whom welcomed her with happy and triumphant greetings, hugs, and kisses. Sembado swayed on his feet as he walked out of the water and onto solid ground for the first time. It did not feel all that different from the halls of the complex, although pushing around in the sand was already making his calves tingle. He averted eye contact with the welcoming islanders and quickly made his way to his grandfather's side. The old man wore a smile as his good arm took handfuls of sand and slowly rubbed them through his fingers. He continued to scoop the powdery white grit as he protested with his attendants who were trying to fit him with an oxygen tank.

"Get that damn thing off me," he snapped. "I did not just escape from that underwater cage just to be fed more canned air."

Mahana was now coming over to translate the old man's protests and shoo the medical attendants to the side. Sembado was at his grandfather's other side now, helping the old man scoop the sand into his hand. They had worked their way down to the saturated grit below, and Grandfather chuckled as he squeezed the wet ooze through his fingers, and let it plop on his chest. Tears were streaming from the corners of his eyes.

The chuckle turned to a cough, and then he was painfully hacking. Only then did he allow a brief shot of oxygen from the tank, but once the cough subsided he pushed the canister away. His eyes drifted around the cloudy sky above, and then to the peak up above his head. He was able to crane his neck just far enough to see the palm trees that flanked the beach. He brought the stare back to his side to look straight into Sembado's eyes.

"You've made me happy, Semmy. I never dreamed I'd get back up here, and I'm thankful for it." His other hand was gripped in Mahana's great palms. The dark, friendly man had his head bowed and was whispering quietly to himself, his brow furrowed. Grandfather ignored his friend, but went on. "You will need to help move things on. These people will help you, but you need to help yourself too. This has only just begun."

"I'll do whatever I need to, but I'll still have questions for you," Sembado responded, rubbing the back of the old man's gray knuckles.

"No time, boy. I ain't makin' it off this beach. Wouldn't want to if I could." The old man said. He closed his eyes softly, letting the morning sun warm his face.

"But then what am I supposed to—" Sembado responded more frantically. The old man cut him off.

"My journal, Sem. It's yours now, but you have to go get it. I meant to retrieve it before we left, but we ran out of time." The old man was now speaking in a hoarse whisper; even Mahana's near-silent prayers could be heard over Grandfather's words.

"But why—"

"Those damn...bl...blue orbs. The secret to defeating them is in the journal. It's hidden...in those J-vents. The key...around my neck. It's for the box. Don't forget it—" The old man continued to hold Sembado's hand firmly, though his grip was not as tight as it once was. Mahana's soft words continued as Sembado's tears fell steadily across his grandfather's forehead and face.

Sembado's shoulders heaved slowly with his sobs, and as his grandfather's grip began to loosen, he tightened his own, so that soon he was clenching desperately to the old man's weary palm. Mahana now had a hand on Sembado's head. He gently palmed the back of the young man's scalp and continued his rites.

Sembado had never had anyone pray for him; religion was not allowed in the complex, but he could not deny the warmth and comfort of the wise islander's words. He looked up into Mahana's warm, bright face and received a nod of assurance. His grandfather's grip was completely slack now, and Sembado took the chain and key from around the old man's neck before he and Mahana crossed Grandfather's hands on his chest. Sembado took in his grandfather's peaceful face. His beard had now reached a record length and was down to his chest, streaked gray and yellow. His wrinkles lay in relaxed waves on his face. It was the happiest Sembado had ever seen him. Grandfather's lifeless eyes looked up at the azure sky, the spectacular blue mirrored in his glassy stare. As Mahana gently shut the old man's eyelids, Sembado bent down and kissed his grandfather's forehead for the first and last time.

Chapter Twenty-Nine
Rest and Recovery

That night a great ceremony and feast were held in honor of the sacrifices given by Grandfather and the other fallen soldiers, and in celebration of Mahana and Kaluna's return. Hundreds of nearby islanders turned out with their best food and brightest spirits. Sembado looked on quietly, as he contemplated the bittersweet experiences that the last few days had held. Despite his grandfather's passing, Sembado felt numb than anything else. He tried to think of all of the past few days' events, and what they meant to the old man, but his mind was racing with so many thoughts he could not concentrate on a single one.

Throughout the day Sembado stayed close behind Kaluna. She was willing to accommodate him considering his loss, and she had even made an effort to comfort him on a few occasions. In reality, Mahana had become very busy with council meetings, and Linx was immediately recruited into the islanders' fighting ranks, so Kaluna was the only one left that Sembado was even remotely familiar with. Luckily, the majority of the islanders tended toward Mahana's disposition and making friendly acquaintances was no difficult task. In fact, many of them had heard of

Sembado's role in Mahana and Kaluna's escape, and the islanders were willing to bend over backward for Sembado's most minor of needs. That afternoon, a man had pulled off his shirt and quickly knotted it into a roughly fashioned hat to keep the sun off Sembado's pale and delicate neck. By that evening's events, Sembado had memorized a handful of names and faces. Despite this preferential treatment, he found that he still favored Kaluna's company. Something about their exploits together, and his memories of Grandfather that were associated with her, brought comfort to Sembado even if she was not particularly talkative.

The two young adventurers were now sitting next to each other at the feast. There were dozens of long tables set around the beach, but Sembado and Kaluna, like many others, were sitting on low cushions around a large bonfire. They watched young men and women dance, and listened as the entire group sang one, long song. Some played small stringed instruments that Sembado had never seen. They had a happy, playful sound. The bonfire was new as well; any type of open flame was prohibited in the complex, even for cooking. The sight was mesmerizing; his thoughts were lost as he focused on one ember and then another. Here and there, he saw random nails glowing orange on the burning timber. He quickly developed a fondness for the sporadic popping that sent embers and sparks high into the air. The embers would land harmlessly in the sand or sometimes they would settle on the leg or arm of an inattentive bystander. Even with the dancing flames ten feet away, Sembado could feel the heat full across his face. He rejoiced quietly at the penetrating warmth. It touched deep in his skin and bones, but it also touched his heart and his soul. Along with the heat, the music and singing warmed his insides even more.

The mood of the gathering changed as a separate fire was stoked with carefully selected logs. The song that was being sung now slowly transitioned to a melancholy hum, as a board carrying some bulky mass was hauled out by intricately clothed islanders. Mahana was at the head of the procession. The form on the board was covered in chains of beautiful flowers. The rosy petals glowed yellow and orange in the flickering flames. Blues appeared green, and whites looked gold. As the train of islanders moved between Sembado and the ceremonial fire, he could see the silhouette of the form for the first time. It appeared to be the profile of a person lying on his back. Just as the realization struck Sembado, he felt a small, soft hand cover his own. He looked down to see that the golden brown fingers belonged to Kaluna. His eyes rose to meet hers; they were welling with tears, but her mouth formed a rare and subtle smile.

"He was a great man." It was barely a whisper.

Further understanding hit Sembado in the pit of his stomach as he watched his grandfather's mortal remains carried closer to the pyre.

He stared, immobilized, as the funeral fire was stoked higher, and then expertly collapsed into a perfect platform—an eternal resting place.

As it collapsed, Sembado squeezed Kaluna's hand, and she returned the gesture. His sorrow guided his movements, and he found his cheek pressed hard against her shoulder. Through his emotional stupor, he could sense the most delicate embrace against his head.

"You do nothing now. My brothers will do the heavy lifting. It is your job to mourn. That is the heaviest job of all."

Mahana led the farewell chant, and despite the mournful tone of the song, its sound was still uplifting and comforting. Sembado pivoted his head toward the fire, keeping it braced against Kaluna's shoulder, and his paralyzed stare transformed into a stoic one as the lyrics of the song became louder and elevated. The tears streaming down Mahana's cheeks were highlighted and glistening in the funeral flames. He cried out the beginning to the final verse, and the farewell began. Grandfather's flowered plank was carefully, but quickly, lowered into the flames. The board, flowers, and light cloth that wrapped the corpse began to smolder and catch. The sweet smelling oils of the blossoms were amplified as more and more petals were thrown into the blaze. The burial cloth caught fire and the dry material burst into flames. As it did, Kaluna's hand squeezed Sembado's, and the two were unaware that the each other's eyes were closed tight. Then the song the islanders were singing shifted again to a triumphant melody. It grew in brightness and in pitch, and Sembado opened his eyes to see Mahana, embraced in the arms of the other pallbearers, wearing a brilliant smile across his face, which was still shining from the dried tears on his cheeks. Sembado's emotions were held captive by the music, and his brief sadness had been diverted to a place of comfort. The music told him that his grandfather would not want him to feel sorrow but pride, and not to linger on what could have been, but to go forth with purpose of what will be. He thought of the fact that his grandfather had made it back to the surface, let alone to solid ground, and the old man's absolute satisfaction brought Sembado solace. As his spirits climbed with the surrounding mood, his thoughts of the old man did not go away; they changed character. The ceremony was a celebration of an influential man's life, not his death.

Kaluna was now singing along with her people, and had let go of Sembado's hand so that she could start playing one of the small stringed instruments that Sembado had learned was called a ukulele. She played along with the two or three basic riffs that were buzzing around them. She continued to look at her fingers as she played; they danced across the strings as she strummed to a quick, lively pace.

An islander tried to hand another ukulele to Sembado, and after much resistance, they forcefully pushed one into his arms. He watched Kaluna for a long time before cautiously attempting his own note. Despite his concentration, the first attempt was quite sour, and all of the islanders around him burst into laughter. Sembado was only mildly embarrassed; he had learned from Mahana that it was not a mocking laughter, but a joyous one that celebrated all of the simple, fun things in life that the majority of the denizens of the complex would have overlooked. Sembado smiled with the islanders, and tried to adjust his fingers on the neck of the instrument. But before he could pluck the strings again, Kaluna's hand appeared on his fingers, pushing them down half an inch before returning to her own song. That little half inch had made the difference, and the sweet, cheery note elicited a small cheer from the surrounding crowd. He worked on that note, strumming to the steady, double-note pace that the surrounding song had evolved into. After many measures of the one note, he risked changing it up. He quickly slid his fingers farther down the neck about an inch, and with much surprise, the note came out bright and sharp. He plucked the strings two more times before returning to the first note. Soon he was playing the two notes to the quick but steady pace. He would frequently make mistakes, but found that humming the lyrics, which he did not know, helped him relax enough to play more consistently. He continued to play along until his fingers became so raw they were nearly bloody. By this time, platters of food were being passed around. He ate a pile of sweet grilled fruits and vegetables, as well as several types of the strange canned meat he had seen in the refugees' safe house in the complex. Every flavor was as bright as the music, and after three and a half plates, and one too many shots of multicolored liquor, Sembado felt lethargic and sleepy. His eyelids grew heavy, and it took everything he had to stay awake as the fire died to ash. The music had slowed to a more relaxed pace, and Kaluna had taken up the ukulele again. She played freestyle notes and made up soft, easy words. When she could not think of a rhyme, she would simply hum along. This relaxed Sembado further, and he was soon in a very heavy sleep rich with fire, music, and Kaluna's sharp, bright eyes.

Chapter Thirty
The Defender

Sembado's entire body was in pain. Before he even opened his eyes, he was aware that every square inch of his exposed skin felt like it was on fire. As the previous night's festivities had died down, the islanders had failed to notice that he had passed out behind one of the long benches. As it was nearly noon, the sun had had little difficulty finding him, and had been searing his skin for several hours. He struggled to open his crusty eyes without crying out. As he squinted through the pain and bright, white sand, he saw shadows of passersby. A group had slowed as they noticed him. He wished they hadn't.

"Look at the little flounda' squirmin' in the sun!"

This elicited a chorus of laughter.

"His burned skin's the same color as his flamin' hair!"

"You should only come out at night, pale one!"

The laughter began to burn more than Sembado's skin as his stomach turned from the embarrassment and its memory of the fruity liquors from the night before. His vision improved enough to make out the jeering faces and pointed fingers. Suddenly, a pair of hands appeared and gingerly fitted a pair of sunglasses over his eyes.

"Is that the best you can do?" The voice was familiar, but loud and angry, unlike its usual melody. The husky tones were resolved and purposeful. "A sunburn? Are you really that pathetic?"

The young men tried to continue with their catcalling, but had no opportunity.

"He's been through more than any of you, and is twice the man! We were raised to be warm and inviting, not a bunch of mocking pigs." Kaluna's voice had become sharp and personal, like Sembado had never heard it.

The young men were now becoming bristling and defensive, but the gathering crowd also brought them embarrassment. Sembado began to stand, fighting back the urge to cry out at his pain. Mahana stepped through the crowd to the front of the group as his fiery niece continued.

"You've all become lazy, spoiled hotshots up here, and you know nothing of honor!" Before anything else could be said, she grabbed Sembado forcefully by the hand and marched away, practically dragging him along. Mahana could be heard continuing the lesson in humility behind them.

When they had reached a shady stretch of palms, she slowed her pace, letting his hand fall to his side. She continued to lead the way to a pair of small canopies that stood where the beach met the thicker trees. Three old island women sat under one canopy, each hand-making a small trinket. The other canopy stretched over a table strewn with jars and containers of every size and shape.

Kaluna led Sembado to the second canopy and motioned for him to use one of the benches next to the table of jars.

"Try and sit down," she said. She conversed briefly with the old ladies, and they all looked over at Sembado, grimacing at his severe sunburn. One of the ladies shook her head and pointed to the table of jars, offering her wisdom to Kaluna.

Kaluna went over to the table and searched through the containers, selecting two of them. She sat on the bench behind Sembado, having him remove the island garment that had been lent to him.

"This will make a mess if you leave the shirt on," she instructed.

Sembado's humiliation continued to throb along with his burnt skin. In his frustration, he offered a sarcastic observation

"I don't understand why you're so helpful all of a sudden. No offense—but it doesn't seem like you," he said, looking off to the ocean beyond. It was obvious the old ladies only spoke their own language, offering him some unintentional privacy. Kaluna said nothing but began to spread the contents of the first jar across his crispy shoulders. The radiating pain was cut with a cold blast of comfort. His audible relief was ignored by the old women. After several quiet moments, Kaluna responded, continuing to work gingerly across his neck and shoulders.

"What I said to them was true, about my people being warm and tolerant. Inviting. If I do nothing to help you then that is just as unwelcoming as their laughter and teasing, no? Besides, I was alone on the other side of the surface once, and your world was just as foreign as mine." Her response was honest and genuine, and it made Sembado's stomach burn for being so accusatory. He sat quietly, trying to think of the right thing to say, as he desperately wanted the conversation to continue. To his surprise, she carried on without being prompted. "I knew your grandfather for some time you know? He visited Mahana regularly, and always noticed me when no one else did. So do you. In that way, you remind me of him. I am very sorry he is gone."

"Me too. At least he got to see the surface again. To pass on firm land." Sembado was surprised about her existing past with his grandfather, but was more interested in continuing to hear her speak. As she finished with the first salve, he realized that his back, neck, and shoulders were again glowing, but this time with the icy sensation the ointment provided. She continued with the second substance, retracing her pattern across his ears, neck, and shoulders. This time, the tingling sensation was eliminated, and soon his skin felt nothing. Sembado made another suggestion, this time in a more complimentary fashion.

"You know you're a leader, Kaluna, don't you? Whether you want it or not. They respect you, even if they're afraid to show it. Mahana respects you too. And is proud."

For the first time during the treatment, she paused, her fingers entwined in the curls of his scalp as it turned into his neck. She then let out a deep sigh and continued.

"What difference does it make if they are going to be afraid to show it? Then it doesn't actually mean anything, does it?"

"It will. When the time comes, it will."

She continued the remainder of the application in a peaceful silence. The old ladies continued to chat quietly as their nimble fingers made steady progress.

Soon Kaluna was finished, and she helped Sembado carefully slip his tunic back on. She returned the containers to the table and wiped her hands on her skirt. She gave him a sideways glance and said, "Call me Luna."

"Okay."

"And, Sem?"

"Yeah?"

"Stay out of the sun."

"Okay."

Every inch of Sembado's skin, sunburnt or not, began to glow again, radiating from head to toe and back again. And for the second time that morning, his stomach seemed to turn upside down.

Chapter Thirty-One
The Simple Life

The next few days found the beginnings of a routine on the island for Sembado. He woke regularly at dawn and departed *The Beluga*, the permanently docked cruise ship that he now called his home. The islanders had renamed the ship when they took it over. Sembado could still make out the faded name, *The Gray Drake*, underneath the roughly stenciled letters the islanders had added. Sembado was part of a slowly growing group of displaced citizens of the complex, or "tankers" as the islanders had come to call them. A handful of escapees arrived each week.

Sembado left his room and walked down a hallway to the stairwell. Eight doors and on the right. He jogged up the steps. The third landing was open to the air outside. He paused to take in the morning sun and the busy islanders and crashing waves. It was 6:45 a.m., and preparations for the morning meal would start soon. Sembado jogged around the deck to the landside ramp that zigzagged to the dock below. His morning run took him past a group of islanders who were cutting additional holes in the side of the ship with torches. These holes were to accommodate the large guns and cannons that the island defenders were continually outfitting onto the ship. From a distance, this side of the ship now looked like it was covered in small black quills.

He slowed to a walk as he approached the sprawling outdoor kitchen where a number of men and women gathered each morning, afternoon, and evening to make large feasts for the workers, islander and tanker alike. He had made a habit of helping prepare breakfast. Although he never had the chance to cook at home, in the limited time he had spent around the islanders' stoves, he had learned so much about seasonings and oils and how to chop fruit consistently and efficiently. Very often though, he would cut a piece too big on purpose, making sure to get his fill. The older women could not stop laughing at how continuously he ate.

After breakfast Sembado found a few hours of time before his island defense duties would occupy the remainder of his day. He tried to practice the ukulele with Kaluna as often as he could, and the two had become noticeably closer. Sembado was happy for a companionship after being away from his friends and family for so long. He learned that Kaluna was much more talkative around other young island women, and that she did not prefer the company of most men.

By the afternoon, Sembado would train with Linx and the island guard. The watchmen concentrated a great deal of their time and effort reconfiguring, equipping, and reinforcing their own boats and any submarines they had commandeered from the complex. Their arsenal and fleet grew bigger nearly every day with shipments that refugees were ferrying in from the complex. They also had several watchtowers to operate, and the extra eyes that Sembado, Linx, and the other tankers offered were well received. The technologies they employed were more developed than that of the complex refugees; relatively powerful aquatic radar could even be used to scan for incoming boats and subs.

After just a couple weeks of preliminary training, Sembado and Linx had been integrated in with the rest of the watch. They sometimes were on duty together, but often found themselves paired with more experienced islanders.

Chapter Thirty-Two
A Weasel in the Henhouse

Over a month had passed since Sembado had come to the island. This afternoon, Sembado was posted in a concrete watch tower with an islander named Ba'ia; they were reviewing the procedures and techniques used to monitor the radar system. The young man had a lighthearted way of life, but he took the defense of the island very seriously.

Ba'ia was pointing out a pod of whales at the edge of the radar when the blips on the screen continued to multiply. Sembado looked to him for direction, but Ba'ia's wide-eyed expression did little to calm Sembado's nerves. Ba'ia quickly regained composure, and began stepping through the proper process of signaling an alert. Soon three of the older island watchmen were in the monitor room assessing the signals on the radar, which were moving in toward the island, but in a direct fashion.

"Those ain't any whales." The first man to speak identified the radar blips as nonsurfaced submarines.

"They ain't stickin' togetha'," another added.

"Looks to be 'bout thirty or so," Ba'ia said. He then addressed the fact that the submarines had come from the direction of the complex; this surprised no one, including Sembado. "They aren't stickin' to a formation like the Pens normally do." He added.

"They aren't too close yet, but keep yer eyes peeled, huh?" the first leader ordered.

Sembado and Ba'ia continued to monitor the progress of the blips, and the islander showed Sembado how the color of the blip signified the depth of the object. Some of the subs had surfaced. Others were roaming around aimlessly, but in general, the blips were steadily making their way toward the island.

The first of the strange submarines finally passed the line that designated the islanders' security perimeter. This was the same line that Sembado and his mates had passed that caused the islanders to come out, investigate, and eventually save them from the IFCG officers. Ba'ia sent out the signal to the dispatchers who made the orders to send the interceptor submarines out. Sembado looked out the window to see half a dozen boats cutting quickly over the waves. The radar showed three times as many submarines flanking the boats. They raced straight out to the first of the unfamiliar crafts that were now steadily leaking across the security perimeter. Sembado and Ba'ia continued to monitor their progress. It took over an hour for them to intercept all of the incoming subs, and in that time, Sembado and Ba'ia were visited four times by supervising watchmen and other curious guards. Linx even stuck his head in to offer an anecdote about sinking Pens, but he was promptly ordered to leave. Sembado recognized the full gravity of the situation when a call went across the radios for the intercepting group of islanders to arm their weapons. Several more tense minutes passed as the patrol reached their weapons' range of the intruders. Sembado watched the choreographed corralling on the radar as the islander vessels flanked and surrounded the intruders, slowing them to a stop and encircling them. The group of submarines that had made it through the perimeter numbered ten; the remaining submarines were still wandering outside of the islander's security range. After a very long wait, some confusing radio messages were sent back. The only part of the garbled message that Sembado could understand was the word "unarmed." He wanted to ask Ba'ia for a clarification, but the islander was too engrossed in his radar duties. The blips, including the intruders, were reforming and heading back toward the island at cruising speed. They would return in just a couple hours, and Sembado resigned to waiting until their arrival for more information.

The time waiting for the submarines' return seemed even longer than their first trip. Two and a half hours passed slowly for Sembado, who felt as if he were waiting alone because of Ba'ia's unwavering concentration. They would have typically signed out for the next shift, but when their replacements arrived, they remained at post. Ba'ia shared his radar duties with the new arrival, who Sembado recognized as Ba'ia's younger brother, Pa'ulo. The sun was falling in the sky when the returning submarines arrived within eyesight of the guard tower's high vantage point.

The other islanders were not out to greet the submarines like they did when Sembado and the others had arrived, because there were no returning island refugees reported aboard the boats. Mahana and Kaluna's return was the biggest news the islanders had received in some time, and without the appeal of returning kin, very few islanders cared to greet the incoming vessels.

The incoming boats and submarines could be spotted in the water. Sembado decided to see the incoming strangers firsthand as his current companions were of little help or conversation. He slipped out of the guard tower and worked his way down to the docking bays around the back end of the point that flanked one side of the bay. He walked along a palm-lined path with the bay on his right and the hills of on his left. The lights that crisscrossed the path had just popped on as the sun fell closer to the horizon. He followed his shadow to a concrete structure set back in the cross of a hill where the point met the foot of the island's main mountain. This structure was the entrance to a tunnel that worked back through the hills to the cove where the island watchmen kept their fleet. He plodded along through the tunnel as the click of his footsteps echoed in the concrete tube. The bright lights that lined the tunnel highlighted the red, flaky skin on his sunburned forearms. His body was finally starting to adjust to the sunlight. As he brushed and picked the dead skin away, a tougher, darker layer showed through. It was a big improvement from the persistent blisters and scabs that had plagued him for his first few weeks on the surface. He reached the end of the tunnel. It passed into another concrete structure that transitioned into the mouth of the cove beyond. Several boats and submarines had been hoisted out of the water near the dock, and the islanders present were busy hammering and welding away on their hulls. Sembado continued on past these workers with some greetings following him through hatches. Most of these men knew of him because of his recent endeavors. He had gained a decent reputation as a hard worker and for having relatively accurate aim with a gun. Being a part of the watchmen reminded him of his time with the Elephants.

As he walked down past the maintenance area and onto the dock, he saw the first of the returning patrol boats rounding the corner into the cove. They sped past his position and began their routine docking procedures. After them came a mix of modified submarines that Sembado recognized as islander subs, and a random group of civilian-grade submarines that he could have seen on any given day in the complex. He watched with excitement as the islander subs guided the newcomers into port. The hatches on the submarines opened, and the islanders who had commandeered and piloted the crafts exited. After exiting, they each turned around to assist several others out of the subs. Dozens of people came pouring out of the ten submarines, much more than they were rated to hold. Some seemed to stick together as families, but others were standing alone once they reached the dock. The one thing that they all shared was the same look of stress, fatigue, and utter confusion at their surroundings and predicament.

Sembado recognized the various brands and types of clothing that they wore. These people were regular citizens of the complex. Sembado could not believe his eyes.

But how did they get out?

As the people finished piling off, Sembado watched dumbfounded as his best friend, Meligose Feldman, stepped out of the closest submarine wearing a look of bewilderment. This look was amplified when he caught sight of Sembado. Meligose ran forward to embrace Sembado, but just before he could reach his friend, Sembado recognized another face as a man stepped out of the submarine behind Meligose. It was the haggard face of Gerard Hutch.

Hutch took in the highly organized industrial operation around him before he locked eyes with Sembado, and before Sembado could react, Hutch was elbowing an island guard in the throat and grabbing his gun. Meligose had just wrapped his arms around Sembado and did not understand why Sembado was struggling to get away. He continued to fight to hug Sembado, while behind him the assailant Hutch produced a small round object from his pants. He pressed the button on the grenade, threw it in the water next to the dock where Sembado and Meligose were struggling, and dove back into the submarine he had just left. A spray of bullets came out of the sub, and several guards and civilian tankers outside the submarine collapsed in a bloody spray. Sembado had picked Meligose up around the waist, and was trying to move him, but a second later the grenade exploded in the water, and Sembado and Meligose were thrown into the cavern wall behind them.

Chapter Thirty-Three
Darkness

Sembado awoke with a soft kiss on his chapped and bloody lips. He struggled to open his eyes, but could see nothing but a foggy light through the gauze wrapped around his head. His thoughts were foggy too, a black cloud as he struggled to make sense of the sensations his body was sending his brain. Another kiss. He fought to swallow around the tube in his throat, but failed. All he could taste was blood. His labored breathing made him gurgle and choke as the oxygen tubes in his nose cycled fresh, dry air into his chest. His left leg itched, but he could not lift his arms. The itch grew to a terrible sensation and he started to struggle against the pain. He flexed his knuckles into fists and they popped painfully. He could not move his arms. Sembado cried out at his pain and frustration and gritted his teeth as he focused all his energy into picking up his right foot. He managed to lift it a few inches. He slowly rotated it over where he could scratch his left leg with it, but when he brought it down to the itch, it came to rest on the surface he was sleeping on, not his left leg. The pain from the leg grew. He started to thrash his right leg around in frustration. A pair of hands grabbed each of his limbs; he heard muffled words in his ears. Another soft kiss on his cheek. A cold liquid entered the syringe in his arm, and he drifted back into an uneasy sleep.

Chapter Thirty-Four
Guess Who's Back

Sembado came back to consciousness with a bright, warm light shining in his eyes. The bandages across his face had been removed. He turned his face away from the window. Throbbing pains shot down his back and into his legs. He blinked a few times. Kaluna was sleeping in a chair next to his bed. He took in his surroundings. He was in one of the villager's homes. They were typically warm, happy interiors, and this one was no exception. In the corner, a terrarium held a large branch. Sprawled across the branch was a large iguana that was soaking up the heat of a large, red bulb. Sembado recognized the lizard as Min'na, Kaluna's pet iguana that she had left on the island before leaving for the complex. Kaluna had introduced Sembado to the large female lizard before, and he had even fed her insects from time to time. He was lying in Kaluna's bed. He looked over again at the small young woman. Her brown skin looked like wild animal stripes in the shadows that the window shades were casting on her arms, legs, and face.

Sembado closed his eyes, and his head began to spin as it did the morning after the celebration for Grandfather's passing. He opened his eyes again and tried not to wretch. His mind slowly started to work beyond his current surroundings, and he pondered how and why he was in Kaluna's bedroom, and why he was so sore. He clenched his teeth as his last memories flooded his brain. Meligose, Hutch, and the explosion overwhelmed him, but it all seemed like a bad and distant dream.

His left leg suddenly itched furiously. He lazily reached to scratch it with his right leg, but as he dragged his lower limb under the covers it did not find what it was looking for. He moved his right foot back and forth near the discomfort, but again, nothing. His confusion spread as he looked down at the lumps his body made underneath the otherwise smooth bedding. His right leg made a long smooth ridge finished with a small peak that was his foot. On his left side, the smooth ridge stopped halfway down. He blinked stupidly while trying to roll his left foot up so that he could see the lump that it should have made, but the short extremity slid to the right with nothing else to show. Sembado strained against his pain as he sat up and off the pillows to put his hands where his lower left leg and foot should be, but his palms landed in empty bed. His panic spread as he worked his way closer to his knee, and finally found a rounded end to his thigh. He was not ready for the pain of cupping his bandaged stump. He fell back against the pillows, growling through gritted teeth. He tightened his fists, punching one side of the bed hard.

Kaluna was up and at his side. Her sleep-filled eyes were underlined by layers of dried tears.

"Be careful. Don't strain," she said. It was more pleading than her normal demanding tone. She touched his forehead, and her soft fingertips drew Sembado's pain away as he concentrated on her cool touch. She held his face for several quiet moments until the tension in his body went away. When he opened his eyes again, she was sitting on the edge of the bed. She was looking at his eyes, his mouth, his face. Sembado swallowed hard.

"What happened to me?" he asked with an unfamiliar gravelly voice. "What happened to Meligose?"

Kaluna looked out the sunny window. The warm shadows cast one of their window-shade stripes right across her eyes and the bridge of her nose. She looked mysterious and troubled. Her eyes were bloodshot.

"There were government agents on the rescued subs. One of them recognized you."

"Hutch," Sembado muttered under his breath.

"They escaped after the explosion. The island guards got one sub, but the other one got back to the complex. They always knew we were here, but now they know what we're up to, and that you're here."

"The explosion," Sembado repeated flatly.

"It took many lives," Kaluna added. "They could not save your—" She looked away to the window again. Tears were welling in her eyes. She had placed a hand on Sembado's leg, but it did not hurt like before.

"Where's Mel?" he asked. She did not answer right away. "My friend, Meligose. Where is he?" Kaluna got up off the bed and crossed the room. She stuck a finger through the terrarium mesh and slowly tickled Min'na's crusty tail. The lizard turned its head from the heat lamp and blinked contentedly.

"Mahana and the elders have decided to undock *The Beluga*. They will have it armed, and sea-ready in a week or two, but they fear an attack from the complex will come at any moment." The distraction did not work.

"Where is Meligose?" Sembado asked firmly.

"The Government doesn't know about *The Beluga* yet. Mahana thinks it's our only hope. I have heard that the rescued tankers say the complex is one giant prison now." Her voice was becoming higher and more broken.

Sembado's next exclamation was almost a bark. "Kaluna!"

She spun around from the window. Tears were streaming down her face. The streams cut through the light layers of dried tears that were already on her face.

"What do you expect?" she cried. "His body was the only thing that kept you alive!" She threw herself on the bed, and hugged his right leg through the covers, sobbing loudly. Sembado let his head fall back against the pillows. It fell too high and made a dull thud on the wall. He put his hand on Kaluna's head and closed his eyes tight.

***

Several days later found Sembado's severed appendage stitched and scabbed. He was now using a wheelchair. His arms had started to overcome their initial weakness, and he found himself thankful for his lifetime of swimming that had strengthened his upper body more than he had previously appreciated.

On occasion, Kaluna would push the wheelchair, and despite not needing the help, Sembado never rejected the offer. She would walk behind the chair and give Sembado the most up-to-date information on the islanders' embattlements or how many more escapees had arrived from the complex.

Their current conversation was on the topic of Grandfather's journal, and how Sembado expected to get back to it in his current state. They discussed his possibilities quietly as they took part in the preparations for that morning's breakfast for the workers.

"Well, it's not like you'll need your leg for a lot of the travel; the subs don't require a lot of leg work," Kaluna offered. She was very good at cutting out unnecessary worry when discussing these kinds of options. "Besides, I'm sure you'll be on crutches by then," she added halfheartedly.

"Yeah, that'd be great. Me hobbling around the complex while it's crawling with Fabian's finest."

Just then, Linx came careening up in an old golf cart. Despite his convenient ride, he was nearly breathless when he spoke.

"Come on you two. You won't believe who we just pulled out of an escaped sub."

Sembado and Kaluna exchanged looks as she got up and pushed his chair away from the table.

"Who is it?" Sembado asked as Kaluna pushed him quickly over to the little cart.

"Just get in."

Sembado stood on one leg and hopped to the front seat. Kaluna folded the chair and pulled it into the back of the vehicle with her.

"Who is it?" Sembado demanded.

"Jonah Feldman," Linx said with a dark smirk, and he motored away as fast as the cart could take them.

Chapter Thirty-Five
Friend or Foe?

Mr. Feldman had arrived with a submarine full of other random escapees, and Linx had promptly pointed him out to the islanders. By the time Sembado had arrived at the islanders' small detention facility, Mr. Feldman had been checked in and fed. The islanders were very serious about not sinking to the same standards of care as experienced in Fabian's facility, and Sembado was glad for it. He had decided that dignity should be unconditional for anyone.

As Linx had already explained Sembado's experience with Mr. Feldman to the islanders, they had agreed to allow Sembado to interview Mr. Feldman in the hopes that Sembado could get what valuable information the traitor might have.

Sembado was directed to a room with a table. He wheeled his chair right up under the end facing the door and waited. After a few minutes, the door opened, and two islanders escorted in a very haggard Jonah Feldman. He saw Sembado, and his eyes and shoulders dropped. He was shuffled to the chair opposite Sembado and plopped down. The island guards locked his legs down and left the room, indicating that they would be ready when Sembado was done.

They sat in silence for a long time. Mr. Feldman sat with his eyes fixed on the table. Finally, he spoke.

"I can't say I'm surprised to see you." He paused. "But I'm happy you're okay."

"Am I?" Sembado asked. Mr. Feldman responded with a furrowed brow. Sembado pushed himself away from the table, and Mr. Feldman recognized the wheelchair for the first time. His furrowed brow turned to a genuine look of concern. Sembado pushed himself around the side of the table just far enough for Mr. Feldman to catch sight of his missing leg.

Mr. Feldman's mouth fell open.

"My word! Sembado?! What happened?"

"Didn't Hutch tell you?" Sembado asked, genuinely curious as to how familiar or comfortable Mr. Feldman may have become with the other members of Fabian's ranks.

"Who?" It was sincere confusion. Then the realization hit his tired, dreary eyes. "Gerard Hutch? Are you serious? Wait, did he do this to you?"

Sembado was angry at Mr. Feldman's cluelessness, even if it was genuine. Hutch getting loose and eventually finding his way to that dock with that grenade was all Mr. Feldman's fault.

"You realize it's your fault he got out, don't you?" All of the emotions that had built up over the last few weeks started to boil over as the memories of the events—from

Mr. Feldman's betrayal to Hutch's attack and Meligose's death—flooded over Sembado's heart. Before he could let loose, Mr. Feldman made his best attempt at a rebuttal.

"Sembado, please, you don't understand." He ran his fingers through the little hair he had left. "They got to me after the prison escape. They really have our best interests in mind. Things have just gotten a little out of control. And they...they threatened my family. Meligose. What was I...?"

Sembado couldn't listen anymore.

"Well a lot of good that did you, because he died anyway! Hutch got him along with my leg! Your boy Gerard killed Mel, you fool!" Horror and despair spread across Mr. Feldman's face.

"I'm done!" Sembado shouted as tears started streaming down his face. The island guards appeared immediately, pulling a struggling, desperate Jonah Feldman out of the room. His screams about his son continued all the way down the hall.

Chapter Thirty-Six
A Leg to Stand On

Several days had passed since Mr. Feldman's return, and Sembado's thoughts had returned to his preoccupation with getting back to the complex to retrieve the journal. He woke one morning to a strange sensation; someone fiddling with his left leg. He opened his eyes and found Kaluna strapping some metal apparatus to his stump. He smiled.

"You couldn't wait until I was awake to do that?"

She didn't look up, but continued making adjustments as she responded.

"I couldn't wait forever. You sleep more than my tutu," she said.

"Tutu?"

"My grandma."

"Oh. Hey! Is that what I think it is? Where'd you get it?"

"One of my cousins smuggled it back from the complex just for you. It's supposed to be fairly effective, but you need to wear this on the back of your neck." She handed him a tight-fitting collar with a sensor on the back. It fit like a choker, with the receiver sitting right under the knot on the back of his head.

"That part picks up your brain signals to your—hey!" The nimble rod and foot started flailing as Sembado had started to excitedly think about moving his leg again. Kaluna continued to wrestle with the leg and finished with a couple adjustments on the ankle.

"Okay. I think that's it," she said. "Get up and try it out."

Sembado's new leg continued to flail randomly for a few more moments. He soon had both legs hanging over his bed and was standing on both with all his weight. He carefully took his time lifting one and then the other. He walked in a few circles and then right out the door, leaving Kaluna to watch.

He was back in a moment to invite her down to breakfast. They spent the rest of the morning breaking in his new appendage, and discussing how it would fit into their plan to sneak back into the complex.

"This is the difference I needed," Sembado exclaimed. "Thank you so much!" he said for the tenth time, giving her a big squeeze with one arm.

"The difference *we* needed," she corrected. "You won't be going back in there alone, and I wouldn't be caught dead pushing you around in that chair."

"Well, either way. Thanks."

For the second time that week, Linx was speeding toward them on his old golf cart.

"What now?" Sembado laughed. "You guys nab Fabian himself?"

"No, it's Jonah again. He wants to share some info, but he says he'll only talk to you." Sembado gave an exasperated face. Kaluna tried to look encouraging as they hopped on and sped off.

***

For the second time that week, Sembado entered the interview room. This time Mr. Feldman was sitting at the far end of the room, his elbows on the table, his hands covering his mouth. He raised his eyes to meet Sembado's and then dropped them to inspect his leg. He nodded in approval.

"It looks good. Does it work?"

Sembado responded with a sarcastically raised eyebrow.

"Look," Mr. Feldman continued, looking Sembado directly in the eyes. "I've had it. I'm done. I've been playing their game since before Mel was even born. I gave them everything I could to protect him, and not only did he die anyway, but at their hands! That's it. I'm done. I swear on the death of my only son that I will do everything in my power to destroy Fabian and everything he has created."

Sembado had taken a seat across the table with his arms crossed, and was feeling satisfied. The words Mr. Feldman had just spoken guaranteed that no matter what the next few days or weeks or months brought, Meligose's life would not have been lost in vain. He leaned back in the chair and asked Mr. Feldman to continue. They discussed his insights for a very long time. Mr. Feldman would periodically stand and pace. Nothing he said was startling or revelatory, but it confirmed the rumors Sembado had heard of the devolving situation in the complex. It seemed that Fabian had staged a completely successful military coup and was commanding the entire complex under thinly veiled martial law. Their only saving grace was the fact that Fabian consistently used his best and most dangerous men for his personal errands and primary operations. The remainder of his bidding was being carried out by thousands of quickly trained, inexperienced young men. These rookie Pens were now being regularly overwhelmed by even the most basic rioting that the remaining Elephants were helping stage.

"I am fairly certain that if you were to stage an attack from the surface, he would put his most elite defense out directly behind a thin layer of cannon fodder. I've seen him use the tactic time and again." Mr. Feldman finished.

Sembado was completely convinced that Mr. Feldman was now one of their best tactical assets, and his focused rage for his son's vengeance would only fuel his resolve.

It did not take him long to convince the island guard to release Mr. Feldman. Linx was a different story.

Chapter Thirty-Seven
All But Two

The Beluga remained anchored just off shore for several days as it was being laden with weapons, supplies, food, and warriors. Battle plans were continuously being refined as the information and insights that Mr. Feldman provided were integrated into the mass of hints and tips that had already been cultivated from the civilian escapees from the complex. As new details were added and changed, the main objective stayed the same: mount a heavily armored, concentrated attack and penetrate as far into Fabian's defenses as possible.

Sembado continued to familiarize himself with his new leg as the battle logistics were further developed by Mahana and Linx. Linx had become the Elephants' de facto leader on the surface.

Every morning Sembado and Kaluna would jog a couple miles around the deck of *The Beluga*. He had worked the adjustments on his prosthetic to make friction and chafing as manageable as possible. Even with his right leg being as muscular as ever, he had started to notice that the prosthetic was feeling almost too powerful, as if it were going to take off on its own. After a quick break, the leg would cool down and the feeling would pass.

The next day saw a bright, clear morning give way to a stormy afternoon. Mahana called to send *The Beluga* to sea, using the storm as cover. The churning sea was the latest addition to Sembado's experiences on the surface; it proved less pleasant than the others.

With nightfall, the storm got worse, and despite its size, *The Beluga* tossed and turned; its accompanying fleet of subs followed cautiously beneath the surface.

Sembado followed Kaluna down to the belly of the ship, following a summons by Mahana and Linx. They found their leaders in a private room, heads together at a table littered with maps. Mahana looked up and greeted them with his determined smile; Linx continued to study the map.

"You two are looking awfully close." The truth in Mahana's words embarrassed neither Sembado nor Kaluna; both took it as the simple observation that it was. Strangers unfamiliar with Mahana's style would often mistake his greetings and jovial nature as obligated and insincere, but Sembado had known the wise islander to unapologetically wear his heart on his sleeve from the first time they met. When Mahana asked how someone was, or made an observation of their behavior or appearance, he did so with as much truth and honesty as anyone Sembado had ever known.

"We've been training pretty close for this next operation," Sembado responded. "It's best we know each other's moves as much as possible."

Mahana nodded in approval. He turned to Linx who was just finishing the highlights of the suggested route for Sembado and Kaluna to take back to the complex.

"As long as you swing far enough south, you should be fine," Linx suggested, not looking up from the map. "Regardless, though, be on the lookout for Pens. Things have gotten pretty tight lately, you know."

"Yeah, we've heard," Sembado laughed back. "We were thinking it'd be best to leave as soon as possible."

Mahana and Linx exchanged looks of uncertainty.

"My worries are with your departure in the storm," Mahana said, mostly addressing Kaluna. The young lady wasted no time in offering her response.

"That's the whole reason we set off in this storm, wasn't it? For cover and distraction? So let us take off when everyone else is busy watching the winds."

"Kaluna's right," Sembado added. "We will only be down there a day or two. I know where the lock box is, and I have kept the key safe. We just need the distraction from you guys."

Suddenly, they all heard a noise from the adjacent corridor. Linx was the first to react, springing to the door and jumping through. He returned immediately with Mr. Feldman. The worried look on his face showed that Mr. Feldman had heard most, if not all, of the conversation.

"Sembado, I don't think it's a good idea for you to go alone," he offered from Linx's clutches.

"No one asked you, ya sneakin' eel," Linx snapped, roughly depositing Mr. Feldman at the table.

Mr. Feldman ignored the insult and continued to plead with Sembado. "At least let me join you, help you get around."

Linx let out one of his sarcastic laughs. "He doesn't trust you anymore, Jonah. No one does."

"All right, look!" Mr. Feldman snapped, standing up and nearly knocking his chair over. "I've known Sembado for over ten years—most of his life. How about the rest of you?"

The group let Mr. Feldman say his piece. Linx did so with a look of pure disdain spread across his face. Mr. Feldman continued. "You think I'm still a liability, huh?" Now he addressed Linx specifically. "I lost my only son. I lost my only son along with Sembado's leg." Sembado rose at this point and began to position himself between Linx and Mr. Feldman, as the bitter man finished. The sneer on Linx's face was nearly gone. Sembado placed a hand on Mr. Feldman's shoulder as he addressed the rest of the group.

"Look," he said, "Every experience I've ever had with Mr. Feldman stands on its own. These moments of shame that he has had to suffer in front of all of us are not enough to undo a lifetime of guidance and support. So let us put an end to this betrayal, and instead focus on our common enemy."

The silence in the room persisted as the others' pride was actively being broken; each began realizing that this effort was officially bigger than themselves. He then addressed Mr. Feldman quietly, nearly whispering.

"Look. I know what this means to you, and I know how much you want to earn back my trust, so this is how you can do it—by letting me and Kaluna do this alone. An extra body will only make more noise, and someone is much more likely to recognize you." Mr. Feldman dropped his head in defeat as Sembado continued. "My prosthetic is fine. We have trained for this, and we really need to just play this one close to the chest, ya know?"

Mr. Feldman put his hands to his eyes and pressed hard, letting out a sigh. Dropping his hands over his mouth, he nodded in approval. He then looked directly at Sembado with teary, red eyes.

"Please be careful," was all he could say before his voice broke and he pulled Sembado in for a desperate, intense hug. They held the embrace for a long time.

Mahana finally broke the silence. "Let's go find ya a drink, Jonah," he said without his signature chuckle.

After the two left, Linx remained silent, his stony gaze fixed on some invisible point.

"We need to finish packing," Sembado said—a lie. They'd had their gear prepared for a week. Instead, they went to have the last meal they would ever eat aboard *The Beluga*.

They were able to find a quiet corner in the dining facility and ate in near silence. Sembado's stomach danced violently at the idea of returning to the Complex, but ample comfort came from the fact that he would be going there with Kaluna at his side.

Suddenly, a profound boom resonated from deep within the ship. The lights flickered and the ship shuddered. Plates and utensils crashed to the floor. A number of people struggled to their feet and tried to make their way out of the dining center to investigate. The remaining shipmates maintained as orderly a conduct as possible. Sembado and Kaluna waited for the first responders to clear out before departing themselves.

They arrived at Sembado's quarters first, and Kaluna helped him finish preparing for an imminent departure. They collected the remainder of his packs and were just leaving to retrieve Kaluna's things when one of Mahana's men appeared in the door.

"Mahana wants you two down at the dock in five!" the man said breathlessly.

"We're heading there now," Kaluna said flatly. She was much better at keeping her wits about her than Sembado was.

"Was it a torpedo?" Sembado asked.

"Recon sub," the man replied. "We started putting the deck guns to it, so he ran himself right into our side. Small hole—they should have it patched soon."

The man disappeared as quickly as he had arrived. Sembado swallowed hard as Kaluna led him away by the hand.

They passed by Kaluna's bunk quickly and were able to get to the dock in the bottom of the ship within Mahana's requested time limit.

They found him giving out orders as dozens of his sailors were manning two- and three-man interceptors, quickly blowing out of the exit ports cut in the side of the ship.

Sembado and Kaluna followed him quickly over to their prearranged travel vessel as he spoke with the closest thing to a worried tone that Sembado had ever heard from him.

"Ahada gave you my message, I see. It was just a recon sub, but we're picking up some more blips on da radar. For as much as this kills me, this da perfect chance for you two to slip out. I'm sorry you didn't have a chance to say more goodbyes."

Another sailor caught up with them to brief Mahana further. "Those blips on the radar are approaching—in formation."

Mahana grabbed an extra bag off of Kaluna's shoulder and doubled his speed, the others following. The messenger helped the three of them pack the submarine quickly before Kaluna could climb inside. Mahana grabbed her wrist and pulled her back out.

"I don't think so," he said tearfully, pulling her for a farewell embrace. She nearly disappeared in his great size. He reached out a free arm and pulled Sembado in too.

"You betta keep her safe, or so help me God."

"I think she'll end up doing most of the protecting," Sembado retorted between breaths. Mahana's grip was suffocating, but at Sembado's wisecrack he let them go while eliciting one of his great, loud chuckles.

The old islander stood with his fleshy fists on his hips as Sembado and Kaluna pulled off the dock and bobbed toward the exit. Tears were streaming down his golden-brown face.

Kaluna flipped switches and controls as the sub pulled out of the ship's lower hull and rocked away on the waves. They kept the sub on the surface, even keeping part of the visor open so that they could relish the fresh sea air as long as possible. A couple hundred yards out, Kaluna turned the submarine south, and they were both afforded a view of the ship, which was suddenly outlined by a huge blast and fire ball on the far side, followed quickly by the sound of an impact and explosion.

The two exchanged looks as Sembado pulled the windows shut, and Kaluna prepared to dive.

"He'll keep it afloat," Kaluna said, looking away. "This is our only chance," she added flatly. Despite the growing darkness, Sembado could still make out the glistening in her eyes by the glow of the ship's calamity.

She took the nose of the sub beneath the next swell, but it popped back up again, and Sembado quickly took in the starry night as he realized this was the last time he would see the sky for quite a while. With a couple adjustments and a little more power, Kaluna took the sub down for good. Sembado made auxiliary adjustments as they continued to chat diving sequences back and forth to each other.

Soon they were one hundred feet down and leveling off. Despite their uncertain future, they exchanged the reassuring nod that had become common between them and briefly squeezed each other's hand.

Sembado closed his eyes and leaned his head back against the seat, gripping the key that hung around his neck.

Made in the USA
Middletown, DE
05 June 2022

66644330R00176